The Isle of Kernow Fights Back

Cathy-Ann Child

Copyright © 2018 Cathy-Ann Child
All rights reserved.
ISBN: 1726248860
ISBN-13:978-1726248860

DEDICATION

This book is again dedicated to Cornwall,
a county that never ceases to amaze and intrigue.

Other books in this series

The Independent State of Kernow

Chapter 1

Buckingham Palace
It was Friday the 8th of May 2015, and David Cameron was ushered into the reception room where the Queen was already on her feet ready to greet him. He glanced around quickly. Nothing had changed since his last visit; chalk blue panelled walls, immaculate oriental rug, and ornaments perfectly symmetrical on the mantelpiece. He approached her, smiling inanely, unable to shift the grin from his face, "Good morning, Your Majesty," he said with a bow of his head. She shook his hand perfunctorily and returned to the small sofa with gold lacquered legs. Cameron sat on the chair opposite, still trying desperately to quash the daft grin.

"Bloody lucky, if you ask me," she said abruptly.

Somewhat taken aback, Cameron stammered, "Sorry Ma'am?"

"Let's face it, David. No one expected you to be voted back in again. Especially not without that lovely Nicholas."

Somewhat lost for words Cameron stuttered several half sentences, and then gave up, sinking back into his uncomfortable chair.

"Anyway, here we are. So apparently I have to ask you to form a new government. But I must say, I won't like it as much as the last one."

"Um," Cameron murmured, not quite sure how to reply to such an undermining endorsement of his meteoric victory. "Thank you Ma'am. I hope not to disappoint you. You might find that you like it just as much without the Lib Dems?" he added optimistically.

"Hmm, I don't think so. So what have you got planned now you're free to do what you want?"

"I'm not sure I have *that* much power," Cameron said lightly, trying to soften the mood. "We intend to start by creating three million apprenticeships, more help for childcare, helping thirty million people cope with the cost of living by cutting their taxes. Building homes that people are able to buy and own -"

"Did I ask you for your election speech? I asked what are you *actually* going to do?"

Sheepishly he continued, "- well we're hoping we have enough friends left in the party to get the deficit down, and try and get a few more people back into work."

"You and George fallen out with some of the chaps?"

"Nothing that can't be repaired with some nice new cabinet positions now we have extra chairs at the table."

"And what are your plans for the United Kingdom? Are we expecting to see any more parts be sold off, or indeed drift off?"

"We retained Scotland Ma'am, and we expect to see a landslide rejection of leaving the EU when we have the referendum that we promised."

"Well as long as you are sure? I don't want to see any more careless loss of state. Now on this topic, it seems that Charlie wants a word with you before you leave."

Cameron raised an eyebrow as this was not normal for his visits to the palace.

"Yes, he is rather upset by the whole Cornwall fiasco. He was pretty furious when it drifted off, but the whole referendum business, and them leaving to became a British Overseas Territory has left him absolutely fuming. I've not seen him as angry as this since Anne did her horsey thing in the 1984 Olympics, and he wasn't allowed to represent the country playing croquet."

"Well he is the Duke of Cornwall so he has every right to be angry. Of course I will meet with him, Ma'am."

"Good luck with that," she muttered under her breath in a way that Cameron thought was quite sarcastic. 'Ominous' he thought.

The Queen got up to leave and Cameron rose and bowed, retaking his seat as she left the room. How curious, Charles had never wanted to see him before.

The issues to which the Queen referred were two-fold. There was the first improbable event, to become known as the *Drift*, where on the night of the 6th March in 2014 Cornwall broke away from the mainland, splitting off along the river Tamar, and had drifted off into the Atlantic, settling on the same latitude as Spain. The second, and more manmade event, was the referendum held on the 26th September 2014 when the citizens of the newly off-shored Cornwall elected to become a British Overseas Territory. Cameron had found this event especially galling as it turned out that it was Whitehall's own man that had instigated the vote. Roger Stiles had been sent from Whitehall to oversee the Drift disaster, and whilst overseeing the matter he appeared to have gone native, and encouraged the whole separation. The chairman of the Joint Intelligence group, a certain Martin Brownly-Smith, had attempted damage-limitation by putting Stiles in charge of the newly formed overseas territory as the new Governor of the recently renamed Isle of Kernow. Brownly-Smith's logic had been that keeping 'friends close and enemies closer' might be the safest strategy. Cameron still wasn't sure about this, but he had been greatly preoccupied with the general election over the last few months, so now there was time to review the matter, and reflect on how the land lay; literally and metaphorically.

Several minutes later the door opened and Charles entered, hand outstretched with a forced smile.

"Your Royal Highness," Cameron said as they shook hands, and he took another small bow.

"Take a seat, man," Charles said rather impatiently, taking the seat his mother had vacated some minutes earlier.

"I hear you are distressed about the Isle of Kernow, Sir?" Cameron started.

"It's not the bloody Isle of Kernow. It's *Cornwall* for pity's sake. And I'm not distressed, man. I'm damned furious. It was not yours to give away in the first place-" Cameron started to reply but was stopped by a dismissive wave of the royal hand as Charles continued. "So now that wretched communist Clegg is out of the way, you can focus on undoing this godforsaken mess."

Cameron hesitated, unsure how to deal with the insinuation that this was somehow undoable. Before he could construct an answer that suggested that 'he would try but it was probably a legal *fait accompli*,' Charles had started up again.

"And another thing, have you seen what happened to my biscuit sales? If it wasn't for them being available in Waitrose I'd be broke by now."

'Broke? He was the future King of England, not a struggling artisan baker,' Cameron thought. He stifled a sardonic laugh, converting it to a cough for safety sake. "I can imagine how distressing that must be for you, Sir. As soon as I have everything ticking over in the Country I will turn my attention to this matter."

"Well make sure you do, man. And don't shilly-shally around." And with that Charles rose abruptly and was out of the door before Cameron could scramble to his feet.

"Oh Lordy. I wish Ed had won now," Cameron muttered as he left.

Whitehall

"So here's how it stands," Cameron explained to Martin Brownly-Smith, who was lounging back in his chair listening, fingers laced behind his head. "Charles was bloody furious enough about the whole Drift thing – as if we had some sort of control over tectonic shift – but the political break has driven him nuts. He is majorly not happy with Cornwall becoming a British Overseas Territory, and weirdly thinks that we can just repeal it because his biscuit sales have plummeted,"

When Cameron had finished off-loading his hassles of the day Brownly-Smith leant forward, and said in his plummy accent, "Are you just getting this off your chest, man. Or do you actually expect me to do something about it?" he asked incredulously.

"Well, I was sort of hoping you could fix it in some way. You know Roger, you know what makes him tick. Maybe you could talk him down a little, see if he will give us some leeway – like giving up the British Overseas Territory malarkey."

"Dave, you know as well as I do that this was not one man's whim. This was the democratic choice of the Cornish people and it has been ratified now. It's a done deal, old man, Roger is Governor of the British Overseas Territory, now known as the Isle of Kernow. Now I hate democracy as much as the next man, but there's no sweeping this under the carpet, for Charlie-Boy, or anyone else for that matter."

"Well, I've got to do something."

"Or at least look like you are doing something?"

Cameron took a second to get Brownly-Smith's drift. "Yes," he started slowly, "as long as I *look* like I'm doing something that might do the trick."

Chapter 2

Pentwen

Jake was slumped on the massive beanbag, sipping hot coffee whilst watching Mitch sanding a surfboard that he was shaping. They were availing themselves of the hospitality of Ray Jordan who owned the Surf Shack, Pentwen's oldest surf shop. When they weren't at work, or surfing, they were sitting on Ray's porch, on the various beanbags, benches, and most recently a hammock, watching the surf and talking about surf.

Ray was pleased of their company. Even though Ray was older by some margin, it had been Jake, Mitch, along with their friends Sully and Hog, who had kept him going when he thought all had been lost. His livelihood had been threatened by the plans of Royale, a budget cruise company, who intended to dredge the bay to allow for their gigantic cruise ships to dock. Although Jake's parents had been complicit in the plan with Royale, Jake and the newcomer Lloyd Bray, had used a range of equally underhanded methods to scupper it. As a result Ray now had a thriving business, expanded by the Isle's new laws on property ownership.

On the basis of the new legislation, any land that was not being utilised could be appropriated if its use had a positive impact on the community. The condition of any land appropriation was that a percentage of the income was returned to the community, and that the land and any buildings erected on it, could not be sold on, but were returned to the community. There had been a scrap of land adjacent to the Surf Shack that no one seemed to own, which the local surfers had always used as a car park. Ray, and his wife Holly, had used some of the land to build eco-pods; funky looking wooden rooms, each with a shower and kitchenette. All of the power supplied to the pods coming from solar and wind sources. They had become so popular, especially with the more affluent surfers, that Holly was struggling to find the time to run the local backpackers and do change-over on the eco-pods.

Jake was checking his weather app for the following day as all the boys were off work and were planning a surf trip up the coast if conditions were right. He was aware of approaching footsteps, but was too engrossed in his research to look up.

"Where do you guys recommend we paddle out?"

Looking up, through his mop of dark fringe, Jake was astounded to see two gorgeous girls, in their early twenties, wearing wetsuits, and carrying boards that were definitely not hired. Before he could scramble to his feet Mitch was on it. In his seductive Aussie drawl he said, "Well ladies, you've come to the right bloke. I know just about every break on the Isle. So," smiling his widest, whitest smile, "just what is it you're looking for?"

"Some clean, fun, three foot waves to start with I think," said the shorter, curvy girl with strawberry-blond ringlets and a freckled nose.

"Then you've come to the right spot on the right day. In fact," he said glancing at Jake for encouragement, "My mate, Jake, and I were just about to get suited and booted too. Do you fancy some company?" smiling that smile again.

The smile seemed to work, as ringlets-and-freckles referred to her friend briefly before accepting the invitation. The boys were up in a flash, donning wetsuits and grabbing their boards that they left in the rack at the Surf Shack.

"Later, Ray," Mitch shouted over his shoulder. Ray was left standing and laughing to himself at the abandonment of youth.

"No worries," he shouted back sarcastically. "I'll just clear all this mess up," he continued nodding towards the sandpaper and half sanded board, but they weren't listening – they were halfway down the beach.

Mitch had obviously taken a shine to ringlets-and-freckles who turned out to be called Meg. They walked ahead chatting about the North Bay break. Jake introduced himself with a shyly mumbled, "Hi. I'm Jake."

She replied equally quietly, "Hi. I'm Elle."

Neither daring to make eye contact. Jake and Elle walked behind Mitch and Meg in silence, Jake desperately trying to think of something witty or intelligent to say to the tall, slender girl with sleek black hair. "You on holiday?" was the best he could muster.

"Not really. We're students."

Jake nodded, not really understanding whether this mean they were or weren't on holiday.

She must have noticed his bewildered look. "I mean, we're doing a Business and Tourism Management degree and need to find work placements."

"Oh, cool," Jake replied, cringing at his inability to construct a meaningful sentence. "So how long do you do the placement for?"

"A year," she replied. "It's for our Year in Industry module."

Jake nodded, impressed. But if she was a student, then she'd be really intelligent. Now he was slightly worried that she would be out of his league.

"Everyone else on the course has gone to the usual places: London, or theme parks, or bucket and spade seaside resorts. But we thought it would be great to do something where we could catch some surf and some sunshine."

"Logical. So why not try Thailand, or even Auz? Ha, Mitch could give you some pointers of the best places to go."

"No, it has to be in Britain for the module."

"Bummer."

"Yeah, I know. I think too many people were using it as an excuse to party in Ibiza for a year, so they changed it. Britain only."

"I get it. Kernow gives you the best of both worlds."

"Yep. And technically we're still on British territory."

"Cool thinking. I guess you've come to the right place then," Jake replied, not really knowing what else to say as he knew nothing about Universities or industry placement years. To fill the silence he pointed to the best paddle out places, and where to look for rip currents, feeling more in control again.

They had a great surf, the boys showing off their local knowledge, but were equally impressed that the girls could hold their own in the water. Meg was a little ripper, charging around on the waves frenetically, and whooping with fun. Elle was more serene, calm and graceful. As the girls were paddling back out, Mitch paddled over to Jake. "Wow man. I mean how cool are they? And total hotties!"

"I know. Totally."

"I bet they're only here on vacation though, right?"

"Nope! Students on a placement year or something."

"Oh my lord! We better show them the town then."

They arranged to meet the girls later that night in the bar of the North Bay Hotel. Since the Drift the town of Pentwen had been the recipient of eco-town status, and as a result of their drive towards sustainable tourism they were the first whole town to have achieved such status, previously only managed by eco-friendly holiday parks. The North Bay Hotel had spearheaded the eco-town campaign, leading the way for the more nervous business owners to watch, then follow. Eventually they had seen the benefits and had invested in the project. Pentwen had changed beyond all recognition. It had changed visually, through investment in new properties, all of which needed to be built from sustainably sourced materials, and had to be built sympathetically by blending in with the environment. Any proposed new buildings, or extensions to old ones, were scrutinised using new criteria, and the new planning regulations were really starting to make the place look more appealing.

There were also other standards that each business needed to meet, aiming to run to a near zero carbon footprint by employing renewable energy sources wherever it was deemed reasonable. They had built a wind field in an area of the dunes to the north of North Bay. The windmills designed to be sleek and stylish and had been painted to look like giant flowers; green stems with yellow blades. So beautifully had the windfarm been designed that it won an international design award and had featured in many news articles challenging the nimbyism of many UK residents resisting windfarms in their area.

In addition, buildings were temperature controlled through geothermic heat exchanges, which heats and cools without burning fossil fuels. An expensive investment, but it was really starting to pay. Not only was it saving money, but it was saving the planet and not contributing to global warming. This fact alone brought many new visitors to a town that they would never have considered visiting before the Drift.

Jake's parents owned the North Bay Hotel. Dave and Maureen Miller had moved from south London to Pentwen when Jake had been a nipper. They had run the hotel in an old-fashioned style, where their only concern was how to get the customers to spend more.

After the Drift the Millers had been instrumental in encouraging the budget cruise company to buy up all of the seafront properties in order to dredge the bay for docking, and to build a monstrous mall and hotel spa facility. After the deal fell through the Millers saw the light, or at least they saw the cash value of moving towards an ecological approach to tourism. As this was really not their area of expertise they handed the reins over to Jake who had made the North Bay Hotel an eco-boutique hotel, drawing in a whole new sort of customer. This suited Dave and Maureen just fine. They used the increased income to go on holidays and cruises – ironically these cruises were about as tasteful as the ones that Royale had intended to run to Pentwen.

When they were on the Isle the Millers liked to keep their hand in. Dave could generally be found manning the hotel bar where he aimed to keep the customers chatting for as long as possible for two reasons. One, they would spend more. And two, he loved to share the benefit of his extensive local knowledge with anyone that would listen. Maureen could often be found on reception where she took a rather sycophantic approach to the customers. Her obsequiousness was enough to make the skin crawl, and on more than one occasion it had been mentioned that she was not unlike Sybil from Fawlty Towers.

Dave and Maureen used to cover the breakfasts and lunches, but since the overhaul, they employed Jess who had worked at some classy hotels in St Ives. Jess ran a tight ship, her reputation riding on whatever reached the dining room tables, and she was not going to compromise that for anything.

Jake and Mitch were already in the hotel bar. They looked at each other, taking stock. "Nice shirt, but couldn't you have brushed your hair?" Jake said, laughing at Mitch.

"No dice, man," Mitch replied running his hand over his sun-bleached hair. "A comb goes anywhere near these locks and I look like a poodle!"

The girls arrived, fashionably late. Jake and Mitch waved them over to the table, trying to keep their tongues in their mouths at the vision of the two girls. Meg was sporting well-cut shorts and a halter neck top in a shimmering silvery-grey, showing off her curves to the maximum. Elle wore a long sundress in deep turquoise and green cotton. 'Stunning,' thought Jake, concerned that he would not be able to construct a meaningful sentence without stuttering or dribbling.

"What do you lovely ladies want to drink?" Mitch asked jumping to his feet and pulling out a chair for Meg with uncharacteristic chivalry.

"I'll have a lager, please," Meg replied, Mitch's heart melting at her chosen beverage.

"I'll have glass of red," Elle added, Jake crumbling at the worry that she was far too sophisticated for him.

After chatting about the earlier surf Mitch asked about their plans.

"We're on a placement year," Meg explained. "We have to do at least six months working in tourism in Britain."

"Why?" Mitch enquired. "I mean I bet most people on the course have already worked in the tourist industry already. Otherwise they wouldn't have applied for the course, right?"

"Fair point." Meg started. "But we have to do more than just work there. We have to identify an issue and write reports surrounding the issues, possibly working towards resolving the issue."

"Cool," was Mitch's intellectual response.

"So where are you working then?" Jake ventured.

The girls exchanged glances. "That's the first hurdle really," Elle replied. "We kinda came on spec. We don't actually have anything lined up as yet."

"We thought we'd wing it and see what turned up once we got here."

"Risky!" Mitch exclaimed.

"Yes. But I believe all things will turn out right with a positive attitude," Elle said gently whilst catching Jake's eye. Jake just blushed and focused on his bottle of Korev.

"What sort of jobs do you need?" Mitch asked.

"Oh, it literally doesn't matter as long as it's considered part of the tourist provision in the district that you work."

"So what? Waitressing? Chamber-maiding? KP-ing? That sort of stuff?"

"Yes. It can be service, or retail, as long as we can demonstrate links to the tourist economy."

"Well," Mitch started, trying and failing to catch Jake's attention, "we might know some places to start looking, hey Jake?"

"Yes. Possibly," Jake replied cagily, not liking where the conversation was going.

"So how abouts we show you the only other bar in North Bay?" Mitch said laughing, trying to bring up the mood.

All agreed that they should move on, so the boys led the way down the street to the Bay Bar, a 1960s low level concrete building. Formerly ice-cream parlour, it had been converted some decades ago into a bar and live music venue. Story was that back in the day it had been quite a go-to venue, but over time it had become seedy and somewhat unloved. The upturn that the rest of Pentwen had experienced had not impacted on the Bay Bar because Jem Meacher, its unreconstructed hippy owner, didn't have the vision to get involved further than the obvious eco agendas. This said, the boys quite liked the place, despite itself.

The place was buzzing as they entered, evident only from the noise, as the low level lighting made it difficult to see what was going on. They moved past dark coloured velvet-look sofas towards a bar at the back which was slightly better lit than the rest of the room. Two guys with limp shoulder length hair and poor posture stood at the bar drinking from bottles of beer. When they saw Mitch and Jake there were high fives all round. Then Jake introduced Meg and Elle to Sully and Hog. The two men said something that sounded like "owroit" but the girls could not be sure, so smiled and nodded their hellos.

"They're Brummies," Jake offered by way of explanation.

"Cool," Meg replied enthusiastically, although Jake couldn't fathom what was cool about being a Brummie.

The man behind the bar had long, stringy grey hair, evidently well into his sixties, but dressed as though he'd just left the sixties. He handed over four bottles of beer, leering at Elle which made her skin crawl. Jake quickly directed them up a few steps to a booth at the back. There were two long sofas with throw cushions in fuchsia and orange. They curled up on the sofas and took in the sights. There were psychedelic lights creating oil slicks of intense colour across all objects in their path. The décor and light show were somewhat at odds with the music. There seemed to be a random selection playing from occasional late sixties guitar hits from the likes of Clapton, to mid-nineties Britpop.

As the booth also seemed to be lined in dark velvet it absorbed some of the sound allowing for near normal conversations to be held.

"This place is totally mad," Meg offered, giggling.

"I know. It's totally cheesy but it kinda works," Mitch replied.

"Is it like this every night?"

"Mostly, although if you're really lucky they dig up some ancient blues band from the seventeen hundreds who play gigs on the stage over there."

Meg laughed. "Is the owner the bloke behind that bar that totally looks like cat-weasel?"

"Yep. That's Jem. Apparently, he was a guy back in the day. Played for some band that no one's ever heard of, and still thinks he's god's gift to music today."

"Stuck in a time warp more like."

They hung out chatting and drinking for about an hour when Elle said it was about time they left as they needed to be bright-eyed and bushy-tailed for a day spent job hunting. Mitch made nodding motions to Jake who refused to bite. They walked the girls back to the backpackers in the town and agreed that there would be texts exchanged the next day to arrange something if they were all free.

"Oh my lord, as if we won't be free for those little cuties, eh mate?" Mitch exclaimed when they were out of earshot of the backpackers.

"I do have to be at work tomorrow," Jake replied more soberly. "Not like you layabout shapers."

"Yeah, but you are the boss really. You can take time out."

"It's not quite as easy as that. There's still guests to deal with. Someone's got to check them in and pour their drinks."

"Yeah, so why didn't you offer Elle and Meg a job there? I mean you must need someone to help out, what with the season on its way, and all?"

"But it's not totally up to me. And then there's the problem of me having to tell her what to do."

"Yeah, but it's not forever. And if they can't find jobs they may leave." Mitch just left it hanging in the air.

"Don't guilt trip me, Mitch. It's not fair."

"Well at least think about it. And have a word with your old man – I'm sure once he sees them he wouldn't think twice."

"Christ Mitch. The last thing I want is my old man leching at them. Yuck."

Chapter 3

Kernow airport
Martin Brownly-Smith pulled his two enormous suitcases behind him and was almost blown off his feet as he exited the airport. Not only was the wind strong, it was also warm. Surprisingly warm. Reminding him of the Sirocco winds of north Africa, 'God, maybe they've drifted off again,' he said to himself, as he battled against it to find his hire car.

He found his Audi Q7, it's perfect white paintjob masked by a covering of what looked like red sand that had been deposited with the rain. He clicked the fob and saw its light spring into action. Satisfied, he loaded his cases, adjusted the driver's seat, fiddled with the in-car tech until he had located Classic FM and was blasted by ear-splitting levels of Boccherini's Cello Concerto No.9 in Bb major. He quickly punched at the display until the sound was bearable. "Dum dee dur, dum dee dur," he shouted along in accompaniment as he foraged in his bag for the details of his accommodation. He read the document and typed into the Satnav the paltry information that he had been given; THE TREWARGET ARMS, DUMGARTH.

He swished along the Glynn Valley, the Audi hugging the corners like glue. He was overwhelmed by the greenness, the sweeping hillsides and overhead canopy of trees, with the river meandering alongside each time the road descended. This was complemented by Beethoven's Piano Concerto No. 3. Oh, how he loved his job. He reflected on what the week had instore for him. Oh yes, to stay on the Isle of Kernow, all expenses paid by the British tax payer, and to see if he could do anything to appease old Charley-Boy regarding the British Overseas Territory issue. Obviously he could not do this by himself, so he had requested Carlotta, his very *personal* personal assistant, to fly out on Friday and assist him – Mrs B-S would be none the wiser!

An hour later he had pulled up outside an old stone pub, squat and square, with no redeeming features. It was un adorned and slightly austere. 'Why have they sent me to this god-forsaken hell hole,' he muttered under his breath as he entered the main bar. It had a look of old pub about it, but not that of beams and horse brasses, but of faded and slightly grubby magnolia and an inordinate amount of fishing memorabilia.

The man behind the bar was in his mid-forties with sandy, curly hair. "How can I help you?" the barman asked.

"Ah. Yes. I am Martin Brownly-Smith. I believe you are expecting me?" he said hoping to god the answer was 'no' and he could go and find alternative accommodation somewhere more salubrious than The Trewarget Arms.

"Ah, yes Mr Brownly-Smith. I'm Doug Gover, the landlord. I'll just call my wife who deals with the accommodation," he replied, and opening a door behind the bar he yelled at the top of his voice, "Dee! Dee? The man from the Ministry's ere!"

A similar aged woman with over fashioned hair and far too much make-up tottered in, hand outstretched. "Mr Smith, how lovely to see you."

"Brownly, Brownly-Smith," he interjected.

"Oh, of course. Brownly. Very nice to make your acquaintance," she continued in a faux posh accent. "If you would like to follow me?" and she tottered ahead of him whilst he manhandled his two enormous suitcases up the stairs, unaided.

He half-listened to her wittering on about how 'Whitehall keeps the room reserved for any visiting civil servants and the such,' and 'did he know the nice Brian Clough who was the government scientist and the lovely Mr Stiles,' and on she went. He pretended not to know any of the people she mentioned as he did not want them to be aware that he was on the island – for now.

He unpacked and undressed, hanging up his suit in the vast wardrobe and stood in huge white boxer shorts contemplating appropriate attire for a place like Dumgarth. Having decided that he had nothing appropriate he selected casual slacks in beige, a blue and white bold-striped shirt and some navy leather deck shoes. Now he was ready to explore.

Firing up the Audi and turning up the volume on the radio he sped off towards the A38 and the open road. He was heading to a fishing village called Porthissick where he had heard that Roger Stiles had lived before becoming the Governor of Kernow. His plan was to get to know the people there and see if there was any gossip that might compromise Roger's reputation. He might be able to use it as leverage in bringing this whole political debacle to some sort of end, retuning Cornwall to the status quo. He turned off the A38 and followed his Satnav's instructions through country lanes that meandered at will, no sign that a Roman had ever set foot here.

He eventually entered a village square that had not been touched by the 21st century. Classic. He parked in a little carpark by the waterside and wandered about soaking up the atmosphere of the traditional working harbour. The smell of salt water and rotting fish. There was the cawing of the gulls that were hovering above a trawler as it pulled into port, and men busy at the dockside ready to receive its load.

He turned towards the square, noting a grocers, a newsagents, a tourist shop with lilos and beach toys displayed outside, tied together by washing line to stop them blowing away. On the opposite side of the square sat a pub with a traditional hand-painted sign proclaiming it to be The Anchor. There were trestle tables outside and a chalk board announcing the guest beer this week was Atlantic Brewery's Pilgrim ale. 'Just the ticket' Brownly-Smith thought, where better to look for gossip than a pub.

He entered the saloon bar and immediately felt the ambiance of traditional pub. Unlike The Trewarget Arms, this pub had the old-style feel. Dark wood beams and furniture, with red velvet seating. Old photographs depicting the working harbour throughout time, and various sea-related knick-knacks, an anchor hanging in pride of place against the back wall. A tall dark-haired man in his twenties was drying glasses behind the bar. "Afternoon. What can I get you?"

"I'll have a G and T please."

"What sort of gin would you like? We have Trevethan, Caspyn's, and Tarquin's of course."

Brownly-Smith listened, somewhat confused. "Ah. No Gordon's?"

"Nope. Not since the Drift?"

Baffled as to why that should be, he ordered a Tarquin's and found a table by the window so he could look out at the beer garden, which seemed to be prematurely in bloom with pink and purple fuchsias. He looked at his watch, prompted by the rumbling of his stomach and realised that he had not eaten for six hours. He called over to the barman, "Do you serve lunch?"

"We've got some homemade pasties outback?"

Brownly-Smith had never eaten a pasty before, but 'when in Rome' he thought. "Yes, thank you. I'll take a pasty."

Stewie shouted through to Carrie in the kitchen to heat up a pasty, and continued his glass drying. Stewie had recently taken over the running of The Anchor when his Aunt, Aggie Wetherill the village matriarch, had moved in with her partner, Roger Stiles the Governor of Kernow. The saying that behind every great man is a great woman was never truer when it came to their relationship. Roger, sent by Whitehall to manage the Drift, fell hopelessly in love with Aggie, even leaving his wife for her. It was Aggie's honesty and vision that led to opportunities for the people of Cornwall to come together and have their say on the future, ultimately leading to their self-governance. When Roger, somewhat bizarrely, was made Governor, making Aggie the First Lady, she felt that she could not dedicate sufficient time to running the pub.

Her nephew Stewie had been working with her for years, and since his engagement to the beautiful and buxom Carrie Down, it seemed appropriate to hand over the reins to them. Carrie was the daughter of a poacher-turned chicken farmer, who was pathologically protective over his daughter. If it hadn't have been for an unfortunate incident where Stewie threw some over-amorous French fishermen into the harbour for making inappropriate advances to her, Stewie would probably never have convinced Jim Down that he was the man to marry his daughter. The agreement was that they would run the pub together and she would continue to live with her father at Down's Farm until they were 'wed good and proper' as Jim put it. There was many a night that Stewie was thankful to those Frenchies.

Carrie came out with the pasty on a plate and took it over to Brownly-Smith. "Here you go, Sir. Mind though – it hot." She returned to the bar and started to count up the bottles of tonic for restocking when the portly man in the unusually bright clothes returned to the bar.

"I think you forgot my cutlery?" he questioned.

"Yes. Of course, sir. I'll bring it straight over." She and Stewie exchanged amused glances before she took over the requested knife and fork.

She returned to the bar where they supressed sniggers with their hands – cutlery for a pasty – who had ever heard of anything so ridiculous? Carrie pulled her phone out of her pocket and made it look as though she was texting while she surreptitiously took a photo of the ridiculous man eating a pasty with cutlery – she had never seen anything like it before.

Chapter 4

Truro

As New County Hall was situated in Truro, Governor Roger Stiles needed to spend a fair proportion of his time in the city. For that reason he had a small apartment overlooking the river where he and Aggie stayed when there were late meetings or events in the city that required their attendance. Whenever they could they preferred to stay at their tumbledown cottage in Porthissick.

Rose Cottage was the antithesis of anywhere Roger had lived before. In his previous life he had always preferred slick city apartments, with stylish contemporary interior design, not unlike his dress sense, but something had happened to him since he had moved to Cornwall. No more Canali suits or Gieves and Hawkes double cuff classic white shirts. Now it was chinos and casual shirts, except at meetings, and then he would dispense with the tie if he could get away with it.

Today was a no-tie day. Today there was a meeting of the Food Sourcing Network. The Food Sourcing Network had come about as a response to the Drift, when all supermarkets mothballed their stores because the parent companies deemed it too expensive to supply off-shore – essentially leaving the county to starve. To pre-empt the impending food shortage the people of Cornwall took it upon themselves to be resourceful and ensure that they could become self-sufficient, so they would not need to rely on the mainland for anything.

Roger knew that Aggie had been instrumental in the initiation of the network, but had got wind that their means had not always been above board. He had made a point of remaining as ignorant about their methods as possible, so he was in no way compromised. It was the resourcefulness of the network which really made him believe that Cornwall could go it alone.

They walked up Station Road, the headwind blowing Aggie's unruly auburn curls into her face. Roger grinned at her vain attempts to capture the wayward locks and contain them in an elasticated band. Although he had only known Aggie for a year, their romance had been gradual and natural, somewhat mirroring the decline of his marriage to his wife and his job in Whitehall. He and Aggie complemented each other, and he was convinced he had met his soul mate in her. He was not the person he had been when he first met her, and he was sure that some would say she had changed him, but he was more convinced that Cornwall had changed him, and she was indeed part of that. He didn't really care what others thought anymore. He had never been so happy and fulfilled in his life.

They were on their way to the meeting and as they walked past the fenced off Old County Hall Aggie asked, "When is something going to be done with the this. It's such a tragic waste of a building."

"I totally agree. It was sold off for peanuts years ago. Apparently the buyer couldn't raise enough capital to transform it into some up-market hotel and spa. So there it sits, derelict and wasted."

"But can't you do something about it?"

"We are looking into the possibilities. Under the 'vibrant and flourishing communities' section of the British Overseas Territory White Paper we are reviewing whether a minimum residential occupancy criteria can be introduced, and what we can do to manage the abandoned properties of absentee landlords."

"Good to hear," she said demonstratively.

They met, as usual, in the boardroom at New County Hall. Already seated were James and Audrey Sproken-Jones, blow-ins from the Southeast who had retired to Porthissick three years ago and had become integrated into the community there as a result of the Drift. That's not to say that they had been welcomed with open arms. A retired accountant and former PR executive were not the norm in the village, but their resourcefulness and commitment had won the majority of locals round. Audrey had developed the website that the Network relied on for communication and James had been instrumental in some of the less legal aspects of the Network, circumventing official channels to ensure that communities still had access to the basics – although Aggie made sure that Roger had never been made aware of this element of the Network's activities.

In walked five more members of the committee. Four of them were former regional managers from Costmart, the supermarket that had mothballed all their stores and distribution depots as soon as the Drift had occurred. They were kept on retainer from Costmart to keep an eye on their assets on the Isle until Costmart decided what ultimate action to take. Nicolas Nugent, Thomas Wetherill, David Hare and the rather scary Harriet Mallinder were all in attendance based on their understanding of perishable turnover, per capita stock flow and seasonal trends. The last member of their group was Joanne Varcoe, Nicolas Nugent's mousey former secretary who had been instrumental in getting this group together. Since the Drift Joanne had been in charge of sourcing toiletries.

Late to the meeting was Malcolm Roberson and Martin Evans. Malcolm was a second homeowner who, due to his fear of flying, had become stranded after the Drift, and Martin Evans previously the manager of Cotehele Mill, but since the Drift had become Malcolm's business partner. The pair had formed a team ensuring that flour and paper were still milled on the Isle of Kernow so importation could be avoided.

"Sorry we're late," Malcolm apologised, whilst taking his seat.

"Trouble at mill?" Harriet Mallinder said in a mock northern accent, taking the micky whilst studiously ignoring Roger's glare.

Aggie pottered about handing out coffee cups and put a new range of biscuits on a plate that Carrie Down was trialling – happy to receive feedback from the group before she went into production.

"Lovely biscuits, Aggie. Did you make them?" Audrey asked.

"No! I'm not much good at anything except scones. These are Carrie's latest; apple and cinnamon cookies. What do you think?"

"Bloody brilliant," Harriet replied aggressively.

"Absolutely," Audrey agreed. From the way the men were tucking into the plate Aggie guessed that the feedback was unanimous.

"Thank you all for making time in your schedule for the meeting today," Roger started. "So, on the agenda we have the following: drinks, distribution, website and imports. Does anyone have anything else they wish to add?" he looked around and all were shaking their heads.

"Okay. So we'll start with drinks. Where are with this?"

"With respect to alcohol," Audrey started, tapping her gold pen on her pad as she went down the list, "we are all good. With have a good range of brewers of various sizes, more vineyards coming on line with the change in climate, and an increasing number of distillers since we have changed the legal requirements. In fact gin is one of our top exports this month."

"That's all well and good," Harriet interrupted, "but they better leave some of the bloody stuff for us – I mean that's the point isn't it, self-sufficiency?"

"There's plenty left for us, don't panic, Harriet." Audrey continued, "With respect to carbonated drinks we have an increasing amount of suppliers coming on line too, spearheaded by Cornish Orchards there are now quite a few new orchards using their fruit for drinks, especially sparkling drinks."

As part of the Executive Council's health agenda, there were very strict new laws on how much sugar and salt could be added to processed food and drink. As such, fizzy drinks were banned as they did not fall within the new legislative parameters. These were being replaced with sparkling drinks where the sugar came primarily from the fruit, and not from refined sugar.

"How soon will new suppliers be able to supply," David Hare asked. "We are getting closer to summer and we have two unknown unknowns."

"Which are?" Roger asked.

"Firstly, we have no idea how hot we will be in the new climate. If we assume it will be the same as last year then we know it will be hot – therefore more people will want cold drinks, and as we have banned fizzy drink manufacture and importation, the sparkling drinks will probably make up the difference."

Roger nodded, jotting a note down, "And the second unknown unknown?"

"Tourism. We have no idea what's likely to happen. We have had over a year for the Isle to settle so the world can see we are not likely to capsize. The tourist industry has had a year to create a need, and to market that need around the world," David concluded.

"Good point," Audrey interrupted, back in PR mode. "Not only are we a short haul flight to a long-haul island destination, we also have the added bonus of the eco-town and the surf industry."

So far it was unknown what impact Pentwen's eco-town status would have on tourism. The commitment of the Chamber of Commerce and local council, combined with advice from eco-tourism specialist Dr Jeannette O'Loughlin, transformed the town bit by bit to one with a zero-carbon footprint, and all new development had to be sustainable. The entrepreneurs of the town had maximised the opportunity, turning holiday accommodation into boutique eco-pods, offering holiday experiences as beautiful and exciting as the Caribbean, and contributing towards a sustainable environment.

To add to the tourist bounty was the result of the tectonic shift which had left the Isle of Kernow in the path of world-class surf. This had been noted by the surfing fraternity, and North Bay at Pentwen had hosted the first surf tour competition in the winter – to great acclaim.

"I think we need to look into this more. Aggie, can you contact the Tourist Board and establish whether they have any information on bookings for the coming season? I think we may need to circulate findings if there does look like there will be an upturn in numbers."

There was the noise of pencils scratching at pads before Roger continued, "So this will also link to distribution too, I guess?"

"Yes," David Hare continued. "We'll need to know where the hot spots are – no pun intended -" There were groans from around the table. "- and need to reconsider the distribution schedule. We might need to increase deliveries to coastal areas during peak season."

"Do we have enough vehicles to deal with this potential demand?"

Roger was blissfully unaware that the current transportation system, which was essentially the liberation of Costmart's refrigerated lorries and trucks, put to a practical use. Costmart were also blissfully unaware of this arrangement, assuming their trucks were still neatly tucked away in their redundant depots.

"We're all good for transportation, thank you Roger," Harriet said very curtly to prevent any further probing of the issue.

"Okay, so moving along. Website?" Roger said turning to Audrey.

There was a pinging noise and Aggie looked down at her phone, she looked up, somewhat embarrassed and stifling a snigger. "Sorry," she said, blushing.

Roger raised his eyebrows admonishingly. "Sorry Audrey, continue."

"Yes. The website's just about coping so I have asked a local firm to work with some students to review what we have currently, and what our potential needs will be, and see if they can develop something more reliable and fit for purpose."

"What a lovely idea, Audrey," Aggie offered.

"I thought it might be nice, and possibly if we expand we might be able to employ one of the students to keep us technically up to date." A suggestion that was met with much earnest head nodding from all.

They talked at length about their IT needs so Audrey could take this forward.

"Right. Lastly imports -"

There was complex noise omitted from Harriet, a combination of a sigh and a spit. Roger raised his eyebrows in curiosity.

"Imports! Pah, what do we need to import? We don't need help from them miserly bean-counters who left us high and fucking dry. We don't want to line their pockets with our hard earned cash. Screw them!"

There was an uncomfortable silence for a moment, broken by Roger, "- so nothing to report on imports then?"

The group looked at one another nervously, so Roger decided to bring the meeting to a close and deal with imports at another time.

As they were walking back to Roger's office, he asked Aggie, "What were you sniggering about in the meeting?"

"Ha, sorry about that. I forgot to put it on silent," she said as she fished her phone out of her handbag. "But look at this photo that Carrie sent from the pub – it's bloody hysterical!" she said handing the phone to Roger.

Roger looked at the image and stopped in his tracks. "What the bloody hell?!" he exclaimed, possibly louder than he intended, heads of clerical staff turning curiously in his direction. Aggie looked perplexed. It was a funny photo of a tourist in ludicrous clothing eating a pasty with cutlery – what was there to be so angry about?

"You know who this is, don't you?" he said angrily.

"No," Aggie replied tentatively, feeling as if she had done something wrong.

"This is Brownly-Smith! Martin Brownly-Smith."

"The pompous guy from Whitehall? The one that got you the job?"

"Well, the one that recommended me for the role as Governor. What the bloody hell is he doing here. Or more specifically – there? Let's face it, he hardly just happened to be off-shore, and just happened to pop into a pub in a village in the middle of nowhere. My local pub!"

"Maybe he was looking for you, darling?"

"Did Carrie say that he asked for me?"

"Well no. She just thought it was funny that someone would eat a pasty with cutlery."

"Exactly. If he wanted to see me he would have called in advance, and probably demanded a lift from the airport."

"So maybe he's on holiday, I mean this is not exactly office wear," she said pointing at the man's ridiculous outfit.

"I smell a rat. A big, fat, stinking rat. You mark my words." He entered his office and sat heavily at his desk, deep in thought. Suddenly he perked up. "Can you forward me the photo?"

"Sure," she said nervously, knowing he was up to no good.

He picked up his phone and typed:
BROWNLY-SMITH HAS SNUCK IN UNDER THE RADAR. I'M SURE HE'S HERE TO MAKE TROUBLE AS HE HAS NOT BEEN IN CONTACT BUT WAS SPOTTED IN PORTHISSICK
PLEASE CIRCULATE AND LET ME KNOW IF AND WHEN YOU SEE HIM.
PHOTO ATTACHED
and then sent to some of his trusted contacts on the Isle.

Chapter 5

Pentwen

Sully, not known for his dedication or hard work at any of his previous employers, had only taken the job as pot-washer at The Lobster Pot Café in order to spy on the owner, George Tanner. George, and two other local business owners, had been trying to sell their properties and beach access to Royale, the cruise company with all the morals of Attila the Hun. Sully had taken the job at the café to help sabotage their plan from the inside and hadn't quite got round to leaving, even though they had long since ruined the cruise company's evil plan.

One of the organisers of the sabotage team was Lloyd Bray, a reporter for The Times – and now their Kernow correspondent. Lloyd had received Roger's text and had forwarded it on to all of his Kernow connections. It was this text that Sully was holding up next to the café serving hatch whilst trying to establish if the gaudily dressed man eating at one of the outside tables was the same man in the photo – and he was quite convinced he was. "All royt if I take a fag break, boss?" Sully asked George in his native Brummie accent.

"Sure, Sully," George replied, glancing at his watch.

Sully wandered outside, sat on the wall surrounding the café's garden, and lit up a rollie. Casually he picked up his phone and made it look as though he was taking a panoramic video shot as a means of capturing the man's image. He texted the photo back to Lloyd, who forwarded it on to Roger.

Roger replied:
THAT'S DEFINITELY HIM. WHERE WAS THIS TAKEN AND HOW LONG AGO?

Lloyd wrote:
> CAFÉ IN PENTWEN, NORTH BAY AREA. I THINK HE'S STILL THERE. DO YOU WANT ME TO TAIL HIM?

Roger:
> ONLY IF YOU HAVE THE TIME. IT WOULD BE GOOD TO KNOW WHAT HE'S UP TO!

Lloyd:
> I'M ON IT!

Lloyd drove his van up to the layby overlooking North Bay where he could look over the cliff and see which way Brownly-Smith exited, ready to follow him. As he waited he recalled the first time he had been to this very layby, and how what he had witnessed that day had changed his life forever. He had been on a cultural tour of Cornwall, which was focusing on Cornwall in the movies, when they stopped and looked down at the beach. What he saw that day were huge letters drawn in the sand saying *hands off our beach*, and out at sea he had seen a line of people in boats and canoes, and on surfboards and body boards, blocking the access of a survey vessel that was trying to establish whether the seafloor was deep enough to allow in huge cruise ships. Lloyd had taken a picture of the scene and sent it to the Sunday Times, who had published a story on the plight of Pentwen, all playing a part in stopping the cruise ships venture.

His reverie was interrupted by a text from Sully:
> MAN ON THE MOVE!

Lloyd replied:
> CAR OR ON FOOT?

Sully:
> WHITE AUDI. FLASH.

Lloyd:
> CHEERS

Lloyd jumped back in his van ready to pull out after the Audi. He followed the car out of Pentwen, and did his damnedest to keep up with him as the Audi drove at speeds inappropriate for the winding roads. He was relieved as they approached the A30, but on the open road the Audi accelerated off, Lloyd's van struggling to keep up. The old 2001 Renault Trafic was only used to pootle from one surf break to another, or to a slowly evolving news story, not hare after mad civil servants. Luckily Lloyd saw the Audi indicate to pull off at the A38, where he followed him at a distance, ending up in Dumgarth.

Lloyd called Roger. "You will never in a million years guess where he's staying, Roger!"

"So tell me then!"

"Dumgarth! In the very same pub we met at last year!"

"Ah, that sort of makes sense."

"Really? How come?"

"Because I think Whitehall keeps a room on lease there in case they need accommodation at short notice. Do you remember I was with Brian Clough that night we met? He had been brought in by Whitehall to do the science thing, and that is where he stayed before he moved off with Callum."

Chapter 6

Dumgarth

Tired after his day ambling about the Isle, Brownly-Smith was eager to relax. He took a bath back and came downstairs to the bar for dinner as he did not feel like driving again today. He perused the menu with distain. No foie gras or steak tartare. Instead the options were gammon (with a choice of pineapple ring or egg), battered fish, or steak and kidney pie, all served with chips. 'It's just for this evening' he thought, stealing himself for the ordeal. Tomorrow, he and his delightful *personal* personal assistant Carlotta, would be dining together he thought. He made a mental note to spend the morning finding a suitable restaurant, and hopefully a more salubrious hotel room.

The pie was surprisingly nice, served with a thick gravy and a pile of peas. It made him think of meals at his grandmother's when he was a lad; comforting and filling. He approached the bar to order a post-dinner brandy when a woman entered. She was possibly in her mid-60s with refined cheekbones and Mary Quant styled hair, bobbed and in its natural grey. She cut an impressive image.

"After you," he said gesturing to the bar.

"Why thank you," she replied, flashing him an aristocratic smile.

"In fact, let me get this for you," he offered, returning her smile.

"Sorry," Doug interjected from behind the bar. "Let me introduce you. Mr Brownly-Smith, this is Lady Rosemary Du Pont."

"Rosie, please. I hardly call you Mr Gover do I, Doug?" she laughed.

Taking her hand in both of his, Brownly-Smith raised it to his lips and said, "It's an honour to make your acquaintance, Lady Rosie."

She laughed flirtatiously whilst desperately trying to remove her hand from between his fleshy, sweaty palms. "In that case, I will have a glass of your finest, dry white please, Doug," she responded whilst climbing seamlessly onto the barstool. Brownly-Smith decided to join her, struggling to make the transition so smoothly.

As Roger had requested, Lady Rosemary stayed for an hour listening to Brownly-Smith's self-promoting tales of grandeur in the heart of government, liberally sprinkled with references to 'Dave and I'. She smiled at all the appropriate places, looking suitably impressed where necessary. Before she left she offered an open invitation for him to visit Athelstan House and said she would give him a tour of the magnificent gardens. Leaving her card on the bar she made her farewells. As he picked up her card he decided to cancel Carlotta's visit – he had new quarry.

When Lady Rosemary entered the library at Athelstan House, the only lights penetrating the darkness were the reading lights over the green leather Chesterfield. Callum and Brian were curled into each end, deeply engrossed in their reading.

"Hey, Rosie, my little super-sleuth, how did you get on tonight?" Callum enquired curiously. Brian put down his book, also fascinated by her mission.

"Well," she said contemplatively, "creep barely describes him adequately enough."

"He always reminded me of a toad," Brian confirmed.

"Yes, I think that about sums him up."

"So what was the upshot?" Callum asked eagerly.

"Eating out of my hand. Especially when Doug reliably dropped my title into the introduction."

"Predictable," Brian agreed.

"I gave him an invitation to the house so I'm sure we will be seeing more of him soon. You guys will have to keep a low profile though. Especially you, Brian."

Brian nodded in agreement. Brian had met Martin Brownly-Smith several times soon after the Drift. Dr Brian Clough had been seconded to the government very soon after the Drift had occurred, as their chief scientific researcher, to establish how the Drift had happened, and to monitor its consequences. He had since left their employ, and on the invitation of Lady Rosemary, had moved into Athelstan house with Callum in order to start a new life.

At that time Brownly-Smith had been involved in his capacity as head of the Joint Intelligence Group dealing with issues of national security. He had spent time in Cornwall immediately after the Drift assisting Roger Stiles with the aftermath, and then again as the go-between for David Cameron when Roger proposed the change to a British Overseas Territory. Brian was not a fan of Brownly-Smith, indeed most of the residents of the Isle of Kernow who had met Brownly-smith were not fans. He represented everything that was wrong with Whitehall and its disinterest in anywhere outside of the southeast. He was not a man to be trusted, so they needed to keep a close eye on him.

Chapter 7

Porthissick

Aggie stood in the doorway of Roger's minute office in Rose Cottage, which was technically the back bedroom. This is where he had been stationed after the Drift, and it was still his favourite place to work. She watched him staring out of the window, in a trance, tapping a pencil on a pad.

"Writers block?" she asked.

He looked up, evidently unaware she had been watching him. "What's he up to?"

"Brownly-Smith? God knows. But he's a snake in the grass, as you well know, so if he's not been in touch, there's a reason for that."

"That's the problem. If he was on holiday he'd be here with Mrs B-S, or at least one of his floozies. According to Doug and Dee there has been no sight of any floozies at the Trewarget Arms, so a dirty weekend is the not his agenda. Which just leaves one explanation – he's here on business."

"But what sort of business does a man from the Ministry have in a village pub and a seaside café nearly an hour's drive away?"

"Exactly."

Aggie could feel the stress in his voice. She moved behind the chair and massaged his shoulders gently, feeling the resistance in their tension.

"And both of these places have connections to me. I lived at the hotel in Pentwen when I first arrived in Cornwall - until the owners drove me nuts, so I moved here. It's too much of a coincidence."

"Maybe so, but we have the upper hand. He doesn't know that we know that he's here, and he doesn't know that we are watching him."

"Yes. Fair point," Roger agreed. He sat thinking and nodding to himself for some moments.

"You are absolutely sure that was him in Pentwen, are you?"

"Oh yes," Roger confirmed pulling his phone out of his pocket and swiping through photos until he found the one he was after. When he got to the one Sully had sent from the café he passed the phone to Aggie. She looked at it and instantly started laughing. Roger looked at her quizzically.

"Look at how he's eating his cream tea," she said handing the phone back to Roger for contemplation. He looked at the image and laughed.

Chapter 8

Pentwen

Lloyd came up the steps of the Surf Shack to see Meg and Mitch huddled up on the massive beanbag sharing earbuds while watching a video on Mitch's phone. Whatever they were watching was evidently funny as they kept falling about laughing. To the left was Elle laid out on the new hammock, eyes closed listening to music on her phone, while Jake sat on the beanbag below, flicking through a surf mag and occasionally rocking the hammock gently. Jake was the only one to acknowledge Lloyd's presence with a micro-nod of his head. Lloyd continued inside half envious of the youngster's carefree existence.

"Hey, Ray. How you doing?"

"Hi, Lloyd. Yeah, all good thanks," Ray replied as he hung up some sweatshirts on the rail.

"I see love's young dream are alive and well, and living on your stoop."

"I know, what are they like. I worried that if Mitch had actually shaped any boards this week, they would have come out heart-shaped!"

"Ha, you might be on to something there," Lloyd laughed back. "Anyway, I was thinking of going for a beer tonight if you fancy one?"

"I'd love to but I really need to help Holly out. The backpacker's rammed so she's got to do extra hours there, so I'm on eco-pod duty."

"Ah, shame. It looks like the surf comp really put Pentwen firmly on the map?"

"I know. It was a real risk seeing as we don't know how reliable the swell will be, but so far so good. People are risking a lot when they book their flights. It could be millpond flat by the time they get here."

They chatted further about taking a trip to the south coast later in the week to see what the waves were like there, and Lloyd left. As he came outside he noticed that there was movement on the stoop. Both the girls were sitting on the top step putting their sandals on while the boys were lazing in beanbags.

"Hello, ladies, how's it going?"

"Hi. Oh, okay I guess," Meg replied. "We've got money enough to keep us going for another week, and if we don't have a job by then we'll have to return to the mainland and do a stint at Butlin's!"

As Elle replied, "Over my dead body," Mitch threw an evil glance at Jake, who looked away.

"I wouldn't wish that on you. I'm sure you'll find something," Lloyd said optimistically.

"I'm sure we will," Elle replied.

After the girls had set off back to the backpackers Mitch got up and kicked Jake's beanbag, standing above him, hands on hips.

"What?"

"You know damned well what," Mitch spat back. "If you don't do something to get them a job sharpish, then they'll be gone. And then how will you feel?"

"Okay, okay, get off my case. I'll see what I can do."

"See! You better bloody well *do* something, and now."

Jake pushed himself up, grabbed his flip-flops and set off towards the hotel without a goodbye. Mitch decided it was about time he did some work, so he set about sanding a new blank when he felt his pocket vibrate. He pulled off his facemask and took out his phone. Jake's message read:

OK. I CAN OFFER ONE POSITION AT THE HOTEL
BUT CAN'T STRETCH TO TWO

Mitch replied:

IT'S A START

Mitch was still staring blankly at his phone when Ray came out to start closing up. "What's up?"

"Argh, I'm frustrated. If the girls don't get jobs by next week they'll have to go, and I really like Meg. Like a real lot, y'know. I'll be gutted if she has to leave."

Ray had never seen Mitch so bowled over by a girl before. This was obviously the real deal.

"I'm sure they'll find something."

"Jake's managed to create one job, but I'm sure we know who he'll offer that to," he said almost bitterly. He looked pleadingly at Ray.

"Oh no! I can barely afford to keep *you* on, but I will have a word – see if anyone's got anything going."

"Cheers, mate."

Ray was beating some eggs in a bowl when he heard the front door open. "Hi, Holl," he shouted.

"Hi, honey," came the tired voice of Holly from the doorway.

"You look shattered."

"You don't look so hot yourself," she replied, half laughing.

He pushed a glass of Merlot over the breakfast bar towards her, and nodding his head towards the sofa, ordered her to put her feet up. She didn't need asking twice. She kicked off her shoes and slumped on the deep sofa, covered in throws of deep maroons and umber. The room was warm and inviting, the furnishings being a reminder of their travels. Heavy dark wood coffee tables inspired by Thailand, deep-coloured walls reminiscent of Fiji, and animal prints as a reminder of South Africa, her homeland.

Ray appeared above her with two plates of cheese omelettes and salad.

"I love you so much, Mr Jordan," she said grabbing the plate from him. "I'm famished."

"So I see," he laughed watching her tuck into the food. "We can't go on like this. You know that, don't you?"

She nodded with a mouth full of food.

"I think we can safely say, from the advanced bookings on the eco-pods, that they seem financially secure for the next few months."

"Yes?" she replied questioningly, not sure where he was going with this.

"And we are both tired from keeping so many businesses going?"

"Yes."

"So how about we delegate or something."

"And what is this something?" she asked suspiciously.

He used his full mouth of food as a means of gathering enough time to think about how to pose the proposition to Holly.

"Well, we could take on someone to help for a while," half-question, half-statement.

"We could. Did you have someone in mind," she asked suspiciously.

"Well now you mention it, I do."

"Really! And who would this be?"

"You know the two girls that Jake and Mitch have adopted? It seems that if they don't get jobs by next week they will have to leave. And I've never seen Mitch so happy -"

"You old softy, Ray," she interrupted. "What do you have in mind then?"

"I thought you could either give her your hours at the backpackers, or she could do the eco-pods?"

she sipped her wine and thought for a while. "She's a tourism student, right?"

"Yes. The jobs are meant to be like a work placement, or something."

"So let her get to grips with the eco-pods as it's a new venture. See how she gets on for a few months."

"Are you sure?"

"Let Mitch know before I change my mind."

Chapter 9

Dumgarth

Brownly-Smith woke up with a start. He looked around the room quickly trying to orientate himself. He remembered now, he was still in the 'god-forsaken pub'. But what had woken him so abruptly? There it was again, loud scraping and crashing noises. He hauled his sizable frame from the bed and peeked between the curtains. A truck was in the pub garden from which workmen were unloading planks of wood. He shook his head and climbed back into the surprisingly comfortable bed, pulling a spare pillow over his head. He tried to go back to sleep although was vaguely aware of an occasional hammering noise. And then there was warmth, and sand beneath him, and Lady Rosemary, accompanied by a lemur, offered him a cocktail from a coconut shell, warm and relaxed…then judder, judder, judder penetrated his idyllic dream and his pillow buffer. This time the noise was incessant and deafening. He leapt out of bed and looking out of the window saw one man shovelling aggregate into a cement mixer whilst another raked at the ground in boxes constructed out of the planks. This was too much, and it didn't look like they would finish any time soon. He realised that his silk pyjamas were clinging to him with sweat, so he disrobed and went to take a shower – all hopes of sleep abandoned.

As he entered the bar for breakfast he scowled at Doug who was in his usual place behind the bar.
"Ah, yes. Sorry about this racket, but it was the only time they could do the job. I forgot to warn you yesterday," he offered sheepishly.
"What, in the name of all that is holy, are they doing?"
"Laying bases for Dee's latest venture."
Brownly-Smith raised an eyebrow, not in the mood for being fobbed off.

"Bases for the *chalets*," Doug continued with an unnecessarily French emphasis on the word chalet.

"Heathens," Brownly-Smith muttered under his breath as he took his normal seat. 'This morning I think I shall visit with the Lady of Athelstan House' he thought to himself, resigned to the fact that he would have no peace here today.

*

"He's coming! I can see him halfway up the drive!" Colin shouted into the hallway to anyone who could hear him. Colin was Lady Rosemary's gardener of forty years, and Athelstan House was in his debt because the gardens were renowned for their variety and incredible beauty.

"Good man, Colin. Look natural please," Lady Rosemary shouted back. She darted along the landing to the south wing where Callum and Brian lived.

"Boys? Did you hear? That revolting man is on his way so please keep a low profile?"

"Will do," Callum called back.

The old-fashioned doorbell let out a peal of tinny bell chimes, as Rosemary rushed down the stairs. She breathed on the bottom step, smoothed down her hair and pinched some colour into her cheeks. Then slowly and gracefully she approached the great wooden door.

"Well hello, Mr Brownly-Smith. What a wonderful surprise. Won't you come in?"

"Martin, remember. I thought we agreed that we were on first name terms," Martin added, bowing to kiss the proffered hand.

"*Martin*. How are you?"

"Apart from the rude awakening this morning as builders set about the yard, I am very well thank you."

"Wonderful. Have you come for a tour of the gardens?"

"Dear Lady, on such a beautiful day I could think of nothing better to do."

"Give me a mo while I put some boots on," she said disappearing down a corridor.

Brownly-Smith stood in the open hallway, three doors off to the right, and what looked like a bright sunny kitchen ahead. There was an open staircase to the left, and behind him was an open reception area with full length leaded windows through which he could see the sculpted lawn, beyond which was the Atlantic glistening blue. The whole place felt warm due to the worn wood panelling and dark floor boards.

From nowhere came a high-pitched yapping sound and as Brownly-Smith turned he saw a small but quite ferocious terrier alternating from growling to yapping, never breaking eye-contact with Brownly-Smith. He shuffled from one foot to the other, quite uncomfortable, and unsure whether the bark would be worse than the bite.

Upstairs Callum and Brian sniggered to each other, knowing how frightening Tike could be if she had been wound up sufficiently – which Callum had made sure he had done.

"Get down, Tike! Behave!" admonished Rosemary as she re-entered the hall. "I do apologise, she's normally so well behaved."

"Not a problem," Brownly-Smith offered bravely as he made for the door. They turned right out of the front door and entered a former stable yard warmed by the dove grey of the slate facia tiles and the mauve of the wisteria that clung to the side of the building. There were several small cast-iron tables and chairs laid out on the cobbles.

"Do you have a café?" Brownly-Smith curiously, not being able to imagine Lady Rosemary waiting tables.

"Not as such. This is where we entertain some of the guests that attend the Cultural Centre."

"Ah, yes. I have heard about this centre, you must tell me more?"

Brownly-Smith had indeed heard of the Centre when attending his Club in London. There had been a ghastly man, Arthur Du Pont, who had been moaning incessantly about his wife's latest venture, the Cornish Cultural Centre, and 'all of the riff-raff that it would attract'. Rumour at the Club was that not so long after he had been slung out by said wife, Lady Rosemary Du Pont, with a small allowance, and told never to return. Looking at Lady Rosemary now he could imagine that she was not a woman to be messed with.

As they walked up a narrow walled lane he enquired further about the Centre. Entering the gardens through a green wooden gate she explained the purpose of the Centre. "It is really a celebration of Cornwall, past and present. We do Cornish language classes for all levels of learner – they are very popular. And then there are two types of programmes we offer. One is more academic, in-depth classroom based tuition. This is for those who have very specific interests and we tailor the courses for them specifically. We bring in experts and run seminars and workshops for a more interactive experience."

Brownly-Smith listened attentively, nodding occasionally.

"And then we run the trips. They are themed. So we do different historical trips, we do movie trips, we do mythical Cornwall, art trips, all sorts really."

"What a genius idea. I must come along to some of these ventures – you will have to give me a programme?"

"Absolutely. I'd be delighted."

They were weaving through woodland paths, the temperature dropping once they were in the shade. She turned abruptly up a smaller path and Brownly-Smith followed, feeling slightly out of breath. As they came over the brow of the hill they looked down on a Jurassic landscape - a forest of tree ferns in a crater. The ground underfoot felt springy and the air was damp and cool. The atmosphere made their movement soundless. Brownly-Smith felt a shiver go down his spine, imagining pterodactyls hiding, ready to pounce. Rosemary directed him down to the bottom of the crater which did not allay his fears, she pointed out a cavernous rock face down which water cascaded into a slick dark pool. She grinned to herself at his obvious discomfort before directing him up to the top and out on to the open path. The shingle underfoot sounded comforting to his ears and the tall redbrick wall that ran to their right made him feel back in the real world.

The wall ended and they turned into the vast open Victorian walled garden which Colin the gardener had in full production. "We are trying to set up some Cornish traditional cooking courses, linked to the kitchen garden, using all local produce, so we had to step up production here before we could get the courses underway."

"Very impressive," Brownly-Smith said nodding his head in genuine appreciation of the industry and organisation. She guided him to a bench. From the bench the kitchen garden sloped down, offering amazing views of the Cornish countryside; rolling fields in hues of green and brown like a billowing patchwork quilt.

"So what brings you to Kernow?"

"Well to be totally honest with you Rosie, my dear, I am considering a relocation."

"Leave London, and Whitehall?" Rosemary said incredulously.

"Yes, as a matter of fact, I think I have had my fill of the City. I need to slow down and rethink my lifestyle."

"Well you won't see me arguing with you there," she said laughing. "I couldn't live in a city, and most especially I couldn't live in London."

They sat in silence for some moments; Rosemary wondering whether she should probe further to get to the bottom of his plan, whilst Brownly-Smith considered whether he should divulge more to her. He needed an ally, and Rosemary may just have the clout and the connections to help him achieve his goal. As he revealed his plan to her she felt completely outraged, whilst retaining a calm and encouraging exterior – she resolved that it would be better for the Isle to feign friendship than reveal her true feelings.

Chapter 10

Truro

It was early evening and Roger Stiles was waiting in his County Hall office with a sinking feeling in his gut, pacing the room in anticipation. The room had been furnished in a style that complemented the building. Completed in 1966, New County Hall was a celebration of concrete and the modernist movement, as were the interiors. Roger's office was reminiscent of the early 1970s, sleek furniture and intense colours. Lloyd Bray was lying on the long brown sofa, an orange cushion behind his head, trying to appear relaxed.

"Stop pacing Roger, it'll be fine. If you'd contravened any international law Brownly-Smith would have been here to see you directly, or more likely would have summoned you to Whitehall for a dressing down. But no, he's skulking around so he's probably up to no good, like cheating on his wife or doing a shady deal."

"No, there's something wrong. Something doesn't feel right. The man is a total snake in the grass."

The door opened and Callum ushered Brian and Lady Rosemary in and, checking no one had seen them, he closed the door tight behind them. Roger took one look at their faces and knew he was right - there was trouble ahead.

They each pulled up a comfy chair around the coffee table and Lloyd made room for Roger on the sofa. "So here's the deal," Callum said earnestly, "Martin Brownly-Smith wants to challenge your position as Governor of Kernow – he wants the position for himself."

Roger half laughed, sure that this must be one of Callum's jokes. No one cracked a smile. Roger looked at Callum, incredulous.

"Well he can't," he said adamantly. "That's not how it works. He can't just waltz up and say *it's mine*. I've only been in position for six months for chrissake!"

"I think that's the problem. There is no precedent, and I'm not sure who is in charge of setting down such guidance," Callum added gently.

Turning to Rosemary, Lloyd asked, "And you are absolutely sure that this is what he said?"

"I may be advancing in years, but I'm not deaf, nor stupid, Lloyd. He said, and I quote, *I'm going to contest Stiles for Governor of Kernow, he's a fine chap but he's taking this Overseas Territory in the wrong direction.*"

There was a quiet around the room as they all contemplated these words.

"So we have two things going on here," Callum started. "Firstly there is the challenge: is it legal? when and how will he make it? and what can we do to fight it? Secondly, what is this *wrong direction* of which he speaks. Feedback from the council meetings is that the people are generally satisfied, and the economy is really starting to improve."

"More than we can say for the mainland," Brian said bitterly, uncharacteristically cutting for such a mild-mannered man.

Chapter 11

Whitehall

David Cameron had suggested a Skype meeting, but Brownly-Smith had rejected the invitation immediately, letting the civil servant charged with making the arrangements know that he would be on the morning flight from Kernow. He arrived at Cameron's office before eleven, relieved to be back in the thick of it again.

"Ah, Martin. How the devil are you?" Cameron said, hand outstretched in greeting.

"Miserable. And I will not continue this charade unless we dine at Roux."

Cameron rolled his eyes as he pressed the intercom and instructed the person at the receiving end to let Roux know they were coming.

Martin visibly relaxed as he entered the restaurant. He sat and breathed in the air of the rich, whilst getting impatient for the waitress. The relief at ordering a Chablis or Barbaresco without rejection was music to his ears. Martin Brownly-Smith was in seventh heaven just looking at the menu. He ordered quails with asparagus and morels to start.

"So how is it all going, off-shore?" Cameron asked light-heartedly.

"It's a fucking nightmare, if truth be told, Dave. There's nowhere to eat, and their best wine is little more than cooking plonk."

"Oh, I see. I thought they had a nice vintage of their own growing now?"

"Don't believe the hype. It'll never be a Chateau Latour," he replied savouring a mushroom.

"So where are we with respect to devising a plan?" Cameron pressed on.

Brownly-Smith thought momentarily, whilst chewing, Cameron not even sure if he had been listening. Swallowing, he replied, "A plan is starting to develop. I have no devastating intel on Roger as yet, so we might have to play this rather straight."

"Brave move."

"Well in lieu of some gossip, it's all we can do. Although I'm sure there's some jiggery-pokery we can do at this end."

Cameron nodded. "What do you have in mind?"

"First off we need to have something official that states how a governor can be challenged for his position. Now, am I right in thinking that there is no other Governorship model like this one in any of the other overseas territories?"

"Not as far as I'm aware."

"Excellent news. So all we need to do is get the Secretary of State for Foreign and Commonwealth Affairs to draft something that puts me ahead of the game, and even better if they can exclude Roger on a technicality."

"Like what?"

"Oh I don't know. Maybe needing to be of Cornish heritage or some such poppycock," he said flippantly, skewering the last morsel of quail on his fork.

"And are you of Cornish decent, Martin?"

"Probably. Isn't everyone?" he retorted waving over the waitress, eager to have his dry aged duck, cherry, broad beans and Grelot onions to follow.

While they waited for the main course Martin noticed someone walking to their table in haste.

"I think Clegg is making his way over," Martin whispered as he recognised the sycophantic smile.

Although Clegg was approaching from behind, Cameron put his hand up at just the right moment, and without turning to look at him he said, "Clegg, I've warned you about this before. I don't need to talk to you anymore because I don't need you anymore. Indeed, if I have anything to say to you, which I think is highly unlikely, I will call. Do you understand me." He paused without turning to look at Clegg. "Good. So sod off and let us get on with our lunch."

Clegg deflated and turned slowly on his heel and made his way back to his table.

"The man is a complete nincompoop," Brownly-Smith added to punctuate the end of the issue.

"So anyway," Cameron continued, "I have some *friends* on an island one hundred miles due south of my house," Cameron said winking to Brownly-Smith. "Anyway, they have intentions of developing said island into the world's first eco-*island*, and could really do without any competition from Pentwen. So between you and me I have sent some *friends* off down to

Kernow to see what they can do to remove the competition, or at least wing them."

"I'll see what I can do to help," Brownly-Smith said as he shook out his serviette, spying the arrival of the main course.

Between main and dessert Brownly-Smith took out his phone to text his secretary. "Who is in charge of Foreign affairs these days?"

"Phil Hammond still."

"Oh," Brownly-Smith said contemplatively. "I thought you gave him the push some time ago?"

"No. Can't really come up with a suitable reason to."

"I've never known anyone so dull come from Essex before."

Brownly-Smith gave the door a cursory knock, and entered without waiting for a response. Noting that Hammond was sitting at the meeting table Brownly-Smith strode to the desk upon which the computer stood, and nodding his head towards it he said, "Come and get this blackberry or apple contraption heated up, and we can knock this policy out in no time at all."

Philip Hammond stood his ground, tapping his pen on the pad of foolscap in front of him he countered, "I think it might take a bit of planning before we *knock it out*."

"Oh, okay, as you wish," Brownly-Smith with uncharacteristic contrition – anyone knowing him would have been suspicious of his motives at this point.

"So," Hammond started, "I have done some research on the other Overseas Territories, and ultimately the appointment is by the monarch as it's the only way to retain control in the face of a hostile government."

"Well that boat's already sailed," Brownly-Smith said grumpily. "The people spoke in the Cornish referendum and now we have lost the most direct rule we had. Unfortunately our representative is on the side of the people so we're a little stuffed."

"So the option is for the monarch to rescind her appointment of him. Easy." Hammond concluded laying down his pen on his pad neatly.

"Hardly. There would be an uprising. Roger is the man of the people. We need to think of something else which looks like we're not meddling, when we evidently are."

There was silence while both men contemplated the options.

"Ah," Cameron said as Brownly-Smith entered his office. "How did you and Phil get on?"

"The man is beyond tedious. I had to pop out for a mid-meeting snifter," he said patting his inside pocket where a tinny resonance replied.

"Well I hope it oiled the wheels of creativity?"

"Only in how to make the man see my side of the issue," he said tiredly as he slumped into a chair. "Anyway, here's the plan. As Cornwall's population is vast by comparison to any other Overseas Territory, and as its status was due to the will of the people, we are extending their democratic rights to allow them the right to elect their Governor."

"Brilliant, but why would they choose you over Stiles. No offence and all that."

"Naturally. None taken," he paused for reflection, steepling his fingers to add to the conviction of his speech. "They will elect me because I am offering them a better financial package, tax breaks and lower property taxes."

"So in essence, exactly what they would have if they were still part of the mainland?"

"Precisely, but we won't tell them that," Brownly-Smith confirmed.

"Obviously. So what if Stiles offers an equally good package?"

"Ah, yes. That's where I get him on a technicality in the small print," he said with smug satisfaction.

"Which is…?"

"That you need to be Cornish. In that you must be of Cornish descent or married into a Cornish family."

"Excellent. It really sounds like you are giving them more than they could have wished for." Cameron hesitated for a moment. "So," he said slowly, "are you Cornish?" he asked.

"Like I said, isn't everyone?" he replied brusquely. "I have a team of researchers on it as we speak."

"And what about Stiles? How do you know he's not Cornish?"

"I have the security services sending his file over now. If we do find anything I'm sure they can airbrush it out of history for as long as the election period. By then it will be too late."

"Let me never fall out with you, Martin. You are a truly evil man," he said nodding his head in approval.

"Thank you, Dave."

Chapter 12

Dumgarth

"Okay boys, let's put our heads together and work out how we are going to stitch up the delightful Martin Brownly-Smith."

"You are evil, Rosie," Brian said as he pulled up a chair at the sunny kitchen table. Callum put some mugs on the table and poured from the cafetière.

"What's the plan, Rosie?"

"The plan is to give him enough rope to hang himself."

"How?"

"By giving him heritage tours, with our own personal twist."

"Are you up to what I think you're up to?" Callum enquired.

"Probably, and if I keep him close I can feedback whatever his plans might be to Roger, so we can be one step ahead."

"Like I said, pure evil!"

They worked late into the night, meticulously planning each aspect of their scheme. At various points one of them would get up and review the contents of the fridge for sustenance; cold cuts left over from the Sunday roast with pickle and chutney, whilst Brian nibbled on carrot sticks and hummus. After eight this gave way to cheese and crackers, with more pickle and chutney, and inevitably wine instead of caffeine. All of which were necessary to oil the wheels of creativity – never had so much ridden on the back of planning Cornish tours. It was nearly midnight when they felt that they had completed their task. Various trips had been designed especially for Brownly-Smith, and for him alone. The tours were bespoke for a reason, and the intimacy they created was designed to allow Lady Rosemary to get to the bottom of his devious plans whilst setting theirs in motion.

Chapter 13

Truro

The table were in deep discussion about the utilisation of the Old County Hall. It had been derelict for many years and as the landlord could not be traced the building was to be re-appropriated for the sole use of the Food Sourcing Network until contact could be made with the rightful owner.

The Estates Manager was explaining the capacity of the building and what he thought might need to be done before entry could be granted, when Aggie became aware of a faint buzzing sound. She looked around subtly and realised that no one else was responding. She put her hand in her bag and pulled her phone onto her lap, its tinny shudder letting her know a text had just come through. The text was from James Sproken-Jones. It simply said:

CALL NOW. EMERGENCY!!

"Christ," she said inadvertently, surprised by James' tone, as he was not generally an emotive person. She stood, excusing herself quietly from the meeting, and made for the door with purpose, refusing to meet Roger's enquiring gaze. She marched down the corridor, out of earshot of the conference room and dialled James. He picked up instantly.

"What's up?" she said urgently.

"You're never going to believe this, but you need to get to Costmart south depot immediately. You can't tell anyone. Most especially Roger?"

"Okay, okay. I'm on my way," she said pushing the door open to the carpark, switching her phone for her car keys. She slammed her beaten-up old Peugeot 205 into gear, black diesel coughing out of the exhaust as she put her foot down and sped out onto the A390.

Her head was spinning with possibilities. If she was not to mention it to Roger then it must have something to do with the less than legal aspects of the Food Sourcing Network. When the Drift had occurred, and the supermarkets had been mothballed, Aggie, with the help of many local residents, took it upon themselves to source what they needed locally, but utilised the infrastructure of the supermarkets that had left them high and dry. Although, to passers-by, the four superstores were closed, behind the closed doors they were being used as storage and distribution depots. The shelves were stocked with food sourced from around the Isle. Their trucks were used to move stock around at night between the four depots, and a fleet of unmarked vans took deliveries daily from the depots to the local stores.

Once the food stock had been sourced and a steady supply had been organised, the Food Sourcing Network turned its thoughts to other products. As a means of ensuring the residents did not panic at the rate of shop closures, other high street stores were appropriated, and their goods were produced under their slightly altered signage. The residents never noticed that WH Smith had been pluralised, whereas Boots became possessive – Boot's. With respect to stock, they produced their own through the acquisition of a paper mill for stationary, and cooperation from local pharmaceutical and medical supply plants for toiletries.

As the products were sourced legally, the only crimes they were committing were the unlawful use of the properties, trespass, and possibly some element of misleading consumers who had not noticed the addition of apostrophes and plurals to high street brands. It was these less legal aspects that Aggie was concerned about, most especially as she did not want to compromise Roger's position.

Aggie pulled up outside of the Costmart's south depot which looked closed and desolate, the opposite of its night time status, when it was a hive of activity. She opened the padlock on the massive metal gates that led to the loading bay at the rear of the store and, checking that no one was watching her, she pushed them open enough to let the Peugeot through. Cautiously she drove in, pulling up alongside three cars, two of which she recognised as belonging to James Sproken-Jones and Joanne Varcoe.

Mousy Joanne had been the personal assistant to Nicholas Nugent, area manager of this one of the four main stores. It had been Joanne who had called the community's attention to the mothballing of the store, demonstrating how the company seemed happy to let the people of Cornwall starve. In an effort to keep some essence of infrastructure operational, dubious means had been implemented in order to garner the cooperation of the four Costmart area supervisors. No one had been particularly proud of *Operation Infinity*, but it had secured the managers' cooperation, and kept the Isle fed, albeit without the company's knowledge or voluntary assistance.

The third car parked alongside had a sticker in the back window suggesting it was an executive hire car. Tentatively Aggie opened the rear door to the Costmart office block and looked around. All was quiet. She closed the door silently behind her and tiptoed to the office that Audrey Sproken-Jones and the rest of the skeleton staff used as their HQ. Inside Joanne was sitting on a chair in front of the desk, hands wringing in her lap whilst she rocked slowly back and forth. James sat behind the desk with his feet resting on the ink blotter, staring at the ceiling. They turned abruptly as Aggie entered, and she could tell there was panic in the air.

James put his finger to his lips commanding silence from all gathered. Aggie frowned and shrugged intimating her confusion. James pointed towards the back wall of the office, which Aggie took to mean they would talk outside. When they got into the loading bay James again put his finger to his lips and directed them to his Volvo. They climbed in, Joanne getting into the back seat like a naughty child who knew her place.

"What the hell is going on?" Aggie asked angrily, frustrated with the games of subterfuge.

Joanne bit her lower lip and turned her eyes to her lap, no answer would evidently be coming from her.

James looked at Joanne then at Aggie before answering. "It appears that someone, we assume from Costmart's head office, was sent down to check the place out and -" he hesitated, looking towards Joanne again who refused to make eye contact.

"Good grief. What happened? Have they caught us out?"

James continued. "Well, let's say that the situation has been, how shall we put it? It's been *neutralised*."

"What do you mean, *been neutralised*? Did this guy see we were still operational?"

"I don't think he got the chance really," James continued, but looking at Joanne as he spoke.

"God, what have you done to him," Aggie asked urgently, thinking James might have killed the man.

"Don't look at me – I was late to this party. It was your resident ninja here that *dealt* with him," he replied, nodding his head towards Joanne. She sat slumped, having found a cotton handkerchief to wring instead of her hands. Her head was down and a curtain of mousy hair hid her plain features from the gaze of her accuser.

Aggie could feel her distress. Kindly she asked, "What happened, Joanne? What did you do to the man?"

Joanne sniffed, and nothing more than a squeak was omitted.

"Tell her, Joanne," James urged.

"I knocked him out like I saw Stewie do to Mr Nugent that time." *Operation Infinity* had been the post-Drift incapacitating of Nicholas Nugent at the store that he managed, and through menacing means Stewie, James and a select crew of locals had made him call the other area mangers to meet here. The fact that this might have been done against their will, and with a modicum of force applied was a point they chose to overlook since the event. All water under the bridge now.

"You knocked him out! What the hell with?" Aggie asked incredulously, although in retrospect she realised that was not in fact the most important question.

"With a bottle of Camel Valley Pinot Noir," she replied, somewhat embarrassed.

Aggie laughed despite herself. "And where is he now?"

"Hog tied in the cleaning cupboard!" James said.

"You're kidding me, right?"

"I wish we were, I truly wish we were," James said slowly.

"So, who did this hog tying?"

"This is also down to little Miss Billy the Kid, here."

"I used to watch the High Chaparral a lot as a kid," Joanne offered by way of an explanation.

Aggie raised her eyebrows in a mix of respect and surprise. "So, the important stuff - is he okay?"

"He did come round, so I imagine it's just a bad headache."

"Okay," Aggie continued, "Has he seen either of you?"

"Like I said I got here after all the action had happened so he hasn't seen me," James retorted.

"I don't think he saw me. I crept up behind him."

"And during the hog tying?" Barely able to believe the sentence she was uttering.

"No, he was unconscious then," she replied confidently.

"That's good. So how are we going to manage this from here?"

There was a moment's silence while they considered the issues. Aggie continued, "It's not like he's local. He won't feel invested in the same way the local managers did. They lived here and they knew the county would starve if they didn't do something. So I don't think there's any point trying to bring him in on this."

"I agree," James said, "But if he gets wind of what we're doing, the whole Food Sourcing Network is at risk," he added with concern. "If multinational conglomerates move into the market here, the price of food will escalate as there's no competition to keep it in check. We'll lose all of the trading independence that we've built, and," more quietly now, "some of us could go to jail for what we've done."

"Now James, don't get all maudlin on us. You know the pact - we all stand mute - they can't send the lot of us to jail for the actions of the few. Not least, it's not like we've been profiting from our actions, is it?"

James shook his head and there was a further period of silent contemplation.

"Okay. I need a few minutes to think this through," Aggie said as she got out of the car. She could feel all of their hard work teetering on a precipice if she didn't control this situation. She wandered about the car park aimlessly for a few minutes, kicking at stones with the toe of her shoe, and thinking through their options and the possible solutions. When she had decided on a course of action she got back in the driver seat of her car and pulled her mobile out of her handbag and called Stewie at The Anchor.

*

Under strict instructions from Aggie, James Sproken-Jones climbed into his Volvo estate and made off for New County Hall. Pulling on all of his acting skills he knocked at Roger's office, and putting his head round the door, to avoid the seated interrogation he might get if he entered the Governor's inner sanctum, he said, "Aggie asked me to let you know that there's been a problem at the pub and she driven down there to help out Stewie and Carrie." Before Roger got the chance to enquire any further James continued, "So can I pick up the keys and take a recce at the Old County Hall site so I can start to formulate some plans as to how we can best use the space?"

Somewhat overwhelmed by James' intensity Roger nodded, "Sure thing, James. If you go to the estates office to pick up the keys and I'll call ahead to let them know you're coming."

"Cheers, Roger," James blurted, closing the door before Roger could respond.

In time old fashion James was not permitted to enter the property without the Estates Manager accompanying him. When James said that he wanted to look around alone, there was all sorts of tutting and head shaking from the estates crew. James conceded and was accompanied to the semi-derelict building by the Estates Manager. The lack of use had been kind to the vacant building. Grade II listed, the council had continued to maintain it after the aborted commercial venture to convert it into a spa. Now, just over a century old, she stood magnificent in her symmetry and bowed porch, with Tuscan columns welcoming visitors.

The Estates Manager took James to the rear and showed him what keys, from the massive bunch, would allow entry to the building. The official gave James a cursory tour and was hinting that the tour was complete when James had to think on his feet. Pulling out his iPad James said, "I promised the First Lady that I'd take an inventory of accommodation types so she can think about it over the weekend. Save her having to come down herself," James said, rolling his eyes in that *better do what I'm told* manner.

The Estates Manager was convinced, especially at the mention of Aggie in those terms. "Okay. Well if you drop the keys by the office when you're done?"

"Of course," James reassured, palming the bunch quickly and seeing the man to the door. James rushed to the entrance hall and watched the Estates Manager walk down the drive and up the road towards the New County Hall. Once James was happy that he wasn't coming back any time soon he left through the backdoor, securing it behind him, and made down the hill for the city centre. He went to Timpson and asked for duplicates of most of the keys on the bunch to be made while he waited. One hundred and thirty pounds later he returned up the hill and reunited the original set with the Estate Manager's secretary, relieved he did not have to look the man in the face and lie.

Chapter 14

Porthissick

Twilight was drawing in when Stewie turned up at the Costmart depot in his Bedford van, with Arthur Varcoe, Joanne's equally ineffective husband in the passenger seat. Arthur had the look of a worried man. Aggie reassured him that Joanne was fine and wasn't in trouble. All he needed to do was to drive her home, give her a brandy and get her to bed, forgetting the whole affair. This was something that would not be discussed again, for all theirs' sake. Aggie was relieved to see the back of them.

Stewie was at the back of the van, opening the doors he let out his cargo in the shape of the Evans brothers, butchers from the valleys, but three generations on they had not lost their Welsh lilt.

"Aggie." They said in unison by way of a greeting.

"Evanses," she said, nodding at each in reply.

"You need to be out of here," Stewie said earnestly to Aggie. "But you need to be somewhere public when this goes off. You can't be implicated."

"James has told Roger that there was an emergency at the pub so I'll go there and have a drink in the Saloon bar with Carrie. I'll tell Roger that there were *women's problems*. That should nip any further enquiry in the bud."

"Good thinking. We'll give it an hour then."

"Sounds about right," she said looking up at the increasingly darkening sky.

Stewie and the Evans brothers unloaded the van. They took out sacks, rope, cloths and bottles. With balaclavas pulled over their faces they entered the depot silently, surprise being their weapon of choice. They tiptoed to the cupboard that Joanne had described to them. Evans-bother-one was ready with the open sack whilst Evans-brother-two was holding a rag that emitted the noxious smell of ether. On the silent count of three Stewie pulled the door open, Evans-two covered the mouth of the wide-eyed man secreted therein with the rag, and on the count of five the rag was removed, whilst Evans-one covered the man's head and torso with the sack. Stewie went through the man's pockets until he found a set of Vauxhall car keys with the hire company keyring, and pocketed them. The Evanses then took top and tail of the deadweight while Stewie went ahead holding doors open to expedite their escape. They placed their charge in the back of Stewie's van, Evans-one joining him there to prevent him rolling around, whilst Evans-two jumped in the man's hire car and led Stewie out of the distribution centre and off into the countryside.

After being on the road for nearly three quarters of an hour Evans-two drove the hired Vauxhall Insignia to a standstill on the old A30 near the iron bridge, which had since been bypassed by the new dualled road. Stewie pulled the van in behind and got out and went to the Vauxhall's driver door, speaking briefly and quietly to Evans-two. Evans-two nodded, and before Stewie was back in the van, Evans-two had taken off at great speed. When he got to the sharp right hand bend that led over the bridge crossing the new A30, he put his foot down, catapulting the Insignia into the gorse. Stewie had slammed on the breaks and was out in a flash. Evans-two had successfully rolled the car ensuring that it came to rest right side up again. Seeing that Evans-two was fine Stewie breathed a sigh of relief. "Exactly what part of animal husbandry and butcher training gives you these skills?" Stewie asked.

"Mainly the bit where you watch lots of Dukes of Hazard, and you don't just focus on Daisy!"

"Fair enough," Stewie replied pulling Evans-two from the wreck.

They got back to the van and pulled out a bottle of cheap whisky whilst reapplying the balaclavas and gloves. Evans-one had already carefully removed the sack from the unconscious Costmart executive and was opening his mouth to receive as much alcohol as they could get in his system to make it look like the man was drunk at the wheel.

"Feel this," Evans-one said, running his hand over the back of the exec's head.

"Jesus!" Stewie whispered, feeling the egg sized lump, "that girl really packs a punch."

They carried the man as quickly as they could to his car wreck and put him in the driver's seat and belted him in. They then placed the bottle of whisky in the car, first having spread some of the contents liberally around the interior to ensure it smelt of booze. When they were done they closed the car door and jumped in the van.

They headed back to Pentwen where they had earlier secreted the Evan's delivery van in Mitch's lockup. They picked up the van and the Evanses headed off towards Porthissick, high-fiving the Aussie uncomfortably as they left. Mitch and Stewie popped into the Bay Bar for a quick bottle of beer with Jake, Sully and Hog to ensure that Stewie was seen by several casual observers should he ever need an alibi. When he felt enough time had passed he texted Carrie to let her know that he was leaving, and left shouting loud goodbyes to the gathered crowd.

Stewie drove back to Porthissick via the scene of the crash, hoping that someone else had discovered the accident and had intervened, but by the lack of flashing lights and action this appeared not to be the case. As he descended the slope of the bridge he could see the tail of the Insignia sticking out of the hedge. 'What's wrong with these people?' Stewie said to himself as he pulled his van to a halt - either no one passes this way anymore, or they were as drunk as this guy was.

Stewie walked up to the driver's door and opened it, saying, "Are you alright, mate?" The man mumbled something incoherent in reply, and Stewie let out a sigh, relieved that he was still alive at least. He took a quick sniff to check that there was no odour of ether before pulling his phone out and dialling 999.

When he hung up he asked the man what had happened, making it sound like he was trying to keep the man conscious, like he'd seen in movies. In reality he was trying to establish who the man was and what he could actually remember. It was evident from the man's ramblings that he remembered nothing about what had occurred to him, he didn't even recall coming to Kernow. He did recall who he was, "I'm Carl Tarrant, an important man from Costmart. 'Excellent news,' Stewie thought, 'he has no recollection of what happened to him today, but has not been injured so badly that he no longer knows who he is.'

After about five minutes the ambulance arrived with a police car in quick succession. Stewie told the paramedic what he had witnessed since arriving at the crash site, the paramedic already had pretty much made up his mind that this was an alcohol-related crash rather than any medical condition. Stewie repeated his statement to the police. They seemed happy to agree this was drink-driving case, with no reason to suspect foul play as there appeared to be no evidence to the contrary. While waiting for someone from the police to take a statement he texted Carrie to say he had found a car crash and would be late as he had to stay at the scene until they were finished with him. He then left the police with his contact details, reassuring them that he would be available for further questioning if necessary.

*

Aggie helped out behind the bar, slipping into her old role as if it were only yesterday that this had been her home and her livelihood. When the bar was quiet Aggie took the opportunity to ask Carrie how she was getting on in her new role. From the look of her Aggie suspected that it was all a bit much for Carrie. Her normally glowing complexion had become sallow, and there were hints of darkness under her eyes.

"Oh, I'm getting along fine," although Aggie could not hear that in her voice.

"You sure, Pet?"

"Well I am getting pretty tired. What with the cakes and dad, and all."

"You're not telling me you're still supplying cakes for the network as well as working here are you?"

"Well people are depending on me. And the new cookies are so popular."

Aggie shook her head in disbelief.

As if trying to justify herself Carrie continued, "And I mostly do the baking from here while I'm working so it's not too bad."

"Really! And I spent years blaming this oven on my complete inability to bake. Evidently that was not the cause of my burnt offerings!"

Aggie admired the girl's work ethic, but she made a mental note to have a word in Jim Down's ear. His daughter had enough on her plate than to be taking care of him too.

Stewie arrived back at The Anchor and was relieved that Aggie had sent Carrie home to Downs Farm, and was now in the process of closing up.

"Itsh been loverley havin' you back, Aggie me darlin'," Seth Morcom slurred as he was assisted to the door by his son Nigel.

"It's been lovely seeing you too, my treasure," Aggie replied, winking to Nigel as he man-handled his father out of the door.

"Goodnight," Stewie called after them as he locked the door behind them. He looked up to see Aggie was already pouring three large brandies. Stewie looked done in, bags under his eyes, and Aggie thought she saw grey hair at his temples that hadn't been there earlier that day.

"You can come through now, James," she called through to the Saloon bar, as she placed the glasses on a table.

The men's eyes met.

"How did you get on?" James asked, looking as exhausted as Stewie. Waiting for Aggie to confirm that the front door was locked, Stewie replied, "Them Evans boys are heroes. Scary, but heroes nonetheless!"

"Right Pet, how do we stand?" Aggie asked intensely.

"So, the guy seemed fine, no obvious injuries except the bang on the head that they will hopefully put down to the crash."

Before he could continue James asked, "And how did that go?"

"Looked bloody convincing to me. That Evans boy rolled it and still came out sunny side up."

There were relieved looks from Aggie and James, so Stewie continued. "The paramedics seemed pretty convinced that it was drunk driving and the police weren't of a mind to argue so they were pretty chilled about the questioning. I think we're home and dry."

"But did you talk to him?" James asked urgently.

"Briefly, and he doesn't seem to remember much. He didn't say anything about being assaulted, or even visiting Costmart, so hopefully that's been forgotten."

"And if he does think he remembered something, no one will take him seriously after a drink driving charge," Aggie added.

There was quiet contemplation for some moments before James started tentatively, "But one way or another he, or others, will come to check the site out, and in all reality we don't know if that will be in some weeks when they send out a sober guy, or whether it will be this guy with the police tomorrow."

They let the words sink in before pushing their half-drunk brandies into the centre of the table and pulling out their phones.

"I'll see if I can catch the Evanses before they hit the bottle," Stewie said mid-dial.

"I'll see how many of the distribution drivers I can rouse," James added.

"Okay I'll see what fisherman are around to lend a hand. I'll start with Toby Morcom." After she had called a few trusted locals and organised a rendezvous she texted Roger:

SORRY. GOT CAUGHT UP WITH CARRIE. I'M BACK AT THE COTTAGE TONIGHT. I'LL BE BACK TO TRURO TOMORROW. XX

Roger heard the phone ping and picked it up to read the message, glass of red in one hand and mobile in the other. He looked slowly around the tiny living room of the cottage, and thought sadly to himself, 'but evidently you are not'. He left his glass of wine unfinished and went sadly to bed, setting the alarm for six to be out before she got back - assuming she did.

Chapter 15

Truro
James drove ahead to Truro so he could open up the Old County Hall backdoors. He needed to find somewhere near the back entrance where the fridges and freezers could be placed for perishables. Then a terrible thought struck him. He unlocked the door and flicked a switch – "thank god," he said aloud, relieved that there was power to the property. He wandered around considering what would be best placed where. The large kitchens would be best to place the freezers, he then allocated a room to each food type; bread, cake and biscuit products, tinned goods, beverages, and so on. Using a marker pen on paper from the old photocopier he wrote the produce intended for each room and used drawing pins to stick the notices on the relevant doors. Following Aggie's advice, he ensured that all front facing downstairs rooms were left vacant to avoid being caught out by nosy visitors.

   It took them all night to empty the distribution depot, carrying the freezers and chillers full so as not to allow anything to defrost or perish. Many of those helping brought sack barrows to help with the onerous task at hand. Once each vehicle was loaded they had the hour drive to Truro. To ensure that they didn't attract attention to themselves as some midnight retro re-enactment of Duel versus Convoy, they staggered their departure times and divided themselves between the A30 and the A390. Once at the Old County Hall they took it in turns to pull into the back lot and unload before the next vehicle arrived. They marched backwards and forwards, like worker ants, delivering food, cleaning products, toiletries and stationary to their allotted rooms. By five o'clock they were exhausted by lack of sleep and physical exertion.

Aggie stopped unloading when she found boxes containing biscuits and made coffees for all. They sat on plastic-wrapped pallets of beans and spaghetti hoops hugging their mugs, hoping the caffeine would work some magic. Each time someone new came in for a coffee Aggie would get up to take the biscuits round. Dragging a box into the centre of the room, James said, "Aggie put the biscuits here and sit down. People can help themselves to the biscuits."

"Hell James, the moving around is the only thing keeping me conscious."

There was a growing number of helpers filing into the room. Stewie walked in with a driver from Looe to announce that the last of the produce was unloaded. There was a collective sigh of relief.

"Thanks, everyone," Aggie said. "It's been a tremendous effort. Audrey, can you send out a message tomorrow to thank everyone for their help?"

"Will do. I'll leave it vague in case the message gets into the wrong hands."

"Good thinking, darling," added James.

There was silence for a moment, before Toby Morcom asked tentatively, "But do you really think this is the end of it. I mean if they sent a bloke over to look at one depot, don't you suppose that he's here to look at all of them?"

The communal relief evaporated and Toby shifted awkwardly. "I'm just saying, like," he added to break the silence that he had created.

"Toby, I think you are absolutely right," Aggie said to alleviate his guilt. "I was thinking just the same. I think we need to go home, get some rest and meet tomorrow when we can think more clearly about the situation."

"Aggie's right. No one is going to be doing anything for a good forty-eight hours at the earliest, I reckon. This should give us time to come up with a plan."

There were mumbles of agreement.

"Keep an eye on your phones, and I'll send out details about our next move tomorrow afternoon," Audrey said, bringing a close to the conversation.

At this they all started to file out of the room.

"Just leave the cups on the draining rack," Aggie directed as she ushered them out of the kitchen and towards the backdoor. "I'll sort this out tomorrow."

Chapter 16

Porthissick

James dropped Aggie back at the south coast depot at just after six. Dawn had arrived and the perfectly clear sky was starting to tint with swathes of pink and tangerine.

"It looks like it's going to be a beautiful day," Aggie said quietly, almost as if talking to herself.

"I think it is," James agreed, staring at the vista.

Without another word, Aggie got out of his car and crossed the car park to retrieve her car. She sat in silence for a few moments to collect her thoughts. Seeing that she hadn't left, James wondered if her car wouldn't start. He got out and tapped at her window with a questioning shrug. She lowered the window and he asked if she was okay.

"Yes, thank you James. I'm, I'm just thinking," she said tiredly. "Do you think we've done the right thing?"

"Knocking a bloke out cold, and setting him up on a drink driving charge - probably not! But what was the alternative? See the county starve, or be at the mercy of some faceless corporation?"

Aggie laughed lightly, "Big city man rallying against capitalism – if only your old city friends could see you now!" she joked, making reference to his status before retiring to Cornwall.

Smiling at the irony of her quip James continued, "No, on the whole, we did the right thing. We did the right thing from the start, and all we are doing now is protecting our community. This was unfortunate, but what choice did we have. What's more, this will not be the end of it. All we've done is delay the inevitable."

She nodded sadly. They were silent for some time, then Aggie broke it, "I'll see you and Audrey tomorrow at ten at the new HQ then?"

James nodded, "See you then. And please try to sleep. None of us will be any good if we are tired."

Aggie let herself into the cottage that she had grown to love. As she walked through the tiny lounge to the open, rickety staircase she saw a wine glass on the side table. 'Peculiar,' she thought, unable to remember when she might have left it there. Too tired to be concerned about it, she put it in the kitchen sink and collapsed into bed, also too tired to notice it's residual warmth.

Four hours later she was up, showered and driving back to Truro with her damp mop of unruly curls held high in a bayonet clasp. She entered the front door of the Old County Hall, thankful that James had got there first to open up. She wandered through the passageways until she found the debating chamber, which they had agreed to keep free of contraband.

James and Audrey were already there. Audrey held Aggie firmly by the shoulders, looked into her eyes, then hugged her, which Aggie took to mean that she must look terrible to elicit such a silent and sympathetic response from Audrey.

By ten twenty they had been joined by the four Costmart regional heads. "So by now you have heard what occurred yesterday," Aggie started.

"Who knew the spineless whippet had so much fight in her," Harriet Mallinder spat, referring to Joanne Varcoe.

"Well if she hadn't had the presence of mind to do something, god knows where we would be now," Nicolas Nugent replied defensively.

"What's done is done. What we really need to do now is decide how to take it from here," Audrey interjected sternly.

David Hare of eastern region continued, "Do we know who this guy is and what he wants?"

"Joanne checked his pockets once she tied him up. He had business cards in his wallet with his name and position at Costmart on them."

"So she didn't know who he was until she knocked him out." Harriet laughed admiringly. "I told you she was a crazy bitch!"

With a glare Audrey continued, "But this still doesn't tell us what he wants. Why was he here, and why hadn't he been in contact with one of you guys before coming over?"

As they contemplated this they noticed that Nicolas Nugent was now staring uncomfortably at his feet.

"Something you'd like to share with us, Nick?" Thomas Wetherill from western region asked kindly.

Hesitantly, "So after Joanne called me yesterday to say she had knocked out a manager from HQ I thought I better check my emails -"

"- thought!" yelled Harriet in his face. "For fucks sake Nick, you are paid to keep in touch with them. You could have ruined it for the lot of us, for Cornwall!"

"So moving along," Aggie enquired, "what did you find? Have they been in contact?"

"There was one from the London office saying that an asset assessor will be coming down and I should maybe contact him and show him around."

"So this gives us a clue as to what's going on," James said nodding. "It looks like they are considering selling the sites, but," thinking for a moment, "as a going concern or a site for redevelopment. Has anyone else been sent such an email?"

Three heads shook.

"Hmm, so are they testing the water with this site. I mean what would they be selling for? The views aren't great from the site. It's not really near enough to a town or the sea for tourist accommodation."

"It's too near the main road so it would be too noisy for anything upmarket."

"And imagine the cost to demolish such a huge structure."

"Unless they are thinking of a retail outlet, in which case it's ideal," David suggested, bringing the mood down again.

"Good point. But none of this speculation is going to deal with the primary problem," James said.

"Which is?" Harriet asked sarcastically.

"What we do to stop them poking around any further? Can we put them off without any further visits?"

Audrey started, "Well, the first point of intervention is obviously through Nick."

Nicolas Nugent sat to attention at hearing his name.

Turning to address him directly Audrey said, "I think you need to get in contact with this man, seeing as it was you that he was hoping to meet. And work out what his agenda is."

"But how?"

"By replying to his email in the first instance."

"Over ten days late? It seems a bit crazy after all that's occurred since," Nicholas replied.

"Ah, but technically you don't know about anything that's happened since he arrived, as it's not yet in the public domain."

"So how do I go about making contact then?"

"Email a reply."

"Saying what? I've sort of got to explain why it's taken so long to reply. Should I say I've been on holiday and missed his earlier email?"

"No muppet," Harriet admonished, "you're meant to let them know if you'll be away. You'll make yourself look bloody stupid if you do that."

"So more productive solutions?" Aggie asked trying to bring the temperature down.

After a few suggestions David shouted excitedly, "Just say the email has only just come through, and something about terrible reception, poor connectivity or lack of broadband - they don't know the connectivity is absolutely fine -"

"And -" James interrupted, "it suggests that the place is on its knees, without even basic Internet! Brilliant, David."

"Okay, let's go with that," Aggie suggested looking at Nicolas, who nodded enthusiastically as it got him off the hook.

"The only problem is, Nicolas," James continued more soberly, "when you meet him you have to play absolutely ignorant of everything that's happened since he's arrived. Can you trust yourself to do that?"

"I'm sure he can," Aggie interrupted, trying to fill the nervous Nicolas Nugent with some confidence. "You just have to remember to respond only to his questions, and never start a conversation with him. That way, you should stay out of trouble."

There was a lot of all-round agreeing, and as Harriet opened her mouth to explete further, Aggie gave her a withering glance which stemmed her flow.

"That's only one of the problems solved though," Thomas said, almost as an aside.

"Okay smart arse, what's the next problem?" Harriet enquired.

"He might want to have a look at the other sites while he's here and I think Nick, no offence meant mate -" Nicolas nodded in acceptance at whatever offence was about to be made, "- I don't think Nick can stall him, as the man has the right to do what he wants."

"Not least, after what he's just been through, he might feel the need to exert authority as he feels a dick at being caught drink driving when he can't even remember drinking," Harriet added.

"Which means we will have to clear out the other depots just in case," James said exhaustedly. The faces of everyone around the table dropped, especially James and Aggie who had already spent the night clearing out one depot – the thought of three more was too much to bear.

"Yes, I think you're right," Aggie said resignedly.

"I'll get on to the drivers at the other depots and replicate last night's manoeuvres," James replied.

"And I'll see if I can rally some troops to assist," Aggie agreed.

The remaining four sat around helplessly until Harriet shouted, "Phones out scum bags and get some feet on the ground!"

And verily they did.

Chapter 17

Pentwen

Jake watched Elle enter the hotel bar and look around for him. He pulled a cold bottle of Korev from the fridge, topped it and pushed it across the bar towards her. "How did the first day go then?" Before answering she took a long drink from the bottle, Jake amused to note that she had downed nearly half of it in one gulp.

She took a moment to gather her thoughts. "Breakfast service was okay. It's really a case of familiarising myself with the breakfast options and letting Jess know when we are running out of sausages or bacon, or what-have-you." She paused again. "What I didn't predict was how totally exhausting chambermaiding is. Humping around heavy bedding all day. It weighs a ton."

"That's because it's linen, and not cotton."

"What?" she replied bemused.

"The sheets and duvet covers are made from linen, and not cotton. Even the towels are linen," he added proudly.

"And why does this matter?" she said, verging on sarcasm.

"Because it's the best material; ecologically, ethically, economically."

She started to smile. She had never heard his speak so authoritatively on anything before. Settling back on her barstool, she said, "Okay, so tell me more about why this matters."

He looked at her curiously, unsure if she was winding him up nor not. "Why?"

"Because the whole point of us coming here was to do a project on tourism – and this is your niche, ecological tourism – so that's my project."

Jake felt a wave of pride wash over him. At last he felt that he could talk to Elle in an intelligent way about something he knew, rather than feeling like an idiot in her company. He checked the bar for potential customers, before opening a couple more bottles and joining her.

"What do you want to know?"

"First of all tell me why you care about sheets so much. Why you are more than happy to break chambermaids rather than use cotton!"

"Easy. It's all part of the eco-tourism. Part of the eco-tourist agenda is that the community works sustainably."

"Part of? Surely that's it?"

"No. Eco-tourism is a complex system. Yes, obviously the environment is important. Great efforts are made towards being carbon-neutral, from tiny behavioural changes to massive infrastructure developments. But that's not all. It's about the community too. It's about the community working together to educate the tourists about the area. Things like culture and heritage. Even raising political awareness."

"Really?"

"Yeah, I know that makes more sense if we were talking about places like Costa Rica or some jungle retreat, but we've had our share of political upheaval here too, since the Drift. You were aware of the referendum, weren't you?" he said sarcastically.

"Yes – I had to show my passport to board the plane," she said teasing him.

"Well anyway, one of the changes we made was to look at the bedding. If you think about it, bedding is a massive part of the tourist industry. All the hotels, guesthouses, B and Bs, and even the backpackers, they all need sheets, right?"

"I guess so. I never really thought about it before. It's not like we did a module on the Economics of Bed Linen."

"Well, maybe you should."

Laughing, she said she would suggest it to her tutor when she returned to university.

"So why linen and not cotton, not that I even know what the difference is."

"Cotton comes from cotton, and linen comes from flax. We found some farmers up in Camelford that have been growing flax for about twenty years, and now they supply the whole town with their linen. It means we don't have to import, which reduces down the carbon footprint and makes it more economical as it's locally sourced. Not least, the sorts of tourists that come to eco-towns love that local vibe."

A thirty-something couple walked into the bar, dressed-down but still looking classy. All labels, but only if you knew what you were looking for. Several years ago Jake would have thought them smug, but now he saw them as the changing face of tourism. Their interest in engaging with the culture that they visited, preferable any day to the Union Jack short-wearing, full English breakfast eating, binge-drinking brigade. Jake finished serving them their sparkling mineral water and a Chablis before returning to his barstool.

He continued where he had left off, "It's not just that it's locally sourced." He looked at her to check that she was still interested.

She nodded for him to continue.

"It's also more economically sound as it lasts longer. It's really durable, so it is less likely to rip and doesn't need replacing very often. And even if it does need throwing, it's totally biodegradable. Can you imagine what all of the nylon sheets of the seventies are doing to landfill?"

"To be honest it had never occurred to me what the bedding of forty years ago was doing to the planet," she joked.

"Are you taking the micky?"

"Maybe a little. But I love your passion. Go on. What else don't I know about linen?!"

"Cheeky mare. You asked for it! So on top of all of the economic and ecological features, it has a more luxurious feel which improves over time. It can absorb more moisture before it feels wet. And it has healing properties, apparently."

"For real? Such as what?"

"For skin stuff like dermatitis and even arthritis."

"No way."

"Way. That's why the ancient Egyptians used to use it. And hell, they could build pyramids without cranes so I guess they knew their stuff."

"Well obviously if the Egyptians recommend it then it's worth the extra effort when changing the beds then," she said laughing.

They ordered another round of drinks, and Elle sat pensively picking at the label on her beer bottle. "How did you go about making Pentwen eco then?" she inquired, seeming genuinely interested.

"You're not really interested in that, surely?"

With a hurt look she said, "Yes, otherwise I wouldn't have asked."

He looked at her quizzically.

"Remember we're only here because of our course. I have to report on something linked to tourism, so it's obvious that we focus on the eco-town. Nobody else will be doing something as niche as this. I thought I would concentrate on the start-up, you know. The hurdles, the choices, how you got the momentum, like how you won people round."

"That wasn't so easy. It was baby steps really." He had a slug of his beer while he reflected on how the change had come about. There had been great resistance at first. To get the businesses of Pentwen to invest; with their wallets as well as their hearts and minds, had been a struggle. They used tried and tested methods at the outset, such as no plastic bags to be given with purchases, and the replacement of old light bulbs with more environmentally friendly ones, such as LED. The next stage had been to get them to think more specifically about their type of business and what their specific issues were with respect to sustainability. To help with this step they had bought in Dr Jeannette O'Loughlin who specialised in developing eco-parks. She spent time with each business and showed them ways to reduce their carbon footprint and make their businesses more sustainable.

"To take this to the next level the council had to buy in. With the help of some government grants they reviewed their public transport policy to reduce traffic omissions, and are in the planning process of adding foot and cycle paths, away from the roads, to all major routes around the town.

"I can tell you about the little, local initiatives, but Lloyd is really your man for the big stuff. I was really the go-between to help get the trust of the locals – Lloyd is more the brain behind the operation, and Roger was the driving force to help us get things done."

"Roger? Who's Roger?"

Jake laughed quietly. "Roger Stiles. He's our Governor. He came down after the Drift as a government man and turned local! He's cool. He really gets it, like he really cares about what happens here."

"Wow, maybe I should interview him for my project."

"Yeah, he could give you a whole different perspective. I'll ask him if you want?"

"What? You know him?"

"Yeah, why wouldn't I?"

"Because he's like the Prime Minister of Kernow."

"Yeah, but he's cool."

They left the bar enjoying the warm air, despite the ever-present breeze. Neither of them wanted the night to end just yet, so Jake steered Elle towards North Bay for a moonlit beach walk. Elle took off her sandals enjoying the feeling of silky sand between her toes. "What was it like when the Drift happened?"

"God, I don't know. It was all a bit crazy." He paused to reflect. "I mean when I first noticed, I was looking at the webcams early that morning, checking that the swell had arrived overnight, and it all looked wrong. Massive waves in all the wrong directions. So I called the boys and we all hared down here to check it out. It was totally mad."

"But you didn't know what had happened at that point, right?"

"Hell no. So we went for a surf, baffled as to why it was all weird. And it wasn't 'til we got back home later. My mum had left like a million messages on my phone – none of which made sense until I turned the TV on. Then the place went mental for quite some time."

"It must have been crazy?"

"Well first, we were all like – excellent surf, bonus! Then we were all, well nervous I think. We didn't know if it would happen again, or indeed what else might happen. Then there was all sorts of social media hype, like we were going to run out of food, or the Isle would tip into the sea. And all the time the regular media were saying – all is fine, nothing will change. And we really didn't know who to believe."

"How scary."

"It was scary, for quite a time, although I don't think anyone actually said it out loud. We just sort of kept it in, and pretended it was all fine."

They came to a low rock and sat down, gazing out at the black ocean.

"And now how do you feel?"

"We've been settled long enough to feel we won't drift again. But it is still weird sometimes when you think about it. It's like the rest of the country are your parents –"

She laughed at the idea.

"– and like Devon is your really annoying big brother – like your connection with the adult world. And although families can sometimes be really annoying, or they don't appreciate you when you're there, now we've left we sort of miss them, but they seem to have forgotten we existed. And that's a bit hurtful. I think that's why the referendum came out the way it did. We felt that they were pleased to see the back of us, so we might as well break the tie – like a teenager leaving home and becoming independent. And we really have shown them that we don't need them, I reckon. And we've made Devon look stupid 'cos they still live at home while we're all independent and thriving."

She laughed, turning to look at him. "That's so cute. I love your passion for what's happened, and your optimism and drive to turn it into something better."

Taken by the moment, and her smiling upturned face, Jake picked up the courage and kissed her gently, tentatively. When she didn't pull away he pulled her closer and kissed her more deeply.

Jake had walked Elle back to the backpackers, and as he returned to the hotel he felt a growing sense of pride. Not only had he been able to ensure that Elle could stay, by offering her a job, he also felt good at being able to talk to her knowledgably about something. Okay, it was only linen, but this was a fundamental part of what they were trying to create here, and he had been instrumental in making the project successful.

Jake arrived back at the hotel to find Mitch, Sully and Hog propping up the bar. "Hey guys, what's up?"

"All good man, all good," Mitch replied grinning from ear to ear.

Jake shrugged, curious at his mate's beaming joy.

"Bloody Holly only went and got Meg a job! Running the eco-pods! I mean, man, how cool is that?"

There was the slapping of high-fives all round, and Jake pulled up a stool to join them in a drink, or three. The girls would be staying.

Chapter 18

Dumgarth

They started their Cornish Culinary Tour early in the morning – too early for Brownly-Smith, but Lady Rosemary was a formidable character, and when she said they were starting out at 7am, they were starting out at 7am. Lady Rosemary pulled up outside the Trewarget Arms and came in to the bar. "Morning, Rosemary," Doug said from his usual place behind the bar.

"I swear Doug, every time I walk through this door - there you are. Regardless of time of day, fair weather or foul, you are always behind that bar. Tell me, do you ever sleep?" she said jokingly.

"Yes, I do, Lady Rosemary," he replied quite seriously, still pulling through pipe cleaner into a galvanised bucket. "Dee sometimes brings me down a duvet on a cold night," he said, stony faced.

She chuckled at his joke, and pulled up a stool to the bar.

"Do you want a drink while you're waiting?"

"No. I've just had some tea thank you, Doug."

Nodding towards the door he said, "He's only just gone up so I think you may be running a little late today."

"Really? Okay. I'll have an orange juice please?" She paused looking out of the window to the pub garden. "So what are you doing out there," she asked nodding towards the apparent building site where a lawn and picnic tables once sat. "Colin said something about chalets?"

"That's the one. Yep, she's having chalets built."

"But what for exactly?"

"This is Dee we are talking about here, so it's for the prestige, oh yes, and the money."

"How do chalets make money – or even prestige for that matter?"

"It's all these here bird watchers. This really has become a place of importance to them so Dee wants to cash in on it. She's worked out that they are nice quiet men. They don't chat much and are happy with their own company, and more important they seem happy with the basics and aren't inclined to complain. So she thought that she could fit many more in if she used the garden space to build the chalets."

Lady Rosemary craned her head round. On the right hand side there were a few chalets that looked complete, the further left she looked the more they looked like self-assembly kits.

"To be honest Doug, I think they look more like garden sheds. No offence and all that."

"None taken, m'Lady. And indeed there's a very good reason why they looks like sheds."

"Ah. I see," she said nodding.

They headed out on the A38, winding their way through the Glynn Valley before turning left onto the A30.

"So where does our culinary adventure start today?" Martin Brownly-Smith enquired.

"We are starting at the beginning," Lady Rosemary replied cryptically.

"The beginning of what?"

"Of what the County is renowned for, and has been for centuries."

"Pasties?" he enquired tentatively, quite sure that this wasn't the right answer, but unsure what else fitted the bill.

"Not yet. We'll get to them later in the day. No, we are starting with fish, and fishing."

"That makes sense considering the geography. Even before the Drift, the sea was a major feature of the county, I suppose."

"All 290 miles of coastline when Devon was connected. Since the Drift we've acquired another fifty miles of coastline."

"That's a lot of sea."

He looked out of the window – relishing the undulating countryside that flashed before his eyes. Reminding him of a patchwork quilt, adding to his somnolent mood.

"If we are entirely surrounded by sea why are we travelling so far to see some sea?"

"Because not all sea is equal, nor as productive as that of Newlyn."

"Ah," he nodded, not really understanding why Newlyn was so important when they were surrounded by ocean.

It took them over an hour until they turned off the A30 passed Penzance and started down a picturesque, leafy lane into Newlyn. The buildings on the outskirts gave hints as to the area's primary trade, with old stone warehouses with wooden painted signs claiming them to be packers and purveyors of fish of seafood. The road wound further down giving way to rows of stone cottages with tiny front gardens full of palm trees and colourful rhododendrons. The town seemed untouched by modernity, yet bustling with activity.

"Why are there so many art galleries in a fishing village?" Brownly-Smith asked.

"That's their second trade – the Newlyn school."

Brownly-Smith raised a curious eyebrow.

"It was an art colony that emerged in the 1880s. Artists came from all over the world to work here."

"But why? I mean it's quaint and all that, but in the 1800s it must have been the end of the world."

Lady Rosemary thought quickly. "To capture the life of working men. It was all the rage back then."

"Oh," Brownly-Smith replied, unsure why this should be of any interest to anyone. Ghastly fishermen in their oilcloth coats. How would that be appealing? Especially when they could have concentrated on the beautiful countryside.

Lady Rosemary parked up in the carpark by the quay and they got out, relieved to stretch their legs after the ninety-minute drive. Brownly-Smith had yet to have breakfast, but the smell of rotting fish drove away any thoughts of dining. The sky was clear and blue with a hint of an onshore breeze. They walked to the water's edge and looked down into the somewhat murky harbour. "So, Newlyn harbour dates back to the mid-fourteen hundreds," Lady Rosemary started. "It started out primarily for landing pilchards. In the latter half of the year pilchards came near to the Cornish shore so there were watchers, called Huers, whose job it was to watch for incoming shoals, and shout to the fishermen when they were spied."

Lady Rosemary pulled a book out of her bag where she had pasted old postcards, pictures photocopied from books and printed pages from the internet. As she flicked through the images of luggers and drift nets, she explained the complex process of seine netting and why this stretch of coastline was ideal for this way of fishing. Brownly-Smith perused the pictures and nodded his head in interest.

"In another tour we may well go and look at a Huer's hut. There are some quite well-preserved ones around the coast."

As they walked on, southward around the harbour, Lady Rosemary continued. "The pilchards were exceedingly popular with the Italians."

"Really?"

"Oh yes. They were so popular that this trade pretty much made the town. If you weren't at sea then you were involved in the preserving and packing of pilchards to be exported to Italy."

"How did they get the stinking fish to Italy without them going off? I'm guessing they wouldn't have had ice back then?"

"Quite right. No, they were salted and pressed to remove the oil, then put into barrels for the journey to Italy."

"Sounds, to all intents and purposes, like an anchovy."

"Very similar. And considered an absolute delicacy by the Italians."

"Well who'd have thought?"

"The pilchard export made Newlyn a very busy trade route, and a very prosperous town."

Brownly-Smith looked around. Yes, there were definitely boats here – working boats with fishermen busy about their work. But there was a quaintness about the town and harbour which suggested that its reign as chief provider of fish had not lasted forever. Lady Rosemary saw his thoughtful and calculating gaze and was prepared for his next question.

"So what happened?"

"The trade route fell into decline after the 1850s, after the great English-Spanish pilchard war."

"The what?"

"Yes. The great English-Spanish pilchard war – it's not greatly written about, but any Newlyner will be able to recount stories, passed down from their forefathers, about the war."

"By Jove!"

"It started when the Spanish started to intervene in the pilchard's northerly progress to Cornish shores. The northern Spanish fleet would catch the pilchards and market them to the Italians. They could undercut the Cornish price as the export route was so much shorter. There were stories of armadaesque conflicts with disgruntled Cornish fishermen setting off in fleets to confront the Spanish in the Bay of Biscay. Lives were lost – this was a very serious period in Cornish fishing history."

Brownly-Smith was nodding intently, hanging on her every word with rapt fascination. "Well I never. How come I had never heard of this before."

"Because you are not considering who writes history," Lady Rosemary replied choppily. "These were not men of letters, they were probably not even literate. Who writes this history? This is only passed down through family stories and folk song. Sea shanties are the fisherman's history books."

"Yes. I see your point. It never occurred to me before."

Trying to mask her exasperation, she continued. "What history did you study at school?"

"Erm," he thought looking skyward. "I think we did Tudors and Stewarts, and then World War Two."

"Exactly. History is written by the victors, and the victors are those that are in charge. So you studied the reigns of the kings of England followed by international conflict – initiated and perpetuated by those with power."

Feeling slightly embarrassed, and not entirely sure why, Brownly-Smith suggested it was time for a coffee.

As they sat in the chintzy coffee room Brownly-Smith continued. "So what happened after the pilchards?"

"They had to rely on other types fish to make their money." She nodded and smiled at the waitress as she put their mugs on the table. "They rebuilt the harbour to make it one of the safest at the time, and diversified into mackerel fishing. With the advent of the railway it meant that they did not need to export, but sent their catches around the country. The railway was a blessing that also allowed them act as a port, so coal was sent by ship from Newlyn to places like Portugal."

"Fascinating."

"Yes, it has a rich and fascinating history indeed."

They finished their coffee and wandered back up the slope to the carpark. "Where to now?"

"Now we get to deal with the pasty! I'm assuming you've tried one?"

"Yes. I had one in a pub on first day here."

"And?"

"Well it was fine. I mean, well, it was -"

"If you value your life, never let a Cornishman hear such ambivalence about their national dish," she admonished.

"No offence meant, but it's hardly beef wellington is it?"

She kept her eyes on the road, seething at his arrogance. 'I must not let him get to me,' she thought. 'It's for the greater good,' she reminded herself.

They arrived at the Bodmin bakery and the comforting smell of freshly baked pasty filled the air. They were greeted by Geoff the manager and were shown into the entrance where they were to put on hats and overalls.

They were ushered through the double doors into a large open room with a rectangular metal table centre stage and several pasty-makers stood around the table, busy at their trade.

"So here are the crimpers busy making pasties. Here is the skirt beef," he said pointing to trays of beef chunks, "and here we have the vegetables, already seasoned."

"What is it? Potato and onion?"

"And swede. It's important that they are all chunked. All the ingredient goes in uncooked, so it needs to cook at the same rate. Cut your veg too small and we'd have meat and mash."

"Good point," Brownly-Smith replied nodding.

"It's important that the pastry is folded upwards, then the crimp goes along the top edge, like this," he said showing one already prepared. "Our crimpers can crimp about four pasties per minute, it's quite a skill."

They watched the crimpers in action for a few minutes, then Geoff offered Brownly-Smith opportunity to have a go at crimping. He floured his hands and put far too much meat in to his first attempt, the pastry splitting as he tried to crimp it. His second attempt was slightly more successful, which Brownly-Smith laughed off before gratefully being directed out of the bakery and into the café. "So would you like to try one, fresh out of the oven, and I'll give you a bit of history of the pasty?"

Brownly-Smith had been listening to his stomach growl for quite some time and was thankful of its satiation, even if it was through one of these working-class pies.

They sat around a small table by the window and Brownly-Smith looked around for his cutlery. Noting his confusion Geoff called to the waitress for cutlery to be brought.

"The pasty dates back to time immemorial. But really they were the first convenience food, ideal for workers who would not have access to cutlery at lunchtime." Brownly-Smith looked at his loaded fork uncomfortably. "They were produced by tin miners' wives to take to work. The pastry is tough enough to withstand the journey, and the crimp was meant as a handle, so the miners could eat with mucky hands and not end up with arsenic poisoning. They were also popular with fishermen, but obviously theirs were fish-filled."

Brownly-Smith baulked at the thought of a fish pasty.

"The wives were said to have put their husband's initials in the crust," holding his pasty up as an example, "so then they always knew whose was whose."

"Tell him about the knocker," Lady Rosemary urged.

"Well there's tell of the mysterious little folk that live down the mines, called the knockers. They're called knockers because they are said to knock on the mine walls before a shaft collapse to warn the miners to get out."

Brownly-Smith nodded, waiting to the relevance of this to pasties, or whether the man was about to go off-piste and regale them with stories of ancient Cornish myth.

"Story goes that by leaving the crust with your initials on for the knockers, the miners were leaving a treat to ensure that, should there be a shaft collapse, the knockers would know who to warn!"

Brownly-Smith nodded again, forcing a smile. "Incredible," he said whilst thinking that there was only so much quaint story-telling that he could deal with in one day. Rosemary could sense his disinterest, but it was important that she maintained his focus.

"You know," she said, "that the Cornish pasty has Protected Geographical Indication?" she asked, trying to appeal to his political mind.

"No I didn't," he said perking up slightly. "Although I do remember Dave and Georgie-Boy getting into hot water over the pasty tax a few years back."

"Yes. The status was granted in 2011."

"So what does that actually mean? That you can only eat a Cornish pasty in Cornwall?"

"Ah, no." Geoff interrupted. "That's what was so clever about the ruling. If that had been the case then we'd be restricted to only those in the county, leading to a huge drop in revenue. No, this is quite the opposite. The pasty has to be *prepared* in Cornwall to a strict recipe, a minimum of 12 per cent beef, but it can be baked anywhere, see. This allows for an export trade. It also buggered up some of the English bakers as they couldn't sell pasties under the name Cornish pasties unless they had brought them in. Greggs is still mad at us."

"Clever," Brownly-Smith replied, at last interested in pasty-related information.

"You must have noticed the pasty vendors at the major London railway stations? Well this was a genius idea as the trains bring in the chilled pasties ready to be cooked for the daily commuters – fresh and Cornish! Before the Drift we were looking at Cornwall's turnover on pasties being three million pounds a year – that's three per cent of our GDP!"

"Impressive. But this is evidently not the case now I'm guessing?"

"No. We've had to rethink our marketing strategy. The distance now increases distribution costs but we can charge more for them as they are now a foreign delicacy."

"Can't the English just buy them in Devon?" Brownly-Smith asked, somewhat bewildered.

The look on Geoff's face was incredulous. "But Devon is not in Cornwall!"

"But I'm sure they make pasties too, don't they?" he said awkwardly.

"Yes, but not Cornish ones!"

To try to bring the temperature down Rosemary intervened. "There has been a long-held rivalry between Devon and Cornwall as to the origin of the pasty. Cornwall had the oldest documented evidence until an archivist in Plymouth was going through the audit accounts of Mount Edgecumbe, an estate near Plymouth, and there was an account dating back to the sixteenth century of pasties being made there. This predated the Cornish evidence by some two hundred years."

Brownly-Smith made a face that indicated discomfort.

"Yes, exactly. Now that doesn't mean that pasties had not been made in Cornwall before Devon, but it is enough to generate more intercounty rivalry."

"As if we need any more," Geoff added. "It's bad enough with the cream tea debate."

"If we want to get really picky about things," Lady Rosemary continued to distract him from the cream tea debate, "there are writings by a Frenchman in the twelfth century referring to pasties, although interestingly the characters that discuss the pasty are deemed to come from the region that would later become Cornwall!"

"Who knew that the simple pasty could be so contentious."

As they were saying their goodbyes Lady Rosemary's mobile rang, and excusing herself she walked to the car to take the call. When she was finished she re-joined the men. "The car is open, Martin," she said by way of instruction. Taking her lead, he thanked Geoff once more and walked to the car. Rosemary remained, waiting for Brownly-Smith to be out of earshot. "Thank you so much, Geoff. You have no idea how much we appreciate your help today, and what impact that this might have on the future of the Isle."

He smiled back. "It was a pleasure to have been of some assistance."

"What will you do with all of those pasties they made in front of him. Surely you can't sell them?"

"We'll probably give them away. We can't afford to risk our reputation selling top-crimped Devonian pasties!"

They both laughed before shaking hands once more.

Once back at Athelstan House Callum and Brian were waiting eagerly for news, pouncing on Rosemary as soon as she arrived home. "Heavens! Let me get through the door will you? You're more impatient than the dogs!"

They fussed around her, taking her coat and hanging it in the cupboard, finding her favoured fleecy slippers - exchanging her walking shoes for comfort. They escorted her into the sitting room, the dogs running around their legs, excited by her return. Tike jumped up on her lap while Dotty, the older golden retriever sat by her feet.

"Gin or wine?" Callum asked, halfway to the door. She contemplated for a moment, quite enjoying the fuss.

"Oh, gin I think, please, Callum."

She took a long refreshing gulp and was suddenly aware of four pairs of eyes all staring at her; two pairs eager for information and the other two pairs out of canine loyalty. Smiling, she put her glass down and started, "So the day was a raging success, although I deserve some sort of medal for putting up with the intolerable man for so long."

"I'm sure you gave as good as you got, Rosie," Callum chipped in.

"Well, not entirely. I really had to bite my tongue. I didn't want to alienate him until the project is complete."

"Fair point."

"I also had a bit of a genius idea as we drove back," she said, fixing her eyes on Callum.

"Looks like you're in trouble," Brian laughed, punching Callum playfully on the arm.

"Go on, what is it?" Callum asked hesitantly.

"It occurred to me that it is really important that he fixates on our interpretation of Cornish history and culture -"

"So?"

"So we need to make sure that he expresses this version in his election speech. I thought we could help him by introducing him to a scholar of Cornish culture, and that the scholar could help him write the speech."

"Excellent idea, Rosemary!" Brian exclaimed.

Callum sat shaking his head, one step ahead. "And let me guess, I am to be said scholar?!"

"Bingo!"

"Okay, okay," he said resignedly. He got up and returned a minute later with the laptop. "So what we need to do is to make an account of every erroneous thing you told him on each trip so I can make sure that the speech aligns with what you've said." And with fingers poised above the keyboard Callum said, "Fire away."

Chapter 19

Truro

Roger walked down the corridor to the small kitchen where County Councillors heated up soup or made coffee when the canteen was closed. As he approached, the kitchen door opened and Aggie exited turning right, tearing off down the corridor in the opposite direction at a speed of knots. Roger had not asked her about her whereabouts the previous night. Hadn't mentioned that he'd come back to the cottage to surprise her and she had never returned. There were logical explanations possibly. She could have returned to Truro to join him, but then why didn't she call or text to ask his whereabouts? Maybe she was wondering the same about him and too angry to ask. Alternatively, she could have stayed the night at the pub after helping Carrie out. This was the explanation Roger was going with as it was the most innocent. It was the one where his life with Aggie remained constant.

As he reached the kitchen door it opened abruptly and James Sproken-Jones slammed right into Roger. James looked ashen as he faced Roger. "Just getting a coffee," James blurted guiltily.

Roger nodded. Looking towards James' empty hands, he said, "Drank it already?"

Stutteringly James replied, "I forgot my sweeteners," cringing as the words spilled from his lips.

"Wow. I didn't take you for a sweetener man, James. You on a diet or something?"

"Well, you know," he said patting his belly, "You've got to keep on top of it, eh?"

"Looks like it's working for you," Roger replied before squeezing past him into the kitchen. It was true. James did look like he'd lost weight, but not in a complementary way. He looked thin and sallow. He also looked guilty.

Roger pushed this to the back of his mind. He had more important things to focus on right now. He was having a hell of a morning. He had already attended a Harbour Committee meeting to discuss the dispute between the Isle of Kernow and France over fishing quotas and landing rights. But as anyone who had spent time in Whitehall knew Cameron was busy building his retirement home in the Languedoc. This apparently prevented him from carrying out any British negotiations with the French that might contravene his long term plans.

His afternoon had already been interrupted by a petition being lodged, in person, by a group referring to themselves as the League for Postcode Equality. As Roger strained to keep a straight face he was passed a pile of paper which he was reliably informed "had been signed by thousands of marginalised residents of Kernow". Roger asked them to enlighten him as to what this form of discrimination was. It appeared that over half of Cornwall received their post based on postcodes linked either to Plymouth and even some from Exeter. It had not previously occurred to Roger what the origins of PL and EX postcode were, but seeing the distress of the League he promised to get someone to look into it, and ensured that debate would be had over what best to change it to.

Later Roger took the opportunity between meetings to make himself a mint tea in an aim to settle his griping stomach, and as he waited for the teabag to brew he looked out of the kitchen window to the car park below. To his surprise he spotted Aggie, sitting in the passenger seat of James Sproken-Jones' car, deep in serious conversation. He put this curious observation on the mental backburner, as he needed to prepare himself for an arduous afternoon of meetings.

Just when he thought things couldn't get any worse, his secretary buzzed through to say he had a visitor. Before he had the opportunity to ask who it was, his door burst open and the imposing stature of Martin Brownly-Smith filled the frame. Roger had known that it was only a matter of time, but some warning would have been welcomed. At least he still had the element of surprise as Brownly-Smith did not know that Roger was aware of his presence on the Isle over the last few weeks.

Roger got up and came around the desk, hand outstretched. "Martin, to what do we owe the pleasure?"

They shook hands, Martin clasping his left hand firmly over them both.

"I'd like to say I was just passing, but we both know that would be ludicrous, don't we?"

"Indeed. Can I get you something? Coffee or a scotch?"

"Most kind, but no, I'm fine thank you." Brownly-Smith sat on the long, low sofa, left arm stretched along the back, as he quietly scrutinised Roger. "You've changed. Changed quite a bit, I'd venture."

"Well I guess we all have. It has been some time, and life here is very different."

"Yes. Sorry to hear about dear Mrs Stiles. How is she?"

"Very well last time I heard. Met up with an investment banker so I believe."

"And the new Mrs Stiles."

"There isn't a new Mrs Stiles, although I have re-partnered since Melanie and I divorced."

"A bit before that if you believe the jungle drums," Brownly-Smith said guffawing like a public schoolboy.

"Actually not. And I don't listen to tittle-tattle. So what can I do for you, Martin, or is it social call, which I think is unlikely as you've been here for the best part of two weeks."

"Touché. You obviously have your ear very close to the ground."

"I may have happily left Whitehall, but I have not forgotten what that viper's nest taught me. Knowledge is power."

"In some cases, old boy, in some cases. Sometimes power comes through more legitimate means."

"Meaning what, Martin?"

"Meaning that the power you have here only comes from your status as Governor. Unfortunately that little experiment has run its course, and we will soon be relieving you of your duties."

The forewarning that Lady Rosemary had given him had allowed Roger and Lloyd to research the options open to Whitehall in terms of his status. The problem that quickly came to light was that there was no real precedent laid down at any of the other Overseas Territories. One thing they were quite sure of was that he could not be deposed as Governor without an election. Knowing this, Roger asked calmly, "And exactly how do you plan on doing that?"

Brownly-Smith seemed somewhat put out by Roger's calm response to the news. He was a man used to being in the driving seat, and he did not feel that he had full control of this situation. Had he underestimated Roger Stiles? "Well it really depends whether you go quietly, or insist on putting up a fight."

"I think we'll be going for the *putting up a fight* option, if that's alright with you, Martin. Now if that's all you came to say," he said getting to his feet, "I have a very busy afternoon running the Isle of Kernow," he replied gesturing towards the door.

Martin Brownly-Smith knew when to concede, but this was the battle and not the war. "The election will be in six weeks," Brownly-Smith said pushing his portly frame from the low sofa. "There will be an official letter coming soon."

"Good bye, Martin."

As he reached the door, Brownly-Smith turned and said, "This is bigger than you and me, Roger. You might just want to give up gracefully."

Chapter 20

Pentwen

Elle and Meg sat at a table covered in a plastic red and white checked tablecloth, outside the Lobster Pot café. They were stirring coffee and gazing out to sea, the warm breeze intermittently picking up wisps of Elle's hair and blowing it across her face. The sun's heat had increased since they had arrived on the Isle, giving them a hint of what was to come throughout the season. The beach was already busy with dog walkers and families playing beach games.

"Hello, ladies," came a voice from behind them. It was Lloyd Bray, leaning on the back of their chairs. "Can I get you anything else while I'm ordering?"

"No, we're good thanks," Meg replied for them both.

Lloyd returned some minutes later with a black coffee and a croissant. He sat in the chair opposite with his back to the beach so the surf did not distract him. He poured a sachet of brown sugar into his cup and stirred. "So what is it you want to know?" he said, ready for business.

"Jake says you are the man that can explain the bigger infrastructure elements of the eco-town?"

"Well to some degree – I'm no expert, but I can give you the basics and why it works here. If you want the real science you'd be better off talking to Jeanette O'Loughlin."

"I don't think we need anything too sciency," Meg explained. "This is to help us understand about eco-tourism for our uni project."

"Yes. We probably need to get a grip on what the rationale was, the logistics of change. The barriers and stuff."

Lloyd pulled the end of the croissant and dipped it in his coffee before putting it in his mouth. They waited for him to finish chewing.

"Hmm," Lloyd said – thinking out loud, "Where to start?"

"Why not start with whose idea was it?"

"Okay. It probably wasn't one person's idea. It was more like several things coming together at once that led to the idea."

Elle was sat, pen poised over her pad, ready to start scribbling.

"Yeah, initially it was the general disgust felt by the local surfers and some members of the community at the planned takeover of the beach. The Millers from the North Bay Hotel, Jim Meacher from the Bay Bar," Lloyd continued nodding his head to the left in the direction of the bar, "and even George from this café, were all ready to sell up to some hideous budget cruise liner company."

"Why was that so bad?"

"Because they were going to level these old buildings and build a monstrous mall and spa where everything would be in-house so the holiday-makers would not need to go into to the town to add to the local economy. And even worse, they would have to dredge the bay in order to get the liners in and docked. The impact this would have had on the surf, I don't need to explain to you guys, but that wouldn't have been the end of it. The impact that it would have had on the environment, well -" he said exasperated.

"Like what?" Meg asked.

"So this area is predominantly kelp beds. The kelp acts as an ecosystem, offering nutrition and shelter to a diverse range of sea life. The dredging would have destroyed the kelp beds, which may never repopulate with the liners coming and going. This would not only kill off the whole ecosystem, but would have a massive impact on the fishing industry locally."

"Jeez," Meg said. "Not well thought through."

"I really don't think that they cared – it's literally not their business. They are all about maximising the number of people that they can get on a boat and trying to hold them there in order to ensure that all their money goes into the company coffers – hence keeping them hostage at the spa and mall, rather than the cash being spent in the town."

"What gits," Meg continued angrily.

"What stopped them then?" Elle added.

"Ah, well that was a real community effort, but Jake, Mitch, Sully and Hog were instrumental really."

The girls exchanged glances, eyebrows raised. Lloyd continued, "Yes, they looked at other destinations bought by the company and researched what they had been like before Royale Cruises had moved in. Well, what they found was shocking. Perfectly lovely old fishing villages ruined. There was one in Croatia which was decimated by their invasion. It killed off the local fishing industry, so unless the locals worked for the cruise company there was no trade. Their domination of the area chased away the sustainable tourism that had been there before. So, we decided that this was not an option, and made efforts to offer the locals something better."

They spent nearly two hours with Lloyd, learning about the principles of eco-tourism, and how it applied to Pentwen. The lengths that local businesses had gone to with the hope of making a difference.

"No one knew at the outset if it would work. But, bless them, they gradually invested and engaged. And it worked. I mean, that was never guaranteed as nowhere has tried it on a scale like this before. Before us the biggest projects had been eco-parks, which were designed to be ecologically sound and owned by one organisation, therefore automatic buy-in. The success of Pentwen is down to the local businesses that risked all."

"So how do you become an official eco-town? What's the process, or can you just call yourself it?" Meg enquired.

"There are standards we need to meet."

"But whose standards are they?"

"The European Environment Agency have key tourism indicators that should be met, and we voluntarily sign up for The International Ecotourism Society."

"So it's all monitored and official then."

"Oh yes. In fact we have a reassessment coming up in the next few weeks."

"Wow. What will that involve?"

"A team of inspectors will come and look at our provision and ensure that we continue to meet the standards they set. If so, we can continue to market ourselves as the first and only eco-town."

"Pretty important that you meet the grade then."

"Totally."

*

Elle and Meg took a walk around the headland, bracing themselves against an increasing wind, which was blowing the large white clouds out to sea. From the cliff path they spotted a dip in the landscape. Leaving the path they carefully made their way to the hollow where they sat in the soft springy grass that was native only to cliffs. They lay down out of the wind and felt the sun on their face.

"This is heaven," Elle started.

"I know. Everything about here is beautiful."

They sat in contemplative silence for some time. Meg, eyes closed, head tilted towards the warming sun. Elle was engrossed in the activity below. The waves crashing in on the jagged rocks sending fans of white spray skyward. Further out there were a group of gulls sitting in the choppy waters of the bay, bobbing up and down on the wind swell. Every now and then one would take off and soar high into the sky, rising on invisible thermals, giving a loud plaintive cry before dropping at speed to the water again.

"I don't think I can do this anymore," Elle said, turning to face Meg.

Meg, eyes still closed tight said, "Thank Christ you said that. I was thinking the same thing too."

They grasped each other's hand, staring up at the ever-changing expanse of sky.

"What are we going to do then?" Meg asked.

"I don't know," Elle started, emphatically. "But the more I think about the whole situation, the more it seems so wrong."

"Well, we have two days to come up with a solution before we have to meet him and report back."

*

Two days later Meg and Elle caught the bus to Padstow and asked for directions to the harbour. They walked along the harbour edge to the flat car park and scanned it for the white Audi Q7. When they found it they nodded to the man in the driver's seat, and jumped in the back seats as he directed.

"Well hello, ladies," the man said with a plummy, upper class accent, not even turning to meet their gaze, but staring at them through the rear-view mirror. All that the girls could see of him was shoulders clad in a pink and white candy-striped shirt and a sunburnt forehead reflected in the mirror.

"This is all very cloak and dagger," Meg said to the man.

"It bloody well needs to be. I'm too well known here now."

'Hardly surprising,' Meg thought to herself, taking in the man's incongruous attire.

"How is the plan going?" the man asked.

"It's going very well. We both have jobs in North Bay area of Pentwen, and are well acquainted with those who started the whole eco-town project."

"How have you managed that?"

Elle replied, "I am working for one of the guys and we have said that this is part of our uni project."

"We've said this is a placement year, so it's totally fine for us to ask loads of questions."

The man in the front seat grinned broadly. "Well done, ladies. Well done indeed."

"And they are having their annual inspection by European Environment Agency in a fortnight, in order to grant them a second year of accreditation."

"From this we should be able to get a really good understanding of what the inspectors look for, and we can pass this on to you," Meg added.

"Excellent job. Well done." There was a moments pause, before he continued, "So, I've spoken to HQ and there's been a slight change in the mission."

Meg and Elle exchange quick, worried glances.

"HQ are concerned that just getting the lowdown on how to get eco-town status might not be enough. He has decided that -"

"Exactly who is *he*?" Meg interrupted.

"Oh, believe me, my dear, you do not want to know who *he* is. The less you know the better. Shall we just focus on the task in hand?"

The girls retracted slightly in their seats, uncomfortable with his tone.

"It has been decided that not only do we need the intel on eco-towns, and how to get them up and running, and obviously your extra intel on the inspection, but we need more. He's worried that there will be too much competition between Pentwen and his venue, -"

"Which is where exactly?"

"All in good time, all in good time. He requires that not only will you be instrumental in ensuring all is in place for the inspectors at his venue, but he needs you to take out the opposition."

"*Take out?* What the hell does that mean?"

He raised an eyebrow at her response. "It means you need to sabotage the Pentwen inspection."

The girls exchanged horrified glances, then Elle gave Meg a *shut-up* look, and turned back to the front.

"Okay. I think we have gathered enough information to make this possible. I'll research the assessment criteria and ensure that we have enough spanners in the works," Elle said demonstratively. Meg got it, and started nodding in agreement.

"Yes, they trust us so I'm sure we will be able to complete the mission, under the radar, so to speak."

"Excellent news. You will find him to be extremely grateful for the extra assistance."

"How do we report our findings?"

"We will get back to you on this. I think we will wait until you have finished your mission here then take you to the new venue to oversee things there. We'll be in touch."

As they got out of the car he fired up the engine, and had taken off as the last door slammed shut. The girls stood facing each other in shocked silence. "I think I feel sick," Meg said.

"He is truly despicable, I mean, I'm lost for words."

"Hideous creep. And who is the *he* he keeps talking about?"

"I know, that was kind of scary."

"I think we're in too deep, and the whole situation has got way out of hand." Meg said visibly shuddering at the thought.

They walked back to the bus stop in silence, fear preventing them from logical thought. They caught the A5 and sat on the top deck gazing out at the landscape rolling by; blue seas to the right and undulating green fields to the left. The bus twisted and turned its way along the coast road, occasionally stopping to pick up fares.

"I think our way out of this will all come down to timing," Elle mused, almost as if thinking aloud.

"The timing of what? Do you have a plan?"

"I think I do."

"And what if the timing isn't right?"

"Then we're screwed."

Chapter 21

Porthissick

They were sat in the tiny cottage living room, side by side in the ancient over-stuffed armchairs that they had inherited with the house. Between them was an old card table upon which two glasses of gin and tonic sat, ice rapidly melting in the evening heat. They were trying to concentrate on the news, but both were exhausted by stress and late nights brought on by very different reasons.

Obviously Roger had known that at some point there would have been the official challenge to his position but that doesn't take the sting out of it when it happens. He was quite sure he'd caught Brownly-Smith off-guard, which was satisfying. What was still nagging at him was the last comment Brownly-Smith made before leaving – bigger than you and me – what had he meant by that?

Meanwhile Aggie was still concerned as to the welfare of the Costmart exec. Nicolas Nugent had emailed several times but had no reply. They needed to find out if Carl Tarrant was still in hospital or even still in the Isle. "What if he died?" Aggie said to the Sproken-Joneses when they had met earlier in the day.

"Don't be daft," James replied. "We'd have heard something, if that was the case."

"Why would we? Who knows that we even know he's here? We're hardly likely to get a call from the hospital saying *as the ones that abducted Mr Tarrant and set him up in a fake car accident we thought you might like to know that he died in the early hours of this morning.*"

"It would have been on the news surely?" Audrey asked, trying to rationalise with herself more than anyone else.

"Why?" Aggie demanded. "How often do you see the headline Drink Driver Kills Himself in Car Crash?" She paused looking at them both. "No. Never. Because it's not a story."

"Okay. Fair point, Aggie," James conceded. "We probably do need some clarification on this. Who could we ask?"

"Well the last place we knew he was, was in the hospital, so why don't we start there?" Audrey suggested.

"And how do we do that? Can you just ring up and ask if someone is still admitted?"

"Only if you are next of kin."

"But we aren't."

"Obviously, but they don't know that. We could pretend," James added.

"I can't," Aggie replied. "I've been there on charity events too often with Roger. I might be recognised."

"Fair enough. I'm a crap actor, as Audrey will verify."

"What he means is he's a crap liar. He seems to acquire a range of ticks and goes beetroot when he denies eating the last biscuit."

"Okay. So that's sorted then. Audrey, you'll have to go and pretend to be his next of kin."

Audrey deflated, feeling she had been tricked into a blind alley. "Okay," she said, pulling herself together. "I'll do it this afternoon."

It was this call that Aggie was nervously waiting for. Time was ticking by and she was now concerned that Audrey might have been rumbled. Aggie got up and picked up their glasses. "Do you want a top-up?" she asked Roger.

"Yes please," he said distractedly.

As she went into the kitchen Roger picked up the remote to flick to another channel. He heard a ping and looked on the table to see Aggie had received a text. He glanced at the screen to see James' name. Like a flash Aggie was back in the room grabbing her phone and disappeared back into the kitchen again. Roger tried to ignore the rash behaviour but things were really starting to niggle him now. She came back a few minutes later, smiling and bearing the refreshed tumblers of gin.

"Who was on the phone?" he enquired as nonchalantly as possible.

"Oh, it was just Audrey. Just some Network stuff," she replied.

Now Roger was really starting to hear alarm bells ringing. If it was Audrey why had the message come from her husband's phone? It was entirely possible that Audrey had used James' phone to text, it was equally possible that Aggie saved their numbers under one name. But there was the incident in the car park earlier, what was between them that needed to be discussed in cars. There was an increasing doubt nagging at the back of his mind, and everything kept coming back to James.

Chapter 22

Dumgarth
"So, pray, where are we off today, Rosie my dear?" Brownly-Smith said obsequiously, as he bent at the waist, or as much as his girth would allow, and kissed her hand. She squirmed inside, but managed to smile through gritted teeth. Pulling her hand away as quickly as she could, without appearing rude, she gestured towards the old dented Land Rover. She opened the passenger door but before he had put a foot towards it, Tike had jumped in and was barking aggressively at him. 'Smart dog,' Lady Rosemary thought to herself, whilst shooing the terrier out.

They pulled out of the village and headed north on the A388. "Today is the Heritage Tour. So we are looking at Cornwall from the Romans onwards. We are currently shadowing the former Devon border, but we'll talk more about that relationship when we stop off." Martin Brownly-Smith nodded, looking across her he caught occasional sea glimpses, where the now non-existent neighbouring county would once have adjoined Cornwall. To the left were unending green rolling fields. They whipped through small Cornish villages, lined by terraces of tiny stone houses. At Launceston they took the much lesser B3254 until they reached the A39, much to the relief of Brownly-Smith, who was quite terrified at the speed that Lady Rosemary took the winding country roads.

She took a sharp left following signs to the village of Morwenstow. There they entered a whole different terrain. The single track road, if you could call it that, was obviously not well used. There were long tracts of the road that had grass growing down the centre. The road veered left and right, up and downhill, Brownly-Smith growing paler as she went. The trees eventually gave way to open moor, covered in gorse and heather, with the occasional beautifully manicured lawn of cottages situated in splendid isolation. They climbed again, where now the moor gave way to the sea and rugged coastline. As the road petered out into a mere footpath, Rosemary put on the brakes and the Land Rover came to an abrupt halt.

Brownly-Smith sighed with relief. He started to open the window, desperate for air to calm his churning stomach.

"What are you doing, man? We're getting out here."

Looking out of the window at the windswept moor, Brownly-Smith could see no reason to get out as there was patently nothing there to see except heathland and sea. And, well, once you've seen one heath you've pretty much seen them all as far as he was concerned. Indeed, Martin Brownly-Smith was not a nature lover, unless it had been fricasseed and covered in an appropriate sauce. He liked order, the type of order that comes with refinement, and money. He revelled in the reliability of fine wines; earthy local ales had no hold over him. Townhouses with their clean lines, Regency being his favourite, won out over tumbledown picturesque cottages. The countryside was dirty and smelly, and although he appreciated that farmers needed to do their job, and yes that would involve mud and pig muck, at least they did it in the countryside, and did not pollute his darling London. The only use for the countryside, as far as he was personally concerned, was to act as a beautiful backdrop to classical music while speeding from London to their little place in the Cotswolds.

He was considering what value there could possibly be in alighting when he heard the spiky voice of Lady Rosemary, and jumped out before she asked again. He was somewhat relieved for the bracing onshore wind, but also concerned as to what she had planned. He was clearly not the walking type. He was a city man who enjoyed chauffeured cars, or a black cab as a minimum.

"Rosie, I'm not sure that I'm properly attired for this venture."

"Stuff of nonsense. Come on, it's not far."

"What's not far?" he asked pleadingly.

Ignoring his last comment she chided him, "Come on, keep up will you."

The footpath took them to the clifftops where the wind was making his flannel jacket flap uncontrollably. The view was stunning. The cliffs were typical of the Cornish coast, rugged and unforgiving. The sea crashed against massive boulders below, the spray creating momentary white fans.

"What do you think?" Rosemary shouted, competing with the noise of the elements.

"Stunning. Abso-bloody-lutely stunning," he offered eagerly in the hope this would expedite their return to the warmth of the car. Not so. They stood some moments just drinking in the spectacle. The white clouds being charged along by the wind, complementing the motion below them.

"So as breath-taking as this all is, how is this heritage – surely what we have here is just geography?"

"Fair point, but it is a pivotal point in Cornish geography. But first of all take a look at the geology," she said, beckoning him nearer to the cliff edge. Tentatively he followed and peering over he noticed that the beach looked corrugated. He looked at her quizzically.

"I know. Strange isn't it."

"What is it?"

"A sandstone beach by all accounts."

"Amazing, but doesn't look comfy."

She laughed along with him. "The reason we are starting our journey here is because this place bisects Cornish history in two directions. The river that would have been emerging into the sea to our right divided Cornwall from Devon. But this has not always been the case. Although arch enemies now, they were once more reliant on each other."

He nodded and looked at the huge expanse of sea trying to imagine its former neighbour still attached. "I see. So what was the other direction that you mentioned."

"Yes, so if you look directly out to sea, what do you think you might have seen prior to the Drift?"

"Sea?" he replied hopelessly.

She frowned at him, disappointed. "Is that your best effort?"

He shrugged.

"Didn't you study geography at school?" she said sarcastically.

"I am going to have a guess at Wales?"

"Bingo. Exactly. Wales would have been across the channel, or the Celtic Sea."

He looked visibly relieved. In his own domain of Whitehall, Brownly-Smith had incredible power. Power that he abused for his own amusement most of the time. But when he was around Lady Rosemary he was in awe. She was a truly formidable woman. This too confused him slightly – she was not what he was normally attracted to.

Obviously there was Mrs B-S at home, but that did not really count as far as he was concerned. She was his wife because he needed to have someone he could roll out at official events. It had been a marriage of convenience really. Their families had recommended the union and it seemed entirely sensible at the time. There was never any real frisant of passion between them, it had been a very correct engagement with a society wedding. This was followed by two children, but this was more a matter of duty than the consequence of deep love. The relationship worked well. She had the house in the Cotswolds with the bloody horses – the damned things cost a fortune, but they did keep her out of his hair. They also had the London house, which he resided in most of the time, she only using it when beckoned down for a social engagement, or when she felt the need to restock the wardrobe with clothes he never saw her wear. They loved each other in a comfortable, amiable way, where neither made any demands on the other, nor asked questions about their time apart. As far as he knew she was shagging the stable boy, it didn't really matter as long as she left him to his own devices.

Whereas he had a never-ending string of *personal* assistants who were carefully chosen for their legs, their compliance, and the fact that they were young enough to be his niece. Power was such an aphrodisiac it seems, and he believed that it would be a shame not to use it. The problem was that he bored quickly, or they believed that they would be able to woo him sufficiently to become the next Mrs B-S. His view on the rapid turnover of office staff was that it kept the personnel department in employment.

But Lady Rosemary didn't fit into either category – he had never felt so defenceless beside a woman. He noticed that she was talking whilst he had been drifting on this reverie. "Sorry old girl, can you say that again. It's so windy that I'm struggling to catch your drift?"

"So, I was explaining about the historical relationship that Cornwall had with Devon. So during the early Roman period this area was populated by a Celtic tribe, known as the Dumnonii. The area comprised of a united region of the Cornovii, the Cornish," she said gesticulating to the landmass the southwest of them, "and the Dumnonia, later to become known as Devon," now gesticulating to the ocean where Devon once lay.

"So Cornwall and Devon were one county?" he said nodding.

"More of a kingdom really."

"Hardly evident in their recent history, is it?" he said ironically.

"Precisely."

They looked out to sea for a while, Rosemary struggling to keep her hair from blowing in her eyes.

Eventually he asked, "And the Wales thing?"

"Well around this time there were deep connections between Wales as we know it today, and Cornwall. So much so that this landmass was known as West Wales, as opposed to North Wales which was across the sea. It is no coincidence that their names reflect each other," she continued. "The word wealh is Saxon for foreigner, and underpins the word *Wales* and *wall*."

"And the Corn bit of the word?" he queried.

Quickly she responded, "Well exactly what the word says, corn, the land of corn. Not so different from today, agriculture being a major part of the economy."

"It seems to make perfect sense," he agreed.

She stifled a smile, although this was becoming more difficult by the second. "Well it's evident when you consider the name Kernow, this refers to kernels of corn." At this point she turned away, ostensibly to take in the amazing vista, but she could no longer hide her grin.

When she felt able to keep a straight face she turned back and recounted the story of the Battle of Deorham, where in the late 500s King Ceawlin of Wessex successfully gained significant cities through military operations, securing the Cotswolds and important surrounding cities.

Martin Brownly-Smith blanched at the thought of his country residence being party to such an onslaught.

"As a result of their securing the land between Wales and Cornwall, a cultural separation emerged, resulting in the two different languages that we recognise today."

"I'm not sure that I do."

"Not literally speaking," she said as if talking to an insolent teenager.

As they walked back to the car he asked when Cornwall had become a singular place. She explained that in the early nine-hundreds King Athelstan had decreed that the border be set on the east bank of the river Tamar.

"Interestingly," she continued as she fired up the Land Rover, "Cornwall had a rather ambiguous status throughout the early history. There were links in many documents to Cornwall, or Cornubia as it was referred to then, but the same rules seemed not to apply to Cornwall that were applicable to the other counties of England."

"In what way?"

"The surviving documents from Norman times, such as the Doomsday Book and Mappa Mundi show that Cornwall was not subject to the same laws, and the maps show England and Cornubia as separate and distinct regions."

"Well I never. This I did not know. When did it become part of England as we know it then?"

"Difficult to say exactly as there are many references throughout the sixteenth and seventeenth century referring to the three provinces of England, Wales and Cornwall. This was probably perpetuated by lack of a shared language."

"That would serve to separate a nation, I'm sure. I imagine this is where the strong argument for British Overseas Territory originated?" he tested.

"Possibly. But these issues are all purely a matter of perspective. I'm sure if we went back in time far enough, before continental plates started drifting away from each other, then we could argue that Canada is an outpost of Scotland, or Cornwall is an annex of France."

He nodded reflectively. "I think we all probably choose the story which best supports our view of the world."

For a moment Lady Rosemary almost felt that she was starting to make him see the world differently, but only for a second.

An hour later they pulled into Bodmin, parking opposite a huge church. They dodged the traffic, crossing the road to enter its grounds. They wandered around the periphery of the imposing edifice, its sturdy structure more reminiscent of a castle than a house of god.

"Why Bodmin then, Rosie?"

"Bodmin, the word, means *the house of monks* in Cornish, and indeed Bodmin was a huge religious centre for many centuries. The draw being St Petroc, the namesake of this very church. According to historical texts he built a monastery here in the sixth century, although this church dates back to the late fourteen hundreds."

"Not really what I had Bodmin pegged for. All I knew about it was the gaol, and rather unsavoury local references to its inhabitants!"

"Well best you pay no attention to all that gossip. No, Bodmin is steeped in important Cornish history. This was an important place for pilgrimage to worship relics of St Petroc. In the Doomsday Book it was noted that Bodmin was the biggest town in the region. And in 1836 it became the County Town."

They walked across the graveyard, Rosemary leading the way to the ruins of a former chapel in a good state of repair.

"Is this the monastery?" he asked.

"No. This is what remains of the St Thomas Beckett chapel." They stood in its overgrown and eerie silence for some moments. Sunlight falling in shafts through its high arched windows, long since having lost their glass to the elements. Loose leaves blew about the floor in small tornadoes in the breeze. They spent some time wandering the graveyard, looking at the local names reappearing on the gravestones, showing a sense of community and continuity.

They left the car where it was and started walking up the hill, Lady Rosemary leading the way at a pace of knots. When they got to the Shire Hall Martin Brownly-Smith was decidedly out of breath, but tried hard not to show his lack of condition. "This is Mount Folly Square. A place of meetings and events."

Spying a restaurant on the square Brownly-Smith nodded his head in its direction, saying, "Fancy a spot of lunch while you let the next chapter unravel?"

She looked at the restaurant suspiciously.

"My treat, obviously," he added quickly.

They took a seat by the window, watching the locals about their business. Some council workers were inspecting hooks on lampposts for rust before they dared attach the seasonal hanging baskets. Some children were playing a game of tag on the square. Brownly-Smith studied their behaviour for some time and deduced that if a child was touching the railings surrounding the square then they were *safe*, but the same rule did not apply to touching trees or planters. He reflected on his own childhood games, so old that he could really only see them as monochromatic images. He decided that this game really had not changed during his lifetime – and who knows how long before that.

He ordered lambs' livers with a Cornish Blue Hollandaise whilst Lady Rosemary ordered a crab and avocado salad. "So imagine it's the year 1497, and for some time now there has been growing resentment that Cornwall has been subject to a disproportionately large tax levy at a time when there was great poverty."

"There must have been a reason for it? Governments don't just go around raising taxes willy-nilly."

"Some might say they don't go round raising taxes at all," she said sarcastically.

Realising she was having a snipe at the current Conservative stance on raising much needed revenue, he replied, "Austerity measures are an alternative approach to balancing the books. From your tone I suspect that you don't approve?" And without giving her time to respond, he continued. "Dave and Georgie-boy are just trying to save the citizens of the mainland more expense."

"I think we might have to agree to disagree on this one, Martin."

He shrugged.

"And yes, there was a good reason. Henry VII was waging war against the Scots and needed to keep the coffers loaded. The Cornish could see no advantage to them in this war, and the tax compromised some long existing laws, which we will discuss on a later tour."

Their food arrived and Brownly-Smith was suitably impressed with its quality. Not necessarily his usual standard but much better than much he had experienced in this backwater island. They ate in silence, Lady Rosemary picking up the story as their plates were cleared.

"Two men started the rebellion, quite probably from this very square. A blacksmith from St Keverne and a lawyer from here, led the march to London."

"Damned long way from Cornwall!"

"About two-hundred and fifty miles. An army of fifteen thousand marched into Devon, picking up more support along the way. They met no resistance from the English forces along the way, but equally received no message that the King would cede to their wishes."

"No plan B?"

"There was. It was to try and rally the enthusiasm of the men of Kent to join them, but when this didn't work some became disillusioned and returned home."

"Plan C?"

"Not a well-conceived one. There were a mere nine thousand Cornishmen left who could do little with their rudimentary weaponry to match the tens of thousands of the King's men who charged on the 17th June. The Battle of Blackheath was over by 2pm. Many were slaughtered and the long term effects were the seizure of Cornish estates and a lack of future royal support."

"I'm sure there's a message in this tale. Probably linked to death and taxes, and their inevitability."

Lady Rosemary bit her tongue at his insensitivity. "But it does show the Cornish determination and resilience as a nation."

"But not necessarily intelligent determination. Sometimes you have to know when you're beat, old girl."

"And sometimes you need to make a stand otherwise those in power will continue to abuse their position."

"But I think the death of so many was a rather high price to pay."

"Maybe so."

After lunch they retraced their steps and she took him on the brief drive to Lostwithiel, passing straight through the town and out onto yet another single track road with ferns so overgrown that they whipped the window as Lady Rosemary sped past. Martin Brownly-Smith was somewhat relieved that this lane had the benefit of passing-places to reduce the anxiety he felt each time they met a vehicle head-on. The road ended in a small open car park, seemingly in the middle of nowhere and for no purpose. One other car was parked up, and a man had the car boot open and was sitting on the bumper changing out of walking boots while an excited spaniel ran in circles. Brownly-Smith sat in the car with no obvious intention of getting out.

"Chop, chop!" Lady Rosemary chivvied.

"Where, in the name of all that is holy, are we going now," he said almost sulkily.

"Out. Come on, you'll enjoy this one."

"Really? Like I said. I'm really not a country person. I literally don't care whether I see another tree again in my life."

Regardless of his verbal resistance, he had already accepted defeat, and was lumbering his frame awkwardly from the car. The wind had picked up again, and he turned up the collar of his linen jacket to make his point. Oblivious to his moaning Lady Rosemary took the lead, walking towards a small wooden gate.

"I would like to present you with Restormel Castle."

He turned the corner and looked up the hill to a fine looking specimen of Norman architecture, with much of it still intact. "Are we going back to some old battles?"

"Strangely no. We're going to look at something that remains current. I was going to explain about the Duchy."

Brownly-Smith winced slightly, realising that it was the claim of the Duchy that had sent him on this ludicrous mission.

"Fire away!"

"Do you know the origins of the Duchy?"

"No, in actual fact I don't," which was entirely true. It had never occurred to him to look into what rights Prince Charles had over the county.

"So the Duchy came into being in 1337 when Edward III gave Cornwall to his son Edward -"

"The Black Prince?"

"Yes, that's the one. The charter then bestowing the title Duke of Cornwall on the eldest son."

"So what do you get as the Duke of Cornwall?"

"Pretty much the county."

"And the right to make posh biscuits?"

"So it seems, but that seems to be the preserve of this Duke alone."

They walked up the bank to crossing the solid stone bridge, pausing to look into the old moat before entering the castle. The castle was very satisfying, the external wall being perfectly round and complete. Standing in silence, with just the wind as a sound affect, it was possible to imagine hordes of heathens charging the drawbridge with unwieldy swords and clubs.

"Surely this castle is too old to have been built for the Black Prince."

"Indeed. It was passed over to him when he received the Duchy title, and remains as Duchy land today."

"Is there local resistance to the Duchy. I mean they hardly strike me as a bunch of royalists."

"Yes. In many ways. There is the ownership of land that the Cornish don't believe the crown has a right to. There is also the rather contentious fact that he receives the monies of people dying in the county intestate."

Brownly-Smith winced imperceptibly. He was aware of this, and had indeed been party to one of the rather generous donations made to a public school nowhere near the county of Cornwall. He knew that it had not been a popular move, so he decided it was probably best to continue to play ignorant on all subjects Duchy-related. He strolled off, showing interest in a hole in the wall, through which he spied some steps. He took off for the steps, trying to look eager at Lady Rosemary's choice of venue, but immediately regretting his proactiveness when he saw the scale of the climb. She caught him up at the top of the battlements, and they leant over the wall looking down on the vast carpet of fields. "So, well placed strategically?"

"Heavens yes. You could see an enemy approaching for miles. They didn't stand a chance," she agreed, nodding.

"So Charles owns this then, does he?"

"Yes, and many other heritage sites like it."

"Locals not happy about it?"

"As I said earlier, they never have been. Time and distance hasn't weakened that objection."

"Well, at least he hasn't inflicted one of those toy towns on Cornwall like he did on the poor buggers in Dorset," he said chuckling.

"Oh yes he did."

"Ah, sorry. Didn't realise," he said, genuinely apologetically.

Chapter 23

Pentwen

Elle was reversing the cleaning trolley out of one of the two penthouse suites, and as she reached the corridor she felt a presence behind her. A presence that grabbed her around the waist and pulled her close, whispering in her ear that she looked beautiful in her uniform. She turned, and was nose to nose with a soppy-faced Jake. He kissed her lightly on the lips.

"What are you doing?" she said, gently trying to pull away.

"I'm kissing my beautiful girlfriend."

"At work! I thought you said it was inappropriate for staff to be seen getting *up close and personal* at work?"

"Well, I'd say rules are made to be broken." He bent forward to kiss her again, but she pulled back, "Not here. Someone might see. Especially the penthouse residents."

He grabbed her hand, "Come on."

"Where are we going?"

"Up here." He pulled her down the hallway turning into a narrow dimly lit corridor that looked like a dead-end. He stopped and opened a small door and pulled her through and up the narrow staircase. The stairs opened into an attic in the eves with wooden shelving piled high with stuff. He leant her against the wall and they kissed in the darkness and cobwebs. The moment was shattered by the trill tone of Jake's phone.

He pulled away angrily, pulling his phone from his jean's pocket.

"What's up?"

"It's Jess. She never calls unless there's an emergency in the kitchen. I better get down there. But," he said pointing a finger at her and grinning cheekily, "I will be picking this up where we left off later tonight."

She smiled and blew him a kiss as he descended the stairs. She put a hand to her hair and felt where it had come down from her neat bun. As she sought to rearrange her hair she wandered around the attic. The shelves were stacked high with all sorts of items. There were cardboard boxes of light bulbs. There were stacks of bedding; sheets, duvet covers and pillowcases, and piles of towels of all sizes. None of these she recognised as the ones she used on changeover. 'How curious' she thought.

*

Elle had finished her morning shift at the hotel, and wandered over to the Surf Shack to see if Meg was finished yet. Mitch was out front, face covered in a mask as he used a noisy electric sander to sand a board suspended on a trestle table. He gesticulated to the shop door, indicating that Meg was inside.

Meg and Holly were sat on stools at the checkout sorting through a box of friendship bracelets that had just been delivered from South America.

"Hiya."

"Hey, Elle. You look knackered."

"Well you don't look so hot yourself," she joked back. "Anyway I thought you'd be late finishing today. How come you're done so early?"

"Holly and I struck a deal – she helped me with changeover and I'm helping her restock. So here we are restocking," Meg replied, spreading her arms out to indicate how much they still had to do. There were stacks of boxes of various sizes in the small area behind the till.

"Ah, so technically not done yet. Do you guys want a hand?" Elle asked picking up a small box with the words *Toe Rings - India* printed on the side.

"Dig in," Holly replied. "The more, the merrier."

For two hours they opened boxes, as excited as kids at Christmas by their content. After the few lines of beach jewellery they unpacked surf t-shirts from California and a new line of bikinis. Once the stock was unpacked, and they had put out as much as the shop could take, they repacked the remainder into the boxes and carried them to the stock room. "Can you stack them on the far left corner as Ray has a wetsuit delivery coming in tomorrow, and that will take up the rest of the space."

"No worries."

Meg and Elle started carrying the boxes through and stacking as advised. Meg stopped and gazed up at a shelf thoughtfully. "Holly, what are all of these boxes full of?" she asked, pointing to the top shelf of the rickety wooden shelving.

"Hm, it looks like boxes of our old plastic bags. Since going eco we banned the bag, and now only give out the brown paper ones if customers need them."

"Hmm," Meg replied thoughtfully.

They were just finishing up when Jake came in, followed by a very dusty Mitch. "What are you two lovely ladies doing for entertainment tonight?" Mitch asked.

"Nothing special planned? Is there something on?" Meg enquired.

"Sure. We're going down south to meet up with another crew. You wanna tag along? All you need is a bed bag, booze and burgers."

Meg and Elle looked baffled.

"What he means is," Jake explained, "that we are going to have a beach party at a secret spot on the south coast. Lloyd's taking the van so we'll kip in there. Have you got sleeping bags?"

"No. We packed pretty light."

"We've got some you can borrow," Holly offered.

"Ah, cheers, Holly. That'd be great. So what else do we need?"

"Whatever you want to drink and whatever you want to throw on the barbie," Mitch concluded.

"Sounds like a plan. We'll go back to the backpackers and get some stuff together. What time shall we meet up?"

"We'll be by at six."

"Deal."

They drove for nearly an hour, the last leg down a single track road that ended in a shingle car park. There were quite a few cars parked up when they pulled in. They loaded themselves up with disposable BBQs, rugs, bags of shopping and crates of beer, and made their way down the slipway to the sandy beach. As they went Mitch and Jake exchanged lots of high fives with those already gathered.

The sun was still high and warm enough for shorts and t-shirts. The beach was deserted except for their gradually expanding group. People put out rugs in a great semicircle facing the sea. Lloyd and a couple of locals started putting the BBQs out and taking off the wrapping, whilst the rest played football noisily, or lay about on the rugs, drinking beer and chatting.

There was a small clean swell running so a few of the locals went back to the cars to pick up a couple of foam boards so they could lark around in the residual sun. Elle and Meg met new people, chatted, drank and eventually ate, as the red orb of sun dropped, and a spectrum of warm and improbable colours were reflected on the sea. The evening was magical, but there was the looming issue nagging at the back of their mind – how to manage *the situation*.

"I've been thinking," Meg said to Elle when they were alone as they walked back to the van to get more supplies.

"And?"

"What about we tell Lloyd about the situation?"

"Why would we do that?" Elle asked, confused.

"Because he's not stupid. Because he's well connected. Because I think he would help us if we came clean."

Elle considered her answer. "And exactly what would we tell him?" she asked cautiously.

"Firstly be honest about how we got into this mess, but make sure we emphasise what will happen to Pentwen if we don't get this right."

Elle was warming to the idea. She had already considered how incapable they were of managing the situation alone, and in order for their plan to work they needed help. She was also reticent to tell Jake. They were too fond of each other, and at this stage it might ruin their relationship. Yes, Lloyd seemed like the perfect alternative.

"Okay. Shall we do it tonight?"

"No time like the present."

They were walking along the shoreline while the rest of the party lounged on rugs; drinking and smoking. Meg nodded to Elle, who nodded back.

"So exactly what is it you two want to say to me that necessitates us having to walk on chilly damp sand?"

Elle stopped walking and took a deep breath. Lloyd turned to face her, now feeling a little concerned. She started, "What we have to tell you is very hard, but we don't know who else to turn to. We don't know who we can trust. You need to hear us out and promise that you won't tell a soul unless we've agreed it with you."

"Whoa! This is a bit serious for beach party banter. What can't I tell who?" he said, perplexed.

"You can't tell anyone what we are about to tell you. The repercussion will be huge, too huge."

"Hell. That's a big promise when I don't even know what we're discussing here. I'm not sure I can promise that."

"You have to, for the sake of Pentwen," Meg said urgently.

Lloyd held his hands up defensively. "Okay, okay. Why don't you start with what's on your mind and we'll take it from there?"

They nodded eagerly, and Elle continued. "So, where to start?"

"When we got stopped outside the Student Union," Meg suggested.

"Yes, the beginning. So here's what happened. At uni last year we were approached by a guy as we left the Student Union. He said he had the opportunity for a paid internship which was perfect for us. Whoever took the job needed to be a Business and Tourism Management student, female, and be a surfer."

"We were like, student – check, female – check, surfer – check," Meg interrupted. Elle glared at her, and she stopped.

"The man said that he'd looked into us and that we were ideal candidates. We would have a year out of uni for the internship, paid for, and if we were successful in our mission, they would cover our final year fees for us."

"I mean it's too good to be true, hey? But here we are," Meg interrupted again.

"So what was this mission?" Lloyd asked.

"Well that's the thing – it was so easy that we were like, yeah," Meg replied.

Elle glared at Meg again, and continued, "We were to come to Pentwen and try to get jobs in the area and meet the locals. Our cover, which was barely a cover as we are Business and Tourism students, was to find out all we could about eco-tourism."

"Well that seems innocent enough. But," Lloyd hesitated, trying to work something through in his head. "Why couldn't they do that themselves. I mean, if they've got the money to cover your fees and expenses for two years, they must be able to operate the internet and learn in the same way we did."

"That's what we said, but he said he was especially interested in how you get the locals to buy into the project. How do you get it off the ground, and like, where to start."

"Okay. That makes more sense, but it still seems like an expensive way to find out some quite innocuous information."

"Okay, so so far you don't think we did anything really bad?" Meg asked.

"Well, no. Not really. A little underhanded, I suppose, but nothing terrible. So what's the problem?"

"It's escalated. The mission, I mean."

"And we're scared and don't know what to do, or who to turn to."

"We didn't want to tell Jake. I'm too close to him and he might feel totally betrayed," Elle confided sadly.

"Well, he may have a point you know, Elle."

"I know. I get that. And he will have to know at some point, but I only want him to know when we've put this thing right. That's why we need you."

"So explain this mission-drift."

"We met with our contact in Padstow -"

"Which is who, by the way?"

"We don't know. He won't tell us his name, nor give us any contact details. He calls us."

"Hmm, okay. Go on."

"Anyway, we met him last week and he said that now we are not just on a fact-finding mission. Now he wants us to start messing with things."

"Have they, at any point, explained why they want you to do any of this?"

"Yeah, there's this other place, but we don't know where. And they want to go eco too, but they don't know how to start."

"But now they want us not just to pass on useful information, they want us to meddle with Pentwen's chances of passing the assessment, *to remove the competition* as he put it."

"Ah, that makes more sense," Lloyd said, almost satisfied with the logical explanation. Nodding and thinking, he continued, "So why are you telling me? Why don't you just walk away from the situation. Just tell the guy you don't want to be part of his evil plan anymore?"

"Because we're scared. They keep talking about this other guy, the one he works for. Our contact just refers to him as *he*, and *HQ*. And it's all a bit scary."

"Has he threatened you in any way?"

"No. I mean not exactly. It's just his manner."

"Okay. Tell me more about his manner. Is he a thug?"

"Heavens no," Elle replied almost laughing. "He's are the polar opposite. He's, well, posh, I guess."

"Well I didn't see that coming."

"I know. We're scared of posh people. But there's something about his manner, like he has total control. So, I don't know, so arrogant. It feels like if you don't do what you're ordered to, then they will get rid of you, and I don't mean just sack you."

"Yes, like you are expendable. And they are well connected enough to not even care about how they go about it."

"And have they actually threatened this?"

The girls considered the question. "Well, no. Not explicitly. But it's the feeling you get when you're with him."

Lloyd was quiet for a while. "Moving on, what are your thoughts?"

"Well, we do have a plan," Meg said quite excitedly.

"But we can't do it by ourselves," Elle added, nodding at Lloyd, "so we thought you'd help," she continued, grimacing at the audacity of her request.

"I guess I'm in."

Chapter 24

Truro

Roger had had enough. He could not sleep, eat or concentrate on business with the worry that Aggie was having an affair with James. It could not go on, this had to be dealt with here and now. He jumped in the Beamer drove through the deserted city streets faster than the law would appreciate. He pulled into the car park at the rear of the Old County Hall and felt sick to his stomach seeing Aggie's old Peugeot parked next to James' Volvo. He gripped the steering wheel, unsure what to do next. He knew that the not knowing was driving him mad, this really had to end now.

With new determination he got out of the car and marched to the rear door. He grabbed the handle, but it was locked. He shook the door handle furiously, rattling the door in its old wood frame. The door suddenly moved, opening about six inches, enough for him to see Aggie staring out at him in utter surprise. Her hair was wild and dishevelled and she was glistening with sweat, damp patches evident on her tiny vest. "Roger?!" was all she could manage, literally dumbfounded.

He stood with his hand on his hips, equally unsure what to say next. "I thought you said you were going back to the cottage tonight?" was the best he could manage.

She shrugged, "Well, I, well -" as she trailed off the door was opened wider and James stood behind her, equally sweaty, dishevelled and surprised. "Roger!"

"James?" Roger spat sarcastically.

Aggie and James were stood so close, both appearing to be somewhat out of breath. They exchanged a long look with each other. The type of look that conveys complex messages back and forth, but only between those who know each other well enough to be able to read each other's thoughts. Roger watched their conspiratorial exchange with such an intense sadness that he thought his heart was actually breaking.

"Okay. You better come in," Aggie said ushering him in, whilst checking around that no one was watching. Roger was baffled. Maybe she didn't want a scene in the street. He could imagine how the media would love the headline – Jilted Governor punches Lover's Lover in the Old County Hall!

They ushered him through the utility room and down a corridor where several door stood open, through which he glimpsed piles of boxes, stacked high. Roger also fancies he can hear noises; movement and voices elsewhere in the building. He senses something to his right and swings round abruptly to see Evans-two coming out of a room wheeling an empty sack barrow. "Roger," Evans-two says nodding as he passes by.

"Evans," Roger replies, completely confused by this new revelation. Aggies shows him into a room, that if carpeted and furnished with period furniture would have been a magnificent reception room. Its splendour was evident even in its current state of chaos; dusty parquet flooring with a heavy wooden desk beside the window with a chair and computer monitor at either end. There were piles of boxes stacked around the room, and some mismatched dusty or paint splattered chairs were scattered randomly around the room.

James followed them in, and stood awkwardly for a moment. "I'll leave you to it then," he said, half muttering to himself. Aggie nodded to him. She sat down on a rickety wooden dining chair and with a huge sigh put her head in her hands. Roger stood trying to make sense of what was occurring. The noises he could hear echoing around the building confirmed that this may not be the illicit affair that he had been so worried about. But if there wasn't an affair, what were they doing, and why were the Evanses, and heavens knew who else, here with sack barrows.

Eventually Aggie looked up. She looked exhausted. She pulled a band from her pocket and grabbed her wild hair, trying to force it into some semblance of control, wild tendrils resisting the reorganisation. "So what the hell is going on here?" he said at last.

"How much do you want to know?"

"All of it."

"How about I tell you some of it and then we'll review what you need to know?"

Roger had no idea what she was talking about. "Just talk," he said quite cruelly.

"So, this is head office for the Food Sourcing Network," she started.

"I bloody well know that. I gave you the damned building – remember?" he shouted back. She was shocked by his anger, but continued.

"So, I only ever really told you about the community collaboration aspects of the Network."

"Meaning what? There's more?"

"Yes. But there were good reasons for not telling you. I never wanted to compromise your situation."

He shrugged.

"So, there are other aspects that you were not aware of which are, should we say, less legitimate."

"Less legitimate? You mean illegal?"

"Well, not as legal as we would like them to be." She put her head in her hands again for a moment, collecting herself for what she was about to say. "The bits I never mentioned were the logistical factors. Food is easily sourced but getting it to where it needs to be is highly complex and needs all sorts of support. Not to mention storage and transport."

"So what did you do? Steal a lorry?"

"Not one, no."

"Jesus, how many? And who the hell from?"

"We don't like to say stole, we like to say liberated."

"And who are *we*?"

"All of us. James and Audrey, Stewie, the Robersons, the Morcoms, everyone really, the Varcoes –"

"The Varcoes?" he spat, incredulous. "Some real masters of crime you've got there," he said angrily, although not sure why he was so angry. "And who did you liberate these lorries from exactly?"

"From the people who left us to starve. Costmart walked out on us and if we hadn't have thought on our feet we would have starved. You were there at the beginning. You remember what it was like."

"We wouldn't have let you starve. We would have airlifted in for as long as was necessary."

"That's all very well for you to say with the benefit of hindsight, but we didn't know that. We had no idea who to trust." Both voices were becoming raised now, both defensive.

"So we took over their infrastructure to guarantee food supply throughout the county."

"What do you mean, *their infrastructure?*"

"Pretty much everything. We use the depots as distribution centres where our stock is stored, either in the warehouse or the industrial chillers and freezers. We then distribute to the satellite centres using their transport system – trucks and climate controlled lorries."

Roger laughed aloud, but nothing about it sounded humorous. "Yes. That makes total sense. How naïve of me not to realise that the food chain was so fluid." He slumped into a battered old armchair head down, staring at his shoes. Aggie now realised the enormity of what she had done. It was not just that she had lied to him, and kept on lying. It was that they had not trusted him. Not trusted him when he arrived to help them, but they had continued not to trust him.

She went to him, sitting on the arm of the chair trying to hug him to her. He neither resisted nor gave in to her. An hour ago he thought that the worst thing in the world would be that his suspicions about Aggie and James would be true. And now, now what? He did not know. Why did this feel worse. Why would he almost have rather found them in a passionate clinch. Because he felt betrayed by a community.

"Roger, darling. We couldn't tell you. You know that, don't you."

Nothing.

"We couldn't tell you at the beginning because we didn't know who to trust. And then we couldn't tell you later because, because, well because it wouldn't have been fair on you. It would have compromised you. You do understand that, don't you?"

Roger knew she was right, but still felt foolish. Everyone knew but him – idiot. He realised he was being childish, and squeezed her hand to show contrition.

"Okay. I understand the covertness, but, oh I don't know what I feel."

Aggie was relieved with how far they had got with the story so far, but they weren't there yet. Sitting on the arm of the chair with her arm around his shoulder she continued. "And as you were unaware of all of this you can see how efficiently the operation has been running for all of this time."

He nodded, not liking the tone her voice had taken.

"And indeed the operation had been running as smooth as clockwork right up until last week."

"What happened last week?"

"A guy form Costmart turned up. Unexpectedly. At the depot."

"Christ. What did he say?"

She got up and walked over to the long window overlooking the road. She studied the railway line, quiet until the six-fifteen to Falmouth started the days commuting.

"What did he say, Aggie?" he pushed, discomforted by her silence.

"He didn't say anything," she said without turning around.

"What do you mean, he didn't say anything. He must have said something."

"No. He didn't say anything."

"I mean he must have said something. He didn't just stand there mute. So where is he now? Did he go home?"

"He's in hospital."

"He's what?" There was a moments silence. "Aggie, what the hell happened," he said rising from the chair and grabbing her shoulders, turning her to face him. Their eyes locked.

"He had an accident. A drink driving accident. Once he gets out of hospital he will be facing charges."

"How convenient."

She looked away. "Only temporarily. That's why all the stock has been transported here. As soon as he's out of hospital he might want to visit the depot so we've had to mothball it again."

Suddenly the penny dropped and Roger could see the bigger picture, and the enormity of the inconvenient visitor. "What about the other depots? I thought they had a few dotted about the county?"

"They do, which is why we have such a slick distribution system. And that's why we're so worried. If this guy has come to visit one depot, who's to say that he's not visiting all of them. We cleared out the east and south depot, but as you will see there's no space here for any more. We're packed to the rafters as it is. And it's a bit tricky working under the cover of darkness in such as central spot."

Although Roger could see the enormity of the matter he was hit by a wave of relief. So much so that he burst into spontaneous fits of laughter. He was laughing so loudly that James came busting back into the room, concerned for Aggie welfare. "What's so funny?" Aggie called over the noise of his laughter, suddenly quite concerned.

When Roger controlled his outburst enough to allow him to talk coherently, he said, "So you two are not, you know, not having an affair?"

Aggie and James exchanged confused glances, looking back at Roger, she said incredulously, "No. What in god's name made you think that?"

"The texting, the whispering, the not being at the cottage during nights when you said you were. Being so tired the next day that you could barely function."

And then she saw it, how all of this had looked to Roger. The logical conclusion that he had come to. It hurt her to think that he must have been carrying this doubt inside himself.

"Oh god, Roger," James started, patting him on the shoulder. "I had no idea that was how it looked. Honestly, really this is purely professional. Ask Audrey. She's been with us most nights, not to mention half of Porthissick."

"So what do we do from here?" Roger asked.

"If only we knew."

The day's revelations had been too much, on top of the impending election that he had not even had time to absorb. "I need a bit of time to deal with all of this. I'm going for a walk." He strolled down Station Road and wandered into the city, aimlessly. He wasn't sure how much more he could cope with. He needed to prioritise. The most important thing to focus on was the upcoming election and doing the right thing for the Isle, but if any of tonight's revelations got into the public domain the election would be screwed. So, logically, he had to deal with the immediate problem in order to manage the long-term issue of winning an election.

After a long contemplative walk he returned to Old County Hall and they gathered back in the box-strewn boardroom. Roger, having just outlined his suggestion as to how they manage the incendiary situation, sat back and waited for their reaction

"Roger, you cannot be serious?" exclaimed Aggie. "That's a ludicrous idea."

"Well may be so, but do you have a better answer?"

"No, but that's far too risky." She looked at James for confirmation. He sat very still, contemplating the suggestion. Before he was forced into an answer the door opened and Audrey entered. James looked relieved. She started to apologise for being late, when she noticed Roger, and froze in her tracks.

"It's alright darling," James interjected quickly. "Roger knows about the distribution centres we have been utilising, and about the man from Costmart being in hospital from that terrible drink-driving *accident*," his eyes challenging her not to say anything outside of these events, having not mentioned the dubious acquisition of famous high stress brands for the purposes of keeping the citizens calm.

"Oh, excellent," she said breezily. "Good to have you on board, Roger. So where are we at with the next move?"

"Yes Roger, why don't you explain to Audrey your crazy plan for making this alright again?" Aggie said, folding her arms across her chest with a hint of sarcasm.

Chapter 25

Pentwen

Meg glanced, as subtly as she could, over the back of the seat, trying to look out of the bus's back window.

"I still can't see him," she said urgently. "And we're nearly there."

"I'm sure he's on it. He'll have a plan," Elle said, trying to calm her agitated friend.

"But that crappy van of his. It's bound to break down, and then where will we be?"

"Lloyd's too resourceful for that."

"I'm really starting to doubt that."

"Sit down and relax. If he doesn't make it, we'll just be more organised for next time. And we do have a backup plan."

"Hmm," Meg replied, evidently unconvinced.

They alighted and walked slowly along the quayside, subtly scanning the area for any sign of Lloyd. They spotted the man's car but didn't quicken their pace, hoping that if Lloyd was late, their dawdling would give him the minutes he needs to get set up. They reached the man's car, reticent to get in, but knowing they couldn't stall for any longer.

"Hello, ladies. And how are we this fine day?"

"Fine thank you. What should we call you?" Meg asked, as a continuation of their greeting.

"Sir will do just fine. Now how are we getting on?"

They exchanged nervous glances before they started their scripted delivery. As he started speaking Meg nudged Elle and nodded her head slightly to the passenger window. Elle followed her gaze and saw a young uniformed man with scruffy hair walking between the parked cars peering through windscreens and jotting something in a small pad. Elle winked back to Meg. The young man approached their car slowly, and knocked on the driver's window. Their contact pushed a button and the window retracted soundlessly. "Yes?" the man in the driver's seat said curtly.

"Parking inspector," said the young man in a Brummie accent. "And I am inspecting your pay and display ticket," he continued, hand held out ready to receive said ticket.

"What are you wittering on about, man. We've only just arrived."

"I just saws these two arrive," pointing vaguely to the back seats, "But yous been 'ere for ages."

"That's because I was waiting for the young ladies," the driver replied, trying to be more polite now, but it sounded strained.

"Well this is a car park, not a car *wait*. If you was not movin' then technically you was parked, and in such a case would need a ticket, according to the Harbour Commissioner you must pay for the allotted time."

While the driver and the Brummie parried on the finer details of parking tariffs and definitions of parked and waiting, Elle and Meg noticed another couple, hand in hand, near the driver's side of the car. She had long fair-brown hair in a braid, and he was rather scruffy and on the plumper side. They seemed to be happy and in love, taking it in turns to take holiday photos of each other, currently standing with their back to the car - taking selfies.

Meg turned to Elle and winked very slightly. Elle gave a slight incline of her head in response.

Eventually the inspector left satisfied, mainly due to the healthy contribution that the driver had made to the Harbour Commissioner's favourite charity, although no one was under any illusion where the money would end up.

"So, where were we?" he continued.

They got off the bus at Pentwen bus station and were amused to see Lloyd parked up over the road, grinning at them. They crossed and he held the door open for them to jump in. They were buckling up when they heard a rustling from the back of the van, and from under a blanket the day's cast emerged. Sully the Brummie car park inspector, and Jess and Hog the star struck lovers and selfie-takers extreme. Everyone laughed. "Did you get what you were after?" Meg asked.

"It looks like it," Lloyd started. "The photo that Jess and Hog took clearly shows you in the back and it's a really clear shot of him because the window was down, thanks to Sully."

"Sweet."

"Yes. We just need to get back and try out the audio from your phone now, Elle."

"Then drinks are on me!" Sully yelled, waving the twenty pound note that Mr Brownly-Smith had given him as the sweetener.

"Off to the Bay Bar please, Lloyd!"

Chapter 26

Porthissick

The residents of the Isle of Kernow were gradually becoming acclimatised to their new weather system, especially the warmer climate. Even before the Drift they had always had a different weather experience than the rest of the country, which was quite reliable in its uniqueness. The old Cornish winters had generally been wet, which explained their verdant countryside. What was unusual about Cornish rain was that it did not fall downwards, but due to the prevailing wind, it fell at acute angles rendering umbrellas useless.

Cornwall virtually never had frost, and only seemed to have snow if it was a leap year, and even then only for a day if they were lucky. On waking up to snow the entire population of the county would sit, glued with their radios tuned to Pirate FM or BBC Cornwall, waiting to see who would be having a snow-day. *'We are just receiving news that Pentwen High School will be closed, and, we are just receiving incoming information that no traffic can exit Porthtowan as cars are sliding back down the hill on Coast Road...'* Wonderful days, but few and far between.

Spring was the most glorious season, haled in by the magnificent Magnolia trees with their dominating pre-emptive blossom, followed by the gentler cherry. The leaping lambs, and hedgerows blooming with early daffodils creating seasonal optimism. Next came summer, with its balmy, warm days, accompanied by light breeze, fatal to the visitors who were unaware that the breeze masked the most intense sun in the country. This season would swing from Mediterranean vistas of crystal blue sea reflecting a crystal blue sky separated by a ribbon of golden sand, to gusting winds bringing huge billowing clouds which inevitably deposited unseasonal precipitation on a charity fete, undeserving of such retribution.

Within minutes of the schools being back, children ensconced in classrooms, the weather made a change, as if it knew that the only way to get children focused was to remove the allure of the beach. Autumn was also a blessed season. The residents got to see each other through the thinning throngs of visitors, and exchange stories of their season. The countryside celebrated too, with the cliff tops and moorland turning from green and yellow of the summer flowers to the gold, russet and dusky pinks of the heathers.

This pattern had been interrupted since the Drift. There was still a wet and very windy winter, but the spring and summer hit with heat and power not previously experienced. Today was one such summer day. The temperature had built remorselessly, but what was unusual was that the ubiquitous wind had dropped, leaving them in stifling humidity. It was atmospheric heat, rather than contact with sunlight, with very little escape. Everyone was tired and rather grouchy, and for the first time since he had moved into Rose Cottage, Roger was regretting his choice of residence. The cottage was nestled into an inland cliff, which formed the back walls of the tiny garden. The house itself was low lying, allowing no breeze to enter. This was compounded by the minute scale of the rooms, adding to the oppressive feel.

It was too much for Roger, it was early yet but he'd be better waiting for her there, rather than sitting around laying mental bets with himself as to where the next trickle of sweat would depart from.

He pulled up in the car park at Godrevy Towans and sat in the Beamer thinking about his approach again. His night's sleep had been interrupted hourly by his ruminations about how to play today's meeting, and the potential implications of anything he disclosed being taken further. He put the radio on, tuning to Radio 3 in the hope of some uplifting music, only to be met by a sombre Mozart requiem. He let the music swallow him up while watching clouds skid across the blue sky by the return of the wind. The knocking sound made him jump, turning to see the ample bosom of Chief Superintendent Linda Romney, Commander of the Isle of Kernow police force.

This was the controversial plan. Roger believed in going straight to the top. Roger was also more than aware that Linda was more than a little sweet on him. To be fair, anyone who had witnessed them in the same room together would be more than aware of her intentions. Her overt approaches often leaving left Roger slightly petrified.

He smiled, and took a deep breath before pushing open the car door. Linda had her hair down and the thick dark brown locks were blowing wildly around her face. She leant forward to kiss him on the cheek, ensuring that her breasts made solid contact with his chest in the process. Roger blushed slightly.

"Well this is a lovely surprise. You and me on a romantic beach walk together. You and Aggie split up or am I to be the other woman?"

Roger winced, hoping she was playing with him. He forced a laugh. "No, the clandestine nature of today's meeting is not romantic Linda," he said, sounding apologetic.

"A girl can always dream," she said putting her arm through his as they walked across the car park and out towards the expansive beach. They stood on the dune for some moments watching the extreme sport of combining go-carts with kites in high winds. Men were towed across the sand at an incredible rate of knots by the cross-shore winds, their arms being pulled from their sockets.

"Madness," she said nodding towards them.

"Yes," he agreed. "I guess we all do mad things at times, for various reasons."

They continued down the dune to the beach proper and found the level of sand that was not so dry that walking became a chore, but was not too wet that your feet got damp.

"So, if you are not here to sweep me off my feet, you better spill the beans."

'Here we go,' Roger thought before launching into a life changing speech. "Hypothetically speaking, what are your thoughts on anyone that may contravene a law or two?"

She stopped and turned to face him. "Let's get this straight, you're asking me, a Chief Superintendent, what I feel about criminals?! You may be surprised to hear that I feel that anyone who breaks the law should be punished for it."

Not a good start, but in retrospect, probably predictable. "So what if they were doing whatever they were doing for the greater good?"

"As I just said, there is a big book with all the naughty behaviours listed in it. All I do is compare said behaviour to the list in the book, and it dictates the consequences. It's called the British legal system, and has been operating like this for quite a period of time."

"Okay, I'll go with that. But what if someone had done something where no one got hurt, and it stopped an entire community suffering?"

"Then I'd apply the same book to the situation – it's either illegal or not."

"And there's no grey area here? Just black and white?"

"Pretty much."

Roger pondered this. Was there anywhere to go with this if it's just black and white? How much of this could he divulge without getting anyone into trouble. Even if he told her all that had occurred without mentioning names this might trigger an investigation, which would ultimately find a few guilty faces.

"If I tell you something that has not been reported as a crime are you duty bound to investigate it?"

"If it were reported to me in my official capacity as Chief Superintendent, then yes I would."

"Ah, but not in your capacity as fellow beach walker?"

"I don't think it is the job of any beach walker to investigate potential crimes."

Roger sighed inwardly before laying it bare before her.

Chapter 27

Dumgarth

Martin Brownly-Smith pulled up outside Athelstan House in the Audi at the prescribed hour. Feeling that he had been here often enough, and spent sufficient time with Lady Rosemary, he felt it would be fine to knock and enter rather than waiting for the door to be opened. As he pushed the solid oak door open he was repelled by a savage attack from Tike the terrier. Behind Tike stood Dotty the retriever, and something that looked like a ginger Alsatian, a dog he did not recognise from his previous visits here. The welcoming committee was enough to make him retreat to the porch and await Lady Rosemary's appearance.

She came to the door and ushered him in, glancing out to the drive. "The walk up the hill too much for you, old man?"

He could not decide whether the old man reference was to his age and fitness or a term of endearment, so he chose the latter.

"No. I thought I'd be chauffeur today." In reality there was nothing chivalrous about this act. He was pretty terrified by Lady Rosemary's driving skills, she was a fast driver. To be fair, there had never been any near-misses, but his survival instinct had kicked-in during their last outing, and he was going to stick to his guns.

"As you like," she said nonchalantly, whilst gathering her bag and coat.

"Where to today, m'Lady?"

"We're going to Redruth."

He raised an eyebrow. "Really?" he replied, disbelieving that this could be correct.

"Yes. Really, today we are on the Industrial Tour" she replied testily.

As they swept down the A38 he asked what the purpose was of today's trip. She explained how they were visiting Cornwall's' industrial heartland, metaphorical and literal.

They pulled into Heartlands, a cultural centre reinvigorating the Redruth area. They walked across the plaza to a small unit, which looked to all intents and purposes like a giftshop.

"What is this?" he asked.

"It's the Cornish Language centre."

They entered and were met by Marjorie, a lady with a strong Cornish accent, who greeted Lady Rosemary like a long lost friend. She ushered them to a large table and offered them tea, and cakes that resembled industrial strength scones.

"So what can I tell you?" Marjorie asked.

"I thought it wold be interesting to explain to Martin what happened to the Cornish language. She nodded and turned on her stool to face Brownly-Smith, hands cupped cosily around her mug of tea. She sat like this in silence, gathering her thoughts before she began. "So as you may well know, Cornish is a Brythonic language, as is Welsh."

Brownly-Smith shrugged. "No I didn't, but to be honest I don't really know what that means."

"Ah," she said nodding, "It just means indigenous Briton, from the Welsh *Brython*."

He nodded, not really caring what it meant. Not really sure why Lady Rosemary had brought him here at all. It was nothing but a glorified gift shop as far as he was concerned.

"Indigenous Britons, as opposed to the Gaelic or Anglo-Saxons."

He nodded, still disinterested, then caught the laser-beam glare that Lady Rosemary was giving him.

"Oh. How interesting," he forced.

"So technically, this is the original British language. There's a strong case for it replacing English," she continued earnestly.

He raised his eyebrows, not really sure how to reply to the evidently unhinged woman. When she saw his discomfort she laughed, "Only kidding," she said kindly.

Unimpressed with her sense of humour he smiled back politely.

"The murder of the language occurred as far back as 1549. As part of the Reformation, Edward VI instructed that an act be passed that thereafter all church services be held in English. As a way of ridding the church of its connections to Rome, the Latin liturgy was banned and was replaced with the Book of Common Prayer. From that day forth it was decreed that all church services would be held in the English tongue, including Cornwall."

She stopped for a sip of her tea, before continuing.

"Many Cornish did not speak English, so there were obvious technical difficulties. But this was not their issue. Their complaint was the erosion of their culture, being dictated by power in London. Removal of icons related to Catholicism were removed from churches, and pilgrimages were banned. This was too much for the beleaguered Cornish who were suffering from a poll tax on sheep, and inflation that was making their lives more and more arduous.

"Their uprising at having the language of their service changed to English, a language they claimed not to understand, was met with ridicule, based on the point that the services they wished to retain were in Latin, another language that they did not comprehend."

She took a cake a broke it in two, with some considerable effort Brownly-Smith noted, declining her offer of one in favour of his teeth. She picked at the crumbs on her plate before continuing. "Over 5000 people lost their lives in the subsequent uprising. A terrible loss. So unnecessary," she said reflectively.

Brownly-Smith lowered his eyes to acknowledge the seriousness of the event.

"This really marked the end of the Cornish language. For many years it had been the domain of the working classes, the upper-classes long since adopting English as the language of the royal court, trade and commerce. The change was most greatly felt in west Cornwall where it really was the last bastion of the language which ultimately the English chased into the sea."

Brownly-Smith looked at her confused.

"Literally," she said laughing. "The only place that the language existed in regular parlance was on the ships."

She got out some cue-cards and laid them on the table to demonstrate connections between Cornish and English. Brownly-Smith tried to look enthusiastic, but was sure these were part of a children's game, and felt slightly insulted by her manner.

"Is this all that's really left of the Cornish language now?" he enquired, trying to sound interested.

"There was a resurgence in 1904, when a chap called Jenner published a handbook of the Cornish language." She got off her stool and moved to the desk, picking up a well-worn book. "This is a revision of it published about five years ago," she said pushing the text towards him. "You can even get it on Amazon now," she exclaimed.

He flicked through it, stopping occasionally to read a section.

"In recent times there has been a concerted resurgence to get the language recognised and encourage its use before it dies out completely. There are about four hundred fluent speakers in the county and the council is investing money to try and increase its profile, by doing things like adding

Cornish to road signs and the like. In 2002 we received a European Charter for Regional or Minority Languages, so it's definitely increasing in profile. All we need to do now is increase the number of speakers."

Rosemary, who had been quiet throughout, spoke up. "This is why I have been running Cornish language lessons at the Cultural Centre. It's a start. It's mainly locals wanting to learn the basics, but it's definitely building."

After they had finished in the shop, Lady Rosemary guided him over the plaza to the four-story high pump house. "This is Robinson's Shaft," she explained. "It was operational from 1903 until the mid-fifties." They entered the engine house and were met by George Davey, who gave them a tour of the engine works and a potted history of its role in the work of the South Crofty Mine. All considered it was quite a nice little tour Brownly-smith thought to himself. Having no great interest in engineering of any kind, but most especially of that on an industrial scale. He was even more impressed that there was a delightful, although again quite industrial-looking, café to break up the day. They both ordered the soup of the day, and ate it greedily.

They set out again, but little did Martin Brownly-Smith know what Lady Rosemary had up her sleeve at the end of the hour-long drive. As they pulled into the car park he realised that there was more industrial mining experiences ahead. They were greeted by a man who very much resembled the Davey chap from the Heartland's engine room – greying, hair appearing out of a peaked cap, ruddy complexion, and obvious excitement displayed towards any object with moving parts. 'It's obviously a type,' he thought to himself.

Where Heartlands was a small building with only a few elements to be seen, Geevor Mine seemed to be the exact opposite. Brownly-Smith was appalled when given dull blue overalls and a hardhat to don. It was obvious that they had been worn by people before him – what if he caught something. More importantly – why was the attire even necessary? What would they be doing that was so dirty and dangerous. With the air of a sulky child he trudged out of the dressing room looking like a dull smurf to be faced with Lady Rosemary looking quite chic in orange.

They followed the man, who had introduced himself as a former miner, into a doorway hewn from rock, and there started the tour. The man spoke knowledgably about mining work and the conditions, as only can be done by someone who has been there and done it. Despite himself Brownly-Smith found himself being drawn into the stories, the further they progressed down the shafts, the darker and more real the stories felt. He was almost disappointed when they passed through another door to find himself out on open flat ground with the sea in front of them. The contrast from dark and dangerous cavern to bracing sea air was a shock to his system. But this was not the end. The miner took them into the vast sheds where he saw the machinery in action that separated the tin. "Victorian ingenuity as its best, what?" Brownly-Smith said, evidently satisfied with his day's adventure.

The journey home should have taken several hours, but the Audi ate up the A30 at a rapid rate. To pass the time Lady Rosemary explained about Stannary Courts. How King John had made these legislative institutions in Cornwall and Devon in 1201, to protect their 'just and ancient customs and liberties'. Stannary law, a word derived from stannum, the Latin for tin, allowed the Cornish miners to be exempt from British law, Stannary law taking precedence over Common Law, ensuring the equity in favour of the miners.

"But why would the King do that?" Brownly-Smith asked, somewhat confused.

"Because of the importance of tin mining at the time. And indeed for a fair time thereafter."

"I can't imagine it lasted long, surely. I mean it can't be in the best interest of any monarch to have dual systems running?"

"Well essentially it did. Quite amusingly there was an attempt to revise it when the poll tax was bought in."

At the mention of the poll tax Martin Brownly-Smith drifted off momentarily, thinking about Mrs Thatcher and their unreported weekend at Chequers. 'Now that was a woman' he thought dreamily.

"Sorry, old girl, drifted off for a minute. What were you saying?"

"I was saying that a n'er-do-good created a phantom mine, on paper, and convinced people to buy a share in the mine on the basis that Stannary Law would allow them to be exempt from the poll tax, therefore avoiding it."

"Smart man. And were they?"

Laughing at the recollection she said, "No. They were closed down by the Department for Trade and Industry as the company hadn't been registered. Then he did a moonlight flit with all of the money he'd raised."

"What a toad."

Lady rosemary resisted saying out loud what was going on in her head as she watched the squat reptilian man at the wheel racing around the country roads as if he owned them, momentarily reminded of Wind in the Willows.

Chapter 28

Pentwen

Elle and Meg sat at a quiet table in the Bay Hotel bar waiting to meet with the inspectors from the European Environment Agency. Jake entered flanked by two men dressed in suits. It had not occurred the Elle before, but there was a distinct lack of people in business attire in Pentwen. The locals favoured beachwear, shorts, t-shirts and flip flops, and the tourists favoured whatever was in fashion from the mainland, which rarely included pinstripe. Now confronted by the well-dressed men they felt underdressed and a little uneasy.

The girls rose and put out their hands in greeting. "This is Mr Philips," gesturing to the taller and thinner of the two, with wiry grey receding hair and a pleasant smile.

"Oh, please call me Ian," he said stooping to shake hands with the girls in turn.

"And this is Mr Merton," Jake said gesturing to the second man who reminded Elle of one of those FBI men portrayed in 1950s movies, all straight-laced and bespectacled. He did not volunteer his hand. Indeed the man barely met eyes with the girls. The men joined the girls at their table while Jake went to fetch coffees.

"So Jake tells us that you are doing a placement for your degree, business and tourism is it?" Ian asked.

"Yes," Elle started. "We have to do a year in industry within Britain and focus on a tourism-related issue, so we decided on the eco-town due to its relative newness."

Ian nodded interestedly. "And exactly what factors do you think you will be focusing on?"

"I think I will concentrate on the impact on the community. How to get buy-in from those that are resistant, and how they managed to provoke such an change in attitudes," Elle replied.

He turned to face Meg. "I am currently working in one of the new projects, the eco-pods, and I'm really interested in the customer angle. What is it that makes people want to pay more for what is essentially a rather small residence, however well-appointed they are." He nodded, so she continued. "So I thought I might try to establish what the customer motivations are. Whether they live their lives in an environmentally friendly way, so the pods are a continuity of their everyday life. Or whether it's perceived as trendy, so having the kudos to say that they holiday in eco-pods. Or maybe this is so far from their everyday life that it's something they aspire to but cannot achieve."

"Fascinating," Ian said, still nodding. "I think that will give the town's marketing agents something to consider. So how may we be of help?"

Jake arrived with a cafetière and five cups on a tray. He distributed chinaware whilst Meg, Elle and Ian continued chatting, and Mr Merton continued to stare out of the window, assuming a somewhat bored posture. Jake sat opposite Mr Merton and tried to engage him in small talk regarding their journey to the Isle, and other destinations he has visited. Meanwhile the girls pulled out note-taking equipment from their bags. Elle put a gold and bronze covered book on the table opening it up to reveal high quality smooth paper in a warm cream. Meg looked at her own: a bargain reporter notepad and her trusty Bic. She smiled, somewhat embarrassed by the comparison. They quizzed the inspector for some time to get the basics about the process of the initial assessment. "This will really help us get a feel for the procedure the Isle went through at the beginning. All of the sticking points, and how much this may have differed from the way they would have done things before."

"Absolutely. I totally agree. A good foundation from which to develop."

"I wonder," Elle enquired, putting the end of her Parker pen to her lips. "Would it be possible for us to accompany you on your assessment? To get a feel for how the process is viewed from the professionals, as it were?"

Flattery goes a long way, and the slightly coquettish angle of her head when asking sealed the deal. Jake gave her a subtle sideways glance, not entirely happy with the rapport between Elle and Mr Ian Philips.

And so for the rest of the week Meg and Elle accompanied the inspectors on their rounds, pens poised above their pads, no action going unquestioned, as they tried to get the fullest understanding of all elements of the inspection.

The inspectors left on the Friday afternoon flight back to the mainland, and Pentwen gave a collective sigh of relief. Now they had to play the waiting game. There was a hastily arranged meeting at the Guildhall to have a debrief about how all those involved felt the process had gone. Ray and Jake chaired the meeting, not unlike they had done all those months ago when they had presented the idea of the eco-town to the locals of Pentwen.

Ray fed back first with his thoughts. "Mr Merton, the happy-chappy," he said sarcastically to a flurry of chuckles, "seemed about as happy as a man of his disposition can be with the infrastructure projects, wouldn't you agree, Lloyd?"

"Yep, I agree, he was a miserable old sod! But as far as I could tell he was pleased with the readings from both the geothermic heat exchange data, and what we have managed to gather so far from the windfarm."

"It seems that they were a bit of a double act," Jake added.

"Yeah, good-cop and bloody bad-cop if you ask me," Dave Miller interjected, to more laughter.

"Yes, dad. Thanks for that. The Merton guy was all about the big stuff. The stuff that we have had to invest in together as a community. And Ian, the human one, he was about the small stuff. The changes we had made as individuals and business by business."

Ray nodded at Jake's assessment of the men. "So does anyone want to feedback about their experiences?"

There were some mumblings around the room but no one spoke up.

Jake thought he would help things along. "Well I noticed that they did not rely purely on the receipts for things that we bought, like, um for linen. The guys wanted to see the stuff for themselves."

Elle joined in. "Yes, they were really thorough. Like with the linen – they weren't just satisfied looking at a the quilt cover, they checked that all the pillowcases and sheets were genuine, and then they checked all the towels."

"What in each bedroom?" asked Julie Ward, the local fruit and veg shop owner.

"No. They asked to see a couple of different style rooms, so I showed them one of the lower tariff rooms and a penthouse, and then they did a thorough assessment of each."

"That's exactly what they did with the eco-pods," Meg added. "Just two, but went over them with a fine-tooth comb."

Having got the ball rolling they went around the room asking for each of their experiences. As they spoke about their time with the inspectors Elle scribbled anything of interest down in her book. "Why are you taking all this down?" Jake whispered.

"I think it will add something to my report, you know, about how you got the locals on board at the beginning, and how you have maintained that."

Jake blushed a little with pride at her words.

*

"So what's the plan?" Meg asked.

"Well nothing else can be done at this end." Lloyd answered. "Pentwen's fate is sealed, so our concentration is now on scuppering their plans for the new site."

"And we know where it is now," Elle exclaimed.

"You do?"

"Yes. You'll never believe it – it somewhere on the Isle of Wight!"

"No way!"

"I know – it's incredible isn't it."

"Have you got to the bottom of who is behind it yet."

"Not to the source," Lloyd explained. "But thanks to our little troupe of actors I can confirm that we know who the middle man is. He is a slithering toad called Martin Brownly-Smith."

The girls exchanged shrugging glances.

"He's the one that's challenging Roger Stiles for Governor?"

More shrugs and head shakes.

"Christ, you really keep your fingers on the pulse don't you, girls" Lloyd replied sarcastically.

"Technically nothing to do with us. We can't vote. We're just passing through remember."

"Either way, what this suggests is that *he*, the main man, is probably very important. Brownly-Smith is a very important man in Whitehall. He is very well connected. And frankly I'm pretty concerned about what you have got yourselves into."

"Hey, we didn't know what was going on. It seemed like a genuine offer to suit all parties at the outset."

"I know. I know. I think it's all about how to turn this to our advantage now. So now you know where the opposition is, how are you meant to be passing on the knowledge from your spying mission?"

"So this Brownly-Smith guy says we're to go there next week and meet with their organising committee to pass on what we've learnt." Meg explained.

"And," continued Elle, "the beauty of the timing is that Pentwen's report does not get published until after the Isle of Wight's assessment."

"Which means we'll be long-gone before they realise we didn't do our job of scuppering Pentwen's chances of a successful assessment."

"Classic!"

"We learnt a lot from the inspectors, so we know what they really concentrate on."

"And we have some sneaky ideas of our own, but we'll need your help in carrying them out."

"Name it?"

Chapter 29

Camborne

The thin fair-haired man sat on the chair looking uncomfortable and restless. He had the remnants of cuts on his face and a bandage around his head. Chief Superintendent Linda Romney watched him on the CCTV for some minutes, sizing him up. It was a long time since she had done any interrogating and was quite excited about the prospect. She had his measure; he was a man who hid behind the status his suit gave him. No backbone. No balls. She smiled to herself before entering the interrogation room.

"Hello, Mr Tarrant," she said taking the chair opposite him. She got out a manila file and opened it clicking her ballpoint pen into action. "My name is Superintendent Linda Romney," dropping the Chief as she didn't want to panic him too much. "And I am starting the tape at eleven twenty three on 10th June 2015. Here present are Superintendent Linda Romney and Mr Carl Tarrant."

She shuffles some papers and becomes engrossed in one page for several moments while he shifts uncomfortably in his chair. "So, Mr Tarrant," she starts without looking up from the engrossing page, "maybe you would like to tell me what brings you to the Isle of Kernow?"

Bemused, he replies, "I'm on business."

"And exactly what sort of business would that be, Mr Tarrant?"

"I work for Costmart."

"Not very chatty are you, Mr Tarrant?" she continued sarcastically. "What exactly is your Costmart business on the Isle?"

"I'm an asset assessor."

"Oh really. That's very interesting. And exactly what is an asset assessor, Mr Tarrant."

The nervous Mr Tarrant took a breath, but before he could continue, she interrupted, "And if you think that the smart answer to that question is *the assessor of assets*, I recommend you think again."

He hesitated, considering his words carefully. "I, I mean my job is, it's to -"

"Spit it out, man."

"I'm in charge of tracking the values of the properties in Costmart's portfolio," he said quickly.

"I'm in charge of tracking the values of the properties in Costmart's portfolio," she mimicked in childishly. "This doesn't tell me what the hell you are doing on the Isle, does it, Mr Tarrant?"

He looked petrified. She got out of her seat and wandered around the room. He followed her with his eyes, taking in the buxom body squeezed into a navy blue pencil skirt and matching jacket, and the crisp white blouse with at least one too many buttons undone.

She walked behind him putting her hands on the back of his chair, she leant and whispered in his ear, "So if you would be so kind as to answer the question."

"I'm here to assess the sites of our major stores and distribution centres."

"And why would you be doing that?" she said from somewhere behind him.

"Because that's what I was instructed to do."

"And you are so far down the food chain at Costmart that they didn't tell you why to come all the way here to assess these assets? I hardly think that's likely."

He sat uncomfortably, wringing his hands. She took her seat again, and leaning forward so her face was only inches from his, she whispered menacingly, "Now why don't you tell me exactly what plans they have up their sleeves?"

He could no longer meet her glare, dropping his eyes some inches he was confronted by the ample cleavage. To escape, he sat back in his chair and looked up at the ceiling. "The Board think there's money to be made from the sites. We have four huge sites here, not to mention the smaller stores, all of which need assessing for their current market value considering the new circumstances of the county."

"Not a county," she bellowed, "A British overseas territory. And as such we have a different way of doing business, and," an ominous pause, "a different legal system."

Tentatively he asked, "What has all of this got to do with catching the people that did this to me?" he said gesturing to the bandage.

She snorted with laughter, "Did *what* to you? I think the only ones you've got to blame for the trouble you're in is Mr Jameson, or Mr Jack

Daniels. And we have very strong penalties for drink-driving, as you will be finding out very soon."

"You can't believe that I did this on purpose? I was kidnapped or something. I remember being tied up. I even heard voices. You've got to believe me" he continued urgently.

"Back to the plans for the stores. What are Costmart panning to do with them? Sell them or develop them?"

"It depends on my report. They will take action based on their location and market value."

"Interview terminated at eleven thirty-one. Take him to the cells," she called to a constable as she took the tape out of the machine and marched out of the room. The constable came in and helped an astounded Mr Tarrant to his feet, and guided him, dumbstruck, to the door.

*

"I haven't had so much fun in years," Linda said, throwing the cassette tape onto the table where Roger was blowing on his steaming cup of coffee.

He picked it up, looked at it and then up at her. "You know that the police are the only ones who still use cassette tapes, don't you? It's a clever plot to stop anyone else listening to their interviews."

She snatched it out of his hand, clutching it to her chest, "Ungrateful. Come on. Follow me."

He looked at his coffee, "Where are we going?"

"To my car."

He raised his eyebrows questioningly.

"Do you want to listen to this or what?"

Gulping his coffee down he grabbed his jacket and they walked to the café car park where they listened to the recording in silence. "Bloody hell, you were scary."

"I thought that's what you wanted?" she said playfully.

"I'm scared just listening to the poor man squirm."
They sat in silence for some time. "Okay. So what happens now?"

"He's in the cells, although I can't keep him for much longer."

"Can you get rid of him?"

"What are you suggesting, Roger? This isn't the movies, you know. We don't *do over nonces*," she said affecting an east end accent.

"I meant can you get him off the Isle? If he has to leave without looking at the properties, then he can't write his report."

"Possibly, but how does that solve anything? They'll just send someone else."

"Yes, but it would give us some breathing space."

"Okay. I'll see what I can do." As he was about to get out, she continued, without meeting his eye. "Tarrant was adamant that he hadn't been drink driving. He was adamant that he had been kidnapped and framed. You wouldn't know anything about that would you, Roger?"

"He would say that wouldn't he," Roger replied keeping his eyes firmly facing the windscreen.

"It's just, I'd hate to think that anything illegal had gone on here."

"Obviously, what with you being a Chief Superintendent and everything."

"Goodbye Roger."

He got out of the car quickly and she put her foot to the floor as she sped form the car park.

*

It was near midnight when Carl Tarrant found himself being taken from the cell to the interrogation room again. She was already sat at the table, staring into space, clicking the ballpoint pen.

"Ah, Mr Tarrant. So good of you to join me."

"This is an outrage. I've been attacked, drugged, kidnapped, and god only knows what else. I've been in hospital with a cracked skull and a broken rib, and you seem to think that I, -" pointing at himself for emphasis, in case she would be confused as to who he was referring, "that I did this to myself."

Unflapped by his outburst, she continued, "Unfortunately for you Mr Tarrant there is absolutely no evidence of abduction, and there is a great amount of forensic evidence pointing at you as a drink-driver, three time over the limit I might add, causing an accident on the old A30. An accident that has led to the writing off of a car, a car that wasn't yours I hasten to add." More clicking of pen, "But if you are committed to the belief that you were abducted, maybe you can furnish me with the relevant details and I will endeavour to investigate. Please bear in mind that should we find no case to answer, we will also be charging you with wasting police time. Shall we start with the last thing you remember prior to the accident?"

He thought for some time. He reviewed his last recollections before being taken away by ambulance. Everything was very dreamlike and really made no sense. He remembered setting the satnav for the south depot, but passed that he couldn't really remember anything clearly, not even whether he'd arrived at the depot or not. In light of this he considered Superintendent Romney's warning about wasting police time. Between a rock and a hard place.

"And if I can't remember what happened, what then?"

"Then it's just the drink-driving charge. The three times over the limit drink-driving charge." Click, click, clickerty, click went the pen.

He laid his aching head on his arms on the table, miserable and tired.

"So what's it to be, Mr Tarrant?"

He felt his eyes pricking with tears. What would the punishment be for this? He'd almost certainly lose his job, then the house would go, and any hope of holding together his rather strained marriage. Tears were now trickling down his nose and pooling on the table.

"Sit up, Mr Tarrant and act like a man. I'm sure there's a way out of this."

Slowly he sat up, wiping his nose on his sleeve. She pulled a rather grubby tissue from her bag and passed it over the table. He wiped his eyes, but kept them focused on his hands.

"We don't like drink-drivers here, on the Isle of Kernow. We also don't like companies who leave us high and dry when the circumstances don't suit them, only to reappear when they feel there is a buck to be made. So here's what I am offering." She got out of her chair and stretched. She walked over to the window and looked out at the beautifully symmetrical Victorian villa houses opposite, sorry for their view of the brutalist 1960s police station.

"We will escort you to the airport where you will catch the next plane out of here, with the promise that you will never return."

He was already nodding eagerly, this was not prison.

"In addition, you will file a report with your superiors stating that the buildings are in a poor state or repair as they have been left unattended in all this time. You could mention nature reclaiming its own, possibly throw in vandalism for good measure," she said contemplatively, making it up as she went. "You will also say that the locations are inappropriate for any meaningful development. They are, what shall we say?" she trailed off.

"That they are in industrial areas?" he added helpfully.

She turned to look at him. "Excellent, I see you are getting the hang of this thing now. Yes the areas are too industrial for either residential or tourist development."

"But what about the land for industrial development. How should I deal with that."

She pondered. "You can say that there is a moratorium on any further industrial development until the needs of the Isle have been researched and reported on. This process will take at least a year, so they might as well leave it alone for the foreseeable."

He was nodding furiously, manically. He looked at her like an devoted puppy waiting for his treat.

"And in return any reference to the crimes committed here will be put away somewhere secure. If you keep Costmart distracted for another year, I will see to it that the records will be destroyed."

"Yes, oh yes. That's good. Absolutely. Yes, absolutely. Thank you."

She left the room without looking back at the snivelling man, ordering the DS to take him and his belongings, and make sure he was on the next plane off the Isle.

Chapter 30

Dumgarth

Lady Rosemary had arranged to meet Brownly-Smith at the Trewarget Arms. As she entered the bar she noted he wasn't waiting for her. She raised a questioning eyebrow at Doug who was polishing the bar. "He's only just finished his breakfast," he replied. "Fancy a coffee while you're waiting?"

"Oh, why not," she said climbing onto a barstool. She craned her neck to look out into the beer garden. "What's the state of play with the chalets?"

"Don't ask. An absolute disaster."

"How so?"

"Apparently there's all sorts of rules with chalets. Dee thought that as they were technically sheds she only needed to abide by planning regs for sheds, but as soon as you add water, electricity and paying customers to the mix it's a bit more complicated."

"Heavens. I suppose it makes sense though."

"With the benefit of hindsight, yes."

"So, where are they now?" she ventured.

"So we have moved them to the beach."

"What the devil for?"

"Now they are exclusive hides for the birdwatchers. The council gave us permission as part of a community project."

"Excellent solution."

"Not as far as Dee's concerned. Community project equates to the council taking some of her hard earned profit."

"Dee doesn't quite grasp community spirit, does she?"

"Nope. Not when it interferes with her plans for world domination," Doug said laughing.

Martin Brownly-Smith eventually entered the bar donned in white shorts, a floral shirt, and the worst crime of all – sandals with socks. She winced somewhat at the apparition. 'You couldn't make it up' she thought to herself.

He bounded to the Land Rover, excited about the day ahead, and was almost knocked back by the thunderous barking that met him as he opened the car door. Barking at a range of pitches, high from Tike and low from Dotty, and a menacing subsonic growl from the latest of her canine acquisitions.

"Shut up you lot," she bellowed at them, to instant silence. Brownly-Smith looked at her waiting for the signal that they wouldn't attack. "It's fine, they're harmless. Get in, man." He wasn't convinced but got in as instructed.

"Today," she said firing up the rattling Land Rover, "we're off to Pentwen to see some of the more recent cultural sites."

An hour later they pulled off the main road, and started the descent to the beach. Brownly-Smith remembered it as soon as they took the turn, he had come here on his first day and had a snack at a beachside café. She pulled up short on a patch of dirt alongside a surf shop, dust rising dramatically as she did so. The dogs were excited at the sign of the beach, yapping and pacing in the back. They got out of the car, the dogs running round in circles, ecstatic with the potential of the day. Inside Brownly-Smith wasn't sure that he wasn't as excited as the dogs.

As they walked towards the surf shop he became slightly unnerved. She had promised a view of the ocean that he would not have seen before, but surely she didn't mean surfing – he hardly had the physique for such energetic pursuits. He looked at her with a concerned expression. She laughed, "No, don't panic. We're just meeting the guy here that has the boat."

Relief flooded though him. As they entered the shop the dogs started yapping again. "Martin, go ahead without me. I've got to give the dogs a quick run or there will be no peace. You are meeting the lady who owns the shop. She's called Holly. Introduce yourself and I'll be back in a minute."

He nodded and entered the shabby looking shack. It was shady inside with a faint smell of coconut in the air. He walked past racks of pastel t-shirts to his left and wetsuits to the right. The nearer he got to the back of the store the clothing gave way to rows of surfboards of all different shapes and sizes. At the back of the store was an open area with beanbags on the floor and a counter facing him. Leaning over the counter was someone clad in a black wetsuit, their long blond hair falling down their back in a tousled fashion. Excited about the pert posterior that was presented to him he could not resist the gentle slap across the buttocks, as he said, "Well hello, Holly!"

At this point the person wheeled round, and he noticed the wild staring eyes and stubbly chin. The offended man punched Brownly-Smith squarely in the face, to the sound of, "Who the feck are you calling Holly?"

Brownly-Smith windmilled his arms briefly to try and keep his balance before hitting the deck, backside first, his fall broken somewhat by the receiving beanbag.

"What the hell?" came the exclamation in a lilting South African accent. Both Brownly-Smith and his attacker turned to face the willowy woman wearing a long flowing hippy dress.

"This fecker just slapped my ass and called me Holly!" the wetsuit clad man said with a broad Aussie accent, pointing accusingly at Brownly-Smith.

Flustered at the accusation, Brownly-Smith countered with, "Well he assaulted me."

"Only after you sexually assaulted me."

She stood with her hands on her hips, trying to look admonishing, but finding it hard to stifle the smile. "Well let's call it a misunderstanding shall we? Now, I am Holly. And who would you be?"

"This," came the voice from behind her, "is Martin Brownly-Smith, Holly." And Lady Rosemary came into view. "What on earth has been going on?" she asked, baffled by the scene that presented itself.

"It's what we are calling a misunderstanding, Rosemary," Holly replied, lightly kissing Lady Rosemary on the cheek. "Now Mitch, why don't you help Mr Brownly-Smith up?" she said in a tone that did not encourage a refusal.

Martin Brownly-Smith dusted himself down before proffering a hand to Holly. "Very pleased to make your acquaintance, Holly."

"Likewise, I'm sure," she said in a slightly mocking manner. "So, you're up for a tour around the bay and maybe a spot of snorkelling to really get a feel for the sea life that has moved to our shores?"

"Or indeed, your shores have moved to the sea life," he countered, laughing at his own joke.

She smiled politely, and appeared to be eyeing him up. He was somewhat uncomfortable with the situation, when she turned to Mitch and asked him to bring out the North Coast shorty, extra-large. Mitch returned with the wetsuit and pointed sulkily to the changing room. When he was out of eyeshot the women winked at each other.

Some minutes later, and after lots of grunting from the changing room, Brownly-Smith emerged looking rather ridiculous. "Give us a twirl then?" Lady Rosemary asked, which he did reluctantly.

"Do I look completely ridiculous?"

"Well, not completely, no," she joked back.

"You'd look slightly less ridiculous if you had it on the right way, mate," Mitch said, half under his breath.

Brownly-Smith shrugged in incomprehension.

"The zip goes at the back," Holly explained.

Brownly-Smith flounced back into the changing room for another period of grunting.

Martin Brownly-Smith had an amazing morning. Marcus Steele, the local cobbler, had a small inflatable dinghy with outboard motor which he happily took tourists out in if they would cover the cost of his fuel and enough for him to buy a couple of pints on his return. The weather couldn't have been better. The sun shone and there was a very light offshore breeze. Holly had recommended that Brownly-Smith apply some sunscreen before he left 'as these are just the conditions to get burnt to a crisp' she had said, but he had refused.

After a cruise hugging the coastline, with the occasional stop off at inlets and caves to look at the seals, Marcus anchored up in a secluded bay and tuned off the engine. "This is the best spot for snorkelling, bar none," he exclaimed. "Done it before, mate?" he enquired. Brownly-Smith acknowledged that he had and put on the mask with ease. He launched himself off the side of the boat backwards and thought his heart was about to stop when he experienced the water temperature – Belize this was not. Once adjusted to the chill, they both swam off in the direction of some outlying rocks. The sea life was more than he could have imagined, and better than anything visible around the coast of the mainland, of that he was sure.

Meanwhile, on dry land Rosemary and Holly took the dogs for a run on the beach and then went back to Holly's house for a cup of tea. Ray and Jake were there to meet them.

"Ray, did you look at the CCTV footage from the shop this morning?" Holly asked.

"We were watching it real time. Man, I can't remember the last time I laughed so much," he replied.

"You couldn't have planned it. It was epic, man," Jake added.

"Have you saved the recording in case we need it?"

"Oh yeah. Duplicate copies. This is too precious."

"I mean what prat would mistake Mitch for a bird, I mean he's got hairy toes like some sort of hobbit," Jake continued.

"I don't think it was his toes that he was concentrating on."

"Ah, man. You wait 'til I see Mitch. I'm so going to rip the piss out of him about this."

"I'm sure he'll find some way of getting revenge if you do, so go carefully there, my friend," Ray added wisely.

They met Brownly-Smith off the boat, the dogs running circles around them as they strolled back to the Surf Shack to get changed. There was a shower outside of the shop where Brownly-Smith rinsed off and then went inside to dress. He turned to the mirror to see that he was properly attired and he noticed, much to his distress, that his face was as red a lobster. Humiliated again, he exited the shop stooped.

They took a leisurely walk along the beach towards the North Bay Hotel. They paused to look at the menu displayed in the casing at the end of the drive. "This looks nice," Rosemary said. "Hold on here and I'll check that they can fit us in." She entered the hotel and went to the bar beckoning Jake over. "Jake, if I get him to face the hotel can you get a shot of him in his city attire. I think it will be photographic gold."

They sat in the hotel restaurant in seats overlooking the sea. The lunch was fair-to-good, both choosing the Caesar Salad and a glass of Guigal Condrieu. After lunch a scruffy-looking man in his early twenties, with a mop of dark hair came to join them. He was introduced by Lady Rosemary as Jake Miller, the person responsible for Pentwen becoming the UK's first eco-town.

"You know that's not entirely true," he replied, embarrassed by the compliment.

"Well you were the driving force that convinced the locals to change."

"Well maybe."

They chatted for a while and then Jake took them on a tour of the hotel and some of the other local businesses where they could discuss the changes made and the impact that it was having on the community as well as their pockets.

They returned to the bar for a coffee before leaving, and Jake introduced them to a beautiful girl with long dark hair tied back in a ponytail, wearing a hotel uniform. "This is my friend, Elle. She has come from Southampton to work here for a year."

'Oh has she really?' Brownly-Smith thought to himself, 'and I wonder who sent her?' he laughed to himself. He shook her hand, giving her a sly wink, to which she did not respond. They chatted for a while before Lady Rosemary stood, stating it was time to get the dogs home or they'd start eating the locals – a fact that Brownly-Smith did not doubt.

As he got out of the car at the Trewarget Arms, he kissed her hand, and said what a wonderful day he had had. As he started to walk towards the door she lowered the window and called, "You might want to get some moisturiser on your face. Stops it peeling you know." She laughed to herself all the way up the hill.

Chapter 31

Island of Wight

They arrived at Southampton Airport on the first flight of the day and were met by a smart chauffeured car who took them to the Lymington ferry terminal and the brief, but slightly choppy, crossing to Yarmouth. From there they headed west to a small coastal town where they were put up in a faded Victorian hotel and told that they would be picked up the next morning at nine o'clock for their first meeting.

At the hotel reception they were met with a beaming smile by the owner who introduced herself as Maxine. They registered in the book and as Maxine read their entry she became very excited. Calling to the backroom, "John, Johno! Come quick. There's a couple here from Pentwen!" Turning back to Meg and Elle she explained that they used to own a hotel there, some years previously, and asked whereabouts they lived and worked. They chatted with Maxine and John for some time exchanging stories and comparing notes on the town, discussing how it had changed since they'd left.

Once they got settled into their rooms they set about their plans immediately. They then ordered room service, as they were too concerned about being overheard when discussing and revising their ideas. They sat on the floor of Meg's more spacious room, surrounded by plates and paper.

"Are you going to tell Mitch?"

"What? That we were sent to ruin the potential livelihood of the place he calls home? How do you start that conversation?" she replied rather bitterly.

"I know. That's what I've been thinking about all week."

"I've been so worried about getting this trip over and done with, and getting back to Pentwen safely that I haven't started to think about Mitch."

"But you are going to tell him, right?"

"I guess I'll have to. I mean if we stay together I don't think I could keep it a secret forever."

"Me neither," Elle replied distractedly.

"I say let's focus on getting this ordeal over with first. If this is a success, then at least we can tell them how we put it right."

"But do you think they will ever trust us again?"

"Well Lloyd did, and we've repaid his trust, so I'm sure he'll help make a case for us." Meg replied, picking up a folder and putting it in Elle's lap. "So let's make sure we don't screw up this end of the operation by revising our notes."

They were met as promised, promptly at nine, by the same driver as the previous day. They were careful not to say anything relating to their mission in front of the driver as Lloyd had warned them to trust no one. They swept through the beautiful countryside passing redbrick cottages with traditional thatch rooves in the villages, the towns keeping their architecture warm with white stuccoed rendering and red tile rooves. They headed south until they hit the coast road which hugged the Channel. They travelled for some minutes until turning suddenly up a chalky track with no evident destination in sight. Meg and Elle exchanged frightened glances. Where the hell were they being taken? They came over the brow of a hill and descending the track they could see some old farm buildings. A main house, austere and functional; some low-lying buildings with corrugated rooves, probably former cow sheds, and several wooden barns.

The car pulled up in front of the farm house and the driver opened the car door and escorted them to the house. As they entered into the hallway the temperature dropped dramatically, a feeling of dampness in the air. The driver opened a heavy wooden door at the end of the passage and ushered them in. The room was a large kitchen that ran the length of the house. The floor was flagstones upon which sat a huge pine table around which were sat four men on uncomfortable looking wooden chairs. On their entering one of the men stood up and greeted them, showing them to their place at the table.

"Welcome, ladies. May I offer you some refreshment," he said gesturing to the counter. Meg noted the filter coffee jug was full and both opted for this to steel their nerves and take the chill away. They sat at the table, noticing that all the men were dressed in suits, incongruent with the surroundings. The man who had greeted them proceeded to introduce them to the other men sat at the table. "May I introduce you to Mr Oxford," pale grey suit with lilac tie and white hair, "Mr Stafford," Asian and rotund, his buttoned pinstripe suit straining against the force of his belly, "Mr York," beanpole thin accentuated by his slimming black suit and pencil thin black tie, "And I am Mr Warwick," wiry auburn hair with a tie of matching autumn tones.

The girls forced smiles, nodding greetings at each in turn. The evident subterfuge was really starting to concern them. There was only one reason to remain anonymous in such a situation, and that was because you knew you were doing wrong, and wanted to ensure that you could not be traced.

The meeting went quite amiably, despite their initial concerns. The men asked questions regarding different aspects of Pentwen's facilities and provision. Mr Stafford seemed to the most interested in the infrastructure projects and comparisons of scale to Pentwen. Elle pulled some files from her bag where, with the help of Lloyd, they had put together some convincing documentation with figures that seemed entirely achievable but were known not to meet some of the measures that the inspectors would be looking for.

The previous week Lloyd had visited with Dr Jeannette O'Loughlin. It was that chance meeting with his old university friend, Roger Spires at the Trewarget Arms, that had sparked the idea of the eco-town, Jeannette being a specialist in the area, and had just acted as consultant on a eco holiday park. She helped him play with the statistics on a huge range of measures, cooking the books in a way that was not at all obvious unless you were an expert in the matter. It was this that girls were presenting confidently to those gathered.

Mr York seemed most interested in ways of engaging the community. Meg talked passionately about local political figures taking the lead, and having a clearly formulated plan to present, assertively guiding the populace by use of incentives and bylaws. The men seemed impressed with this stoic approach, scribbling away furiously as Meg spoke. "Divide and conquer, you're with us or against us, it was this type of leadership that brought the community together, and this is how they have such a coherent operation today."

"Interesting, very interesting," you could almost hear the cogs turning in his mind as he contemplated who he could bring in to spearhead the campaign.

Mr Oxford was more interested marketing, specifically what could they do that adhered to the eco-town requirements, but would attract the types of tourists they desired. Elle felt queasy at the thought, this is what they were really about, not the development of the town for the community or issues of sustainability, but as a purely economic activity to line the pockets of someone or other. She thought carefully about her response, picking on things she knew they could manipulate.

Once the questions were over Meg ventured to ask what their plans were. The men exchanged glances. "The reason I ask, gentlemen, is that we are more than happy to return prior to the assessment to oversee and help set things up. Under the guise of our supposed university research project, we shadowed the inspectors in Pentwen as they went through each stage of their assessment, and are therefore familiar with the process down to minute levels of detail. They were all very obliging."

The men exchanged more glances, and exchanged slight nods of approval. Mr Warwick clasped his hands, resting them on the table in front of him and considered them for a moment before replying. "A town has been built, not far from here, on the site of a former army base. It is with this venue that we are aiming to initiate our plans, starting with the eco-town as a means to roll this out to the island once they see its success."

"What a wonderful idea," Elle replied, almost choking on her words. "Well as I said, whatever we can do to help?"

"I feel that we may be able to contribute most by working with those at the coal face, so to speak. We can do mock pre-inspections or help venues setting up for their turn."

The men nodded, pondering the offer. "That is very kind of you, ladies. An offer we may well take advantage of."

"Is there a date fixed for the assessment?"

"Yes. We are working to a tight timescale. We have six weeks, so time is very much of the essence."

"I see. Is it possible that we can see the venue?" Elle enquired.

"Not at this moment in time," Mr Oxford said a little too abruptly. Realising his response had been aggressive he attempted a smile, something that did not appear to come naturally to him. "But as Mr Warwick has said, we may very well take you up on your offer nearer to the time."

Goodbyes were quickly exchanged and the girls were ushered back to the car and returned to the hotel. As a gesture of thanks Mr Warwick informed them that the hotel and car had been booked for them for a further two nights, and their food bills would be met if they wanted to stay on. Meg thanked them and for their generosity and said that they would be delighted to do so.

"Why did you agree to stay longer than necessary?" Elle asked curtly, once they were back in the privacy of the hotel.

"To give us the opportunity to have a look around, and maybe get to the bottom of this."

"Who do you think you are? Inspector Morse"

"No, more like Inspector Gadget," she giggled in response.

*

They spent the rest of the day looking for clues on the internet, and Skyping Lloyd. There were a couple of venues that looked like possible sites, and using Google Earth they found a route that would get them to these places, avoiding main roads. They declined the offer of the driver for sightseeing, wanting to stay under the radar as much as possible. Meanwhile Johno arranged to borrow two mountain bikes for the next day; they were now self-sufficient.

They set out early after breakfast with backpacks full of water, fruit and a pack of sandwiches each, courtesy of Maxine. They had taken screenshots of the route which allowed them to turn off all connectivity from their phones. Anything they could do to avoid being traced was worth a try.

Meg was an amazing trail finder, leading Elle with confidence. She soon realised that Elle was not quite so at home in the saddle, and had to adjust her speed to accommodate her. They used drovers trails and farm tracks to crisscross their way south. It took them nearly forty minutes to reach the first venue, which they quickly realised was not the site. So they remounted and continued uphill across more undulating and increasingly woody terrain. Meg checked the screenshots of their route, shouting over her shoulder that it should be over the next ridge. She crested the hill and as she disappeared over the top Elle heard a yelp and some clanking sounds. Elle slowed and jumped off, dropping her bike and running to see what had occurred. She saw Meg in a pile of metal, some of which was bike and the rest appeared to be fencing. Meg was swearing to herself trying to extricate herself from the confusion. Elle rushed to help, pulling the bike off her. Turning back to Meg she looked a little horrified.

"God, are you okay?"

"Yeah, yeah. I'll be fine. What a stupid place to put a fence."

"You know you're bleeding?" Elle said nodding to the gash on her leg.

Meg reached d own and wiped at the trickling blood. "Ah, it'll be fine," she said clambering to her feet.

"Look, that's what cut you," Elle said, holding up some of the fallen fence that was topped with razor wire.

"Jeez, someone really doesn't want people straying onto their land," she replied testing the sharpness of the offending wire. "That's just the sort of behaviour that makes me very curious," she continued, grinning.

"No way. You're not going in are you?"

"Damned right I am."

"But what if you get caught?"

"Then I'll point to my near fatal wound and say that I was looking for my attacker. Possibly with a view to suing."

Elle hopped from foot to foot nervously. "But seriously, with all the cloak and dagger stuff yesterday. I mean it was like Reservoir Dogs, all the Mr Green and Mr Black stuff. These guys are serious and you mean to stalk right in there?"

"Well, not stalk exactly, but have a little peek maybe. Aren't you curious why someone would put a fence across a path? And why you'd feel the need to decorate it with razor wire. They must be pretty clever cows if they need this level of security to keep them in."

Elle looked around nervously, weighting up the odds of being caught. "If they do catch us we could ruin the whole thing. At the moment they think we're on their side. If they catch us snooping what will they think then?"

"Nothing. They offered us the opportunity to spend time on the island, so we are. We've gone for a bike ride in the countryside and hit a stupidly placed fence."

"Okay. What should we do with the bikes?"

"Put them in that hedge over there."

They covered the bikes with branches and carefully negotiated the dangerous fencing. From the perimeter they could not see far enough into the field as they were in a dip, so they skirted the periphery keeping low as they did so. As they came around the side of the raised terrain they could see the place was a hive of activity. There were workmen busy in cranes and diggers, transporting building materials and constructing edifices. Meg pulled some binoculars from her rucksack and surveyed in more detail.

"Hmm," she murmured to herself.

"What?" Elle whispered back.

"The signs on the lorries and construction vehicles aren't English."

"What are they? What do they say?"

"I'm not sure. It look eastern European or something like that."

"Weird. What else can you see?"

Meg looked for a little longer. "Not enough from here. I need to get closer."

"No. It's too risky. We should get back."

"We've come this far. It would be stupid to leave now." And with it said she made a dart across open land to a copse a little nearer the construction site. Elle stood rigid to the spot – too scared to pursue Meg.

Meg lay down at the edge of the copse, hidden by thick bracken, using the binoculars she scanned the site. At the end nearest to her she noticed a pallet loaded high with boxes which the workers were unloading and taking to the different buildings nearing completion. As she was too far away to really see what was occurring she used her mobile to film a tracking shot in the vain hope that they will be able to zoom in later and see what was going on. She put her mobile safely back in her backpack, and looked up to notice a jeep driving across the open terrain making a beeline straight for her. Her binoculars must have caught the sunlight and attracted someone's attention.

Not wanting to learn whose attention, she grabbed her bag and made a dart across the open space between the copse and the fence. As she leapt over it she shouted to Elle to do the same. Elle started off in pursuit, grabbing their bikes from the hedge and made off down the track at a turn of speed, legs pumping like pistons. When they heard voices shouting behind them they gave it an extra boost of energy. Meg leading, turned off abruptly down an old drover's track, not wide enough for a car. They carried on negotiating pitted tracks with occasional puddles and tree roots, relieved that they had mountain and not road bikes. Meg made another unpredictable left turn and they entered a wood of pine trees through a tiny gap in the hedge. Elle overshot the turning and doubled back, looking cautiously over her shoulder – no one to be seen. They pushed their bikes across the carpet of pine needles, no sound could be heard in the peace of the tall majestic trees.

Meg continued into the heart of the wood, and when she found a small clearing she leant her bike against a tree and lay on the floor in dappled sunlight, panting. Elle checked around again before joining her. All of a sudden Elle heard a strange noise, and looking to her left she saw that Meg was laughing hysterically, tears running down her cheeks.

"What the hell's so funny?" Elle asked incredulously.

"Everything. This. I mean, this is like the movies – running from baddies!"

Elle thought about it for a moment whilst still trying to catch her breath. Then she too started to laugh. A quiet giggle at first, and then deeper and more uncontrollable. The girls lay on the carpet of pine needles, side by side, laughing outrageously. When they finally got their breath back they felt the tension from the chase dissipate. Now they needed to consider their next actions.

"We need to get back," said Meg, sitting upright.

"I think we need to cover our tracks. Just in case they suspect it was us. If we don't we could have jeopardised the whole mission."

"So let's do what all girls love to do," Meg said excitedly.

"What's that?" Elle asked quizzically.

"Go shopping! Let's buy bags of stuff, so we can return to the hotel looking like we spent the day at the shops."

They set off on the bikes, but more slowly. In the excitement of the chase they had not really paid attention to where they were going, only ensuring that they were taking routes inaccessible by car. They cycled slowly until coming to a road, then followed signs to Newport. When they arrived at the town centre they locked the bikes to the bike stand outside of the library. They made their way to the high street and went into the first shop that appealed. They both bought a dress that looked very summery, and that it seemed unlikely that someone would be able to cycle in. Having paid the cashier they asked if they might use the changing rooms again as they wanted to wear the dresses now. They swapped their shorts and t-shirts for the dresses, putting the discarded clothes in the carrier bags. As they left they asked the cashier for two more carriers into which they put their backpacks.

They wandered down the street, heads up and shoulders back, girls out on a shopping trip. They popped into a few more shops and bought a few more treats, adding to their bag collection. They then found a café and ordered two coffees and carrot cakes, asking the waitress for the Wi-Fi password. Whilst they waited they switched their phones on. Meg sent an email to Lloyd including the screenshot of the map where the suspected eco-town was being built, along with the photos and video footage she took, then she deleted anything from her phone that could link them to where they had been that morning. Then they sat back and enjoyed their cake before catching the bus back to the hotel.

Maxine raised an eyebrow when she saw them entering, dressed in summery cotton dresses and not the shorts and t-shirts they had left in.

"Long story!" meg replied to her quizzical look. "But we do need to apologise and ask a favour."

"Fire away."

"For reasons too complex to explain we had to ditch the bikes and catch the bus home. They're safe, locked up, but obviously we need to get them back."

"Okay," Maxine said nodding slowly. John stepped out of the office at this point.

"Everything okay, ladies?"

"It's all fine, love," Maxine reassured. "Any chance you could take the Jeep and pick the bikes up from -?"

"They are chained up in the bike rack at the library."

"No worries. Everything alright?"

"We might be in a bit of a pickle, but we don't want to get you guys involved."

"We don't mind, do we Johno? Anything we can do to help."

Elle thought for a moment. "Well, if anyone asks where we were today please can you say that we went out shopping early and were out all day?"

"Of course."

Chapter 32

Pentwen

It was late when they got back to Pentwen and they really didn't feel like talking to anyone until they had met with Lloyd to discuss what had occurred on the Isle of Wight, and what he had found out from the information they had sent him. They dumped their bags on the floor and collapsed on the communal sofa. They exchanged glances. "You alright?" Meg asked. Elle nodded slowly, as if still considering the question.

"Do you think that it was a bit of a close shave?"

"I'm not sure what to think anymore. What with Sir Pompous Git and his cloak and dagger shenanigans here, then the ludicrous meeting with the band of anonymous men at the farm, and then the strange goings on at the eco-town – I'll never watch a movie in quite the same way again," Elle said, half laughing at the ridiculousness off it.

"I know what you mean. Are you scared?"

"Not if I don't think about it – which I'm trying not to."

"Me too. I mean, if they have enough money to send us here, expenses paid and cover our fees for next year, then they are well off, and well connected from what I can see."

Elle nodded. "Text Lloyd and ask him when we can catch up?"

Lloyd was round within the hour. The girls were exhausted but knew they would not be able to sleep properly until they had shared their burden. Lloyd came clutching a bag that clinked satisfyingly. "I'll get some glasses," Meg said on seeing the cool bottle of white being pulled out.

They took him through their time away, step by step, trying to be objective, but Lloyd was keen to press them on their instincts. "If journalists just worked on objective assessments of the facts as they were presented, and didn't follow their gut, or peek over walls, then imagine what stories would have never been uncovered."

"When you put it like that?" Meg said relaxing slightly.

Elle started. "The whole thing was weird from the outset. Even the cloak and dagger stuff by taking us to some deserted farmhouse. I think it was to disorientate us."

"Well it worked. And then the whole naming themselves after English county towns, or whatever the hell that was." Meg continued incredulous. "I mean whoever came up with that has evidently watched one too many Tarantino films – *Hi, I'm Mr Pink and I'm gonna blow your brains out!*" she mimicked in an exaggerated American accent.

"Good point," Elle mused. "If they just wanted to remain anonymous then they could have given themselves entirely normal fake names, so what would be the purpose in highlighting the fact that they were lying about who they were?"

"That's better," Lloyd urged, "Question everything. So why would they want you to know they were lying?"

"To scare us?"

"Yeah, it's like it was some sort of power trip. We know who you are but you don't know who we are."

"And you can't trace us because you don't know who we are."

"I think you're getting somewhere," Lloyd urged.

"And then there was the refusal to let us see the site or even tell us where it is?"

"Yes," Elle continued. "What is the purpose of that resistance?"

"It can only mean they have something to hide at this stage. So have they not applied for planning?"

"I can't think that it would be as basic as that." Lloyd added. "It's not like failing to mention that you've built an extension to your house. This is a massive development, so it must be in line with local planning." He pulled a pad from his bag and started jotting down notes. "I'll see if I can get in touch with the planning officer tomorrow. So if it's not planning, what else could it be?"

There was silence and some sipping of wine.

"I'm too tired to think," Meg said rubbing her temples.

"No, don't stop now. You're on a roll, and it's all still fresh in your heads. Keep going," he urged.

"So maybe it's the land. Maybe who it belongs to, or what was there before?" Elle added.

"That could be it."

"Okay. I'll have a search on the HM Land Registry site tomorrow," Lloyd added more notes to remind himself. "So what we have is money and influence, as denoted by the generous deal they have offered you. We have meetings held in off-track venues overseen by anonymous men in suits, suggesting that there is something underhand at play, otherwise they could have met you at the hotel or at least taken you to the site to get acclimatised. And then there was the security at the assumed site of the eco-town, which suggests that they have something to hide."

They nodded in agreement.

"I'll get on this tomorrow. I'll have a look at the photos you sent and see if it gives us any clues to what we are dealing with here. Then we need to plan the return match."

Lloyd met with Elle and Meg the next afternoon once they had finished their shifts. Jake and Mitch had been hassling them to go for a surf but neither girl felt right hanging out with the guys without coming clean about where they had been and what they had been doing. They had decided not to tell Jake and Mitch about the situation until they felt they had exonerated themselves – which was definitely not yet. They met with Lloyd at Ray and Holly's house to allow them to speak openly and have access to the Wi-Fi. Holly buzzed around the kitchen making a pot of coffee, with a fruit tea for Elle. They were all gathered around the large dark wood coffee table, Holly, Elle and Meg cosied up on the deep sofa, Ray in the armchair and Lloyd on the sitting on the floor tapping at the laptop.

"So here is what we have so far – the who, the where, the when and the what. So the who is someone or something with money and power. They are evidently well connected as they are using Brownly-Smith as a go-between and he, as we are all now aware, is a big hitter and in the pocket of government. This suggests that it's someone in government that he's working on behalf of, or he's moonlighting for another disreputable associate."

"But surely he wouldn't do anything so stupid for a mate, in a place where he's running for governor?" Ray questioned.

"I'm inclined to go with this view, Ray, which leaves us with the more insidious explanation that this is also government business."

A shiver went down Meg's spine at the thought.

"So with respect to the who, all we know is it's people in powerful places?" Holly summarised.

"Yep. So moving on to the where. This we are quite sure of now thanks to the super sleuths," Lloyd continued, nodding at the two curled up on the sofa. "The venue is land previously owned by the Ministry of Defence. It was an old army base, but I'm having difficulty in finding any indication that the land has been sold on to a company or private business."

"So you think this is a government sponsored project?" Ray asked, incredulously. "An interesting diversification – the MOD needing to deal with the austerity measures by turning barracks into amusement parks!"

They laughed at Ray's assessment of the situation. Holly adding to the banter, "Well at least they have the workforce to build the rides – how many squaddies does it take to build a theme park?!"

"Well none by my reckoning," Lloyd added. "There have been no military personnel residing at the site for over three years now."

"So it has essentially been mothballed?"

"It would look that way."

"So no one would miss it if it were closed?"

"Exactly."

Elle leant forward and took her iPad from the table flicking it open. "I did some digging on planning legislation and found this," she said turning the screen to those gathered. "So this is a government document that lays out how planning regulations differ from MOD land by comparison to other land." She scrolled down to the section she was interested in. "This paragraph here stipulates that building on MOD land is not open to the same restrictions or scrutiny as normal planning applications as the publishing of such information would be considered confidential as it might compromise missions and what have you, through the publishing of secure intelligence."

"So let's get this straight," Holly asked, "They can built what they like without asking permission of anyone?"

"Yep. So it seems."

"And with the government's current disposal of MOD land as a way of paring down the UK's military force and budget, it means that they can sell off the land to pretty much whoever they wish," Lloyd added.

"So do you think they, or someone powerful within the government," Meg ventured, "has built an eco-town to their own spec, and of no use to the military, so they can now sell it off to the highest bidder as a finished article?"

"Or if you want to be really cynical, they built an eco-town to someone else's spec, ready to sell to them on completion," Lloyd furthered.

"Or even worse," Ray said, "what if they built it to their own spec as they are going to buy it for themselves – under the guise of some shell company, to feather their own retirement nest?"

"Jeez, that's cynical, but entirely possible," Meg considered, shaking her head in disbelief.

"Well it would explain the scare tactics and the secrecy they seem so keen on using with us," Elle reflected. Meg nodded in agreement.

"I reckon that's covered the what, so it's just the when," Ray questioned.

"So this is the when," Lloyd said, turning to Ray and Holly. "And this is where I think you could help."

Ray raised his eyebrows, curious as to what he and Holly could do to assist.

"After chatting to a journalist at the Island Echo, the Isle of Wight's local weekly, I found out that the new eco-town is due to be opening in a month. There have been a few very cagily worded press releases sent to the Echo but there has been no reply to the journalists' requests for more information. This rather piqued his curiosity so he was very willing to share information on this. The latest release was under the company name of Sustineri Estates, the venue having been creatively named Wight-Green eco-town. Which is strange as they do not appear to be the registered owners of the land – yet." He said turning the laptop screen towards the sofa. "These are the named CEOs Thomas and Fiona Grant." The couple pictured on their slick website in no way resembled the men Meg and Elle had met at the farmhouse on the Isle of Wight. They shook their heads.

"Never seen them before."

"No," Elle added. "The guys we met were nothing like this couple."

"Hmm. I think these are the acceptable front of a more underhanded plan. Anyway, I looked the company up and it's relatively recently founded, needless to say off-shore, and I don't mean Isle of Wight! So no one traceable, but it did give me a contact point."

All eyes were on Lloyd while he paused to top up his coffee and take a sip.

"So I got a colleague at The Times to call them with a very specific request."

"Which was?" asked Holly impatiently.

"That we could send a reporter and photographer along for their test week, as sort of residents, to do an extended article on this new venture for the Colour Supplement Holidays section."

"And still, how does this involve us?" Holly pushed.

"Well the reporter and photographer may look very much like a certain Ray and Holly Jordan," Lloyd concluded, nodding waiting for their excitement about his proposal. All he was met with was bewildered looks from all. Lloyd looked from face to face, "What? Don't you get it? You two will be playing the role of Natalie and Dominic Foster."

"Weren't they the couple from The Times that you called in to help when you needed someone undercover to deal with the budget cruise company last year?" Holly recalled.

"Yes. The very same. But this time you will be going undercover, posing as them."

"But why?" Ray puzzled.

"So you can ask questions and take photos legitimately."

"I get that," Holly continued, "But why don't you get Natalie and Dominic to actually be themselves, doing their actual job?"

"Ah, so you can help Meg and Elle out as they try to scupper the inspection. It didn't seem fair to drag others into this mess."

Around the tables there were slow nods as all digested Lloyd's plan. Logical. It all made sense, and it was good back-up for the girls.

"Why," Ray enquired, "do you always have to make some mystery about your underhanded plans? One day you'll just come right out and say – here's the plan!"

"Yeah, Ray. But where would be the fun in that?"

Chapter 33

Truro

The long awaited day of the hustings had arrived. It was stuffy and overcast which only served to add to the stress that Roger was feeling. They had spent the night in the Truro flat, a choice that Roger was now regretting. He never slept well there. For him there was only one place to be if you wanted to wake refreshed, and this was his tiny cottage in Porthissick. There was nothing better than waking up early and taking a bracing walk across the field to the cliff edge, following the coast path down to the harbour, where inevitably one of the Morcom men would be busy at work on the Helena. From there he would cross the village square, past The Anchor, and return up the winding lane to the cottage. In hindsight this is what he should have done. He'd have had a good night's sleep, got up early for the bracing walk, then drove to Truro. Never mind, too late now.

Aggie was pulling various hangers out of the wardrobe and throwing them on the bed, followed by the occasional expletive.

"What's up with you?"

Through gritted teeth she bemoaned the fact that she never had clothes and shoes that matched in the same place. There then followed a long, and overly complicated explanation, that as she might be spending much of the day standing so she couldn't wear heels, not least she didn't want to look too tall beside him, therefore she needed something flatter, but not so flat that it looked frumpy, so she needed a mid-heel, of which the only ones she had here were either bright red, too tarty, or black, too sombre. She'd have to go with the black, but then to make sure it didn't look like she was ready for a funeral, she needed to find a bright outfit. The only bright outfits she had at the Truro flat were one burgundy suit, which would make her look like a job applicant, a floral dress, probably only suitable for garden parties, and a dark grey Chanel style dress. Before she could rant further as to the rights and wrongs of shoe and dress combinations, Roger pulled out the Chanel dress from the pile and laid it on the chair. He grabbed the black shoes and put them alongside the dress. He moved her gently away from the wardrobe and foraged around inside, eventually emerging with a cerise pashmina and black belt, which he added to the pile. "That," he said pointing to the chair, "with your hair down will be absolutely perfect." His tone indicating that this was not really up for discussion. She perused the collection and decided that this was a pretty good ensemble.

As she picked up her outfit she said, "Well, if it all goes badly today you can always start over as a personal shopper and style guru!"

He was right. She looked stunning with her wild red hair against the cerise. He emerged from the bedroom several minutes later looking handsome in his dark grey suit and black shirt. "No tie?"

"No. I'm not one of them. I'm the Governor who's happy to get stuck in and get his hands dirty. I need to emphasise our similarities, not our differences. I know that many still see me as an interloper, so I've got to show them I'm with them, and not another Whitehall lackey."

"Good point. This will really emphasise the difference between you and that Brownly-Smartarse. God knows what he'll be wearing."

"Probably a top hat and monocle knowing his dress sense." The laughter that this generated was essential to break the tension that was building about the day.

They arrived at the Hall for Cornwall at midday and were ushered backstage to a dressing room. Someone had thoughtfully laid out some refreshments and snacks, alongside a vase of flowers. They sat down on the sofa, and while Aggie flicked through a magazine Roger pulled out some cue cards to peruse whilst they were waiting. A floor manager popped her head round the door. "All good? Got everything you need?"

"Yes, thank you," Aggie said raising her glass of gin and tonic in thanks.

"Needless to say Brownly-Smith has no refreshments in his room," she said smiling. "Anyway, the audience are filing in so we will be calling you onstage in about twenty."

A minute or so later Brian Clough came by. "We're all set with the filming. Callum and I were up to stupid o'clock editing and timing. It's going to be spectacular," he said very excitedly.

"Cheers, Brian. And send our thanks to Callum. We'll catch up with you when it's all over," Aggie replied.

Callum and Brian had been instrumental in helping the plan come together. Lady Rosemary had introduced Brownly-Smith to Callum, claiming him to be a scholar of Cornwall, therefore he could help develop the speech.

Callum was convincing in his approach, speaking Brownly-Smith's language. "One thing the Cornish really respond well to is authority. They like to know who's in charge. A bit like dogs; they need a tight leash and clear instructions."

"Got it," Brownly-Smith said, scribbling down notes. "Take charge and lead from the front. Will do."

"And dress like you mean it. Stand out from the crowd."

"Yes." Still scribbling. "Humour?"

"Absolutely not. The Cornish are a serious nation. You wouldn't want to trivialise the situation."

"Absolutely. Good Point."

"And the media company want some photos to project onto the screen while you're talking. Have you got anything?"

"I believe Rosemary took some while we have been out and about. I'll ask her," adding this to his list.

The stage was laid out almost like a living room, with a large rug in the centre and armchairs to the right and left, with a lectern on a slightly raised podium in the middle. Roger Stiles and Martin Brownly-Smith were ushered onto the stage from opposite wings, with aerial shots of Kernow being projected onto the screen behind them, all very theatrical. Roger thought that all they were missing was D:Ream's *Things Can Only Get Better* being blasted from the speakers, and it would be 1997 all over again.

They took up their seats and the chairman, Robert Ash, Chief Executive of the Council, called weakly for quiet. Roger scanned the auditorium. It was packed to the rafters. Not only was every seat filled, but people were sitting on the stairs, and standing when there was nowhere left to sit. Evidently this was being taken very seriously.

Quiet eventually fell around the auditorium and Ash made a speech about the importance of democracy and letting voices be heard. He explained that there would be an address by each candidate, then questions to both thereafter. Roger was first to speak. He stood up slowly, and looked around the stage. Ash gestured to the lectern, and Roger approached it. Put his cue cards on it, hesitated, and turning his back to it he walked to the front of the stage.

"I stand here before you today, not as your Governor, even though I am honoured to have that role, not even as a politician, but as a man who came to this great County, and threw away everything he had because his love for Kernow was greater. It is as this man that I speak to you today, as I know that every man, woman and child who comes from this great place feels the same, and it is our job to ensure that we continue to make the Isle of Kernow grow stronger and more independent."

Behind him on the screen the drone shots of Kernow from the air changed to footage of the Drift.

"I know I came to this place as an interloper, and there will be some of you out there that think a leopard cannot change its spots. Well possibly not, but it can use those spots to maximise survival elsewhere. And I chose here."

He stopped for a second, and took in the sight. All were silent and waiting for his next words. He felt blessed.

"Having come from the other side," to a ripple of laughter, "it means I know what their rules of engagement are. I fought against those rules to help Kernow become the independent state that you voted for. I never once doubted its ability to go it alone. The resilience of the people, the commitment and dedication when we had been all but left to starve by the mainland. I only wish I had seen your need before, and had helped you on your way to independence." Nodding and sporadic applause. He suddenly felt hot and slightly faint under the stage lights. He took off his jacket and placed it on his chair before walking back to the front of the stage again.

The footage behind changed to a loop that Callum had shot with Aggie, showcasing the Food Sourcing Network; its produce and its producers.

"So here is what I have to offer. I will continue, if it is your will, to make the Isle of Kernow independent of the mainland. During my time as Governor I have been proud to see the economic situation here become stronger. Not something that can be said of the rest of the UK." Some whoops from the crowd and more clapping. "Our exports have significantly increased and we are importing less and less. This is mainly due to the sterling work of the Food Sourcing Network," he said scanning the front row for Aggie. He found her, beaming up at him, holding his hand out so the crowd could see who he was thanking. "This amazing woman and her band of resourceful colleagues have turned the Isle's fortunes around. We are so near to self-sufficiency by your drive to fight against adversity," he was now gesticulating to the whole audience, bringing them into the conversation. "In order to support their amazing work we have now dedicated the entirety of the Old County Hall for their operations in ensuring that we are fed and watered, with proposed satellite offices around the rest of the Isle." Spontaneous clapping. The film changed again to swooping shots compiled from the summer's surf tour. The sun was bright and the sea was spectacularly blue, with bronzed athletes ripping up the perfect waves.

"Another of our great strengths is utilising our change of location to maximise tourism. Even when we did not know what to expect from our new location, some of you decided that sometimes you just have to take risks. The likes of Ray and Holly Jordan were instrumental in bringing the Pro Surf Tour to our coast. Not only does this mean all of those fabulous surfers coming to spend time, and money," he said lightly to laughter, "in our businesses. What this also brings is the reputation that makes us a new go-to surf destination. We're battling it out with the best of them, especially giving Portugal and Morocco a run for their tourist money."

There was now a subtle seamless switch in the film, which concentrated on some of the buildings around Pentwen and their new approach to tourism. This loop showed some of the sustainable technology that had been invested in, and how the local businesses had upgraded their properties and services to meet the new need.

"But this isn't all about the money, as Pentwen has proved. This is about community, and making things better in the future." The D:Ream track sneaking into the back of his mind again. Holding his hand towards Jake who sat alongside Aggie, he said, "It is the innovation and forward thinking of the new generation that will ensure that the Isle of Kernow can sustain its economic position, as well as its natural resources. And this is how it should be. The young making decisions about their own future based on the hard work they have put in to make it possible."

There was applause from around the auditorium. People turning to their neighbours, nodding in agreement. Roger was a little overwhelmed. He turned away from the audience whilst they were clapping and walked towards the back of the stage, wondering what to say next. There was nothing else to say really. He slowly walked back to his position at the front and opened his arms to the audience. "So, what can I say. I have only been with you for such a short space of time, but I hope that you have seen in me someone who genuinely cares about the direction of the Isle of Kernow. I have cut all my ties with Whitehall, as you can imagine, and all I have to offer is myself and my dedication to the cause. I hope you believe it is enough."

He dropped his head and arms, clasping his hands together almost in prayer, or at least thanks, and returned to his seat. There was a momentary silence, then the room burst into applause, many standing with arms raised above their heads. It took Ash some time to calmed the room before he could call Martin Brownly-Smith to the podium.

Wanting to look more like the statesman he took up position behind the lectern, taking his notes out of the pocket of his voluminous Navy blue pinstriped suit.

"Dear people of Cornwall," he started, only to be met, four words in, with heckles of "It's Kernow you fool."

"People of Kernow," he corrected, "Like Roger here, I am not a local, but I think you can tell that I come as one who has spent that last few months getting to know you, and feel I am at one with you." The screen behind changes to a still image of the rotund man sporting white shorts and a floral shirt. From this ridiculous outfit pale white limbs protruded, whereas his face scorched red. To complete the ensemble he was wearing socks with sandals, a fashion faux pas of great magnitude. The auditorium burst into spontaneous laughter, fingers pointing at the image whilst rocking in their seats. Confused, Brownly-Smith turned to face the screen and was incensed by what he saw. Relieved as this image was replaced by a few shots that Brownly-Smith had sent to the media company, of him looking meaningfully out to sea.

He continued. "Not only have I spent time getting to know you – you people of the Corn – but I have been getting to know your ancestors."

The audience were now baffled – 'people of the corn'? what was he going on about. They turned to each other shrugging, the muttering around the auditorium putting him off his stride again. "Does he think that Cornwall means people of the corn?" one man asked his neighbour.

"God only knows. It means people of the peninsula. What an idiot."

"I have seen the challenges that you have had to face. The battles that you have won and lost," Brownly-Smith continued, ignoring the murmuring.

"Not in my lifetime, mate!" Came a heckle form the crowd.

"Maybe not, sir. But your ancestors have suffered at the hands of so many. The losses your people have experienced. The Battle of Deorham, -" he paused for effect. "The Battle of Blackheath, -" another pause, and some nods from the audience. "And the Great English-Spanish Pilchard Wars."

Again the audience were baffled, shrugging shoulders.

"What a miserable way to lose your livelihood, but I shall make sure that those from foreign lands never again deprive you of what is rightfully yours. The Spanish will never take our fish stock again."

There was now hysterical outbursts of laughter coming from areas of the audience that knew their fishing history. To augment the chaos erupting in the audience Callum projected the shot of Brownly-Smith eating a pasty with cutlery in The Anchor. The audience fell about laughing, Brownly-Smith at a loss as to what the problem was.

"Indeed, I feel passionately about restoring this great trade, and, if elected, I am looking forward to spending some time aboard. And I will ensure to bring fish pasties for sustenance."

There was a dramatic intake of breath from the fishing fraternity. "You're mad as a hatter," shouted Seth Morcom, a retired fisherman from Porthissick. "The only thing we have to worry about taking our fish, is the bad luck you'll bring with your stupid fish pasty."

"Not least, we already dealt with the Europeans trying to take what weren't theirs, didn't we Stewie?" continued Seth's grandson, Toby, referring to the incident where some French fishermen were over-amorous with Stewie's beloved Carrie.

"Anyway," Brownly-Smith continued, somewhat confused. "I have been given permission by the Government to rejuvenate the fishing industry with generous grants to refurbish harbours and infrastructure. In addition, we are currently negotiating with Europe to increase the fishing quota for the Isle due to its relocation." A lie, but he'd be in position by the time anyone found out.

There was now a positive mumble around the room, all stupidity forgotten when money was mentioned.

"But how can we trust you?" Toby Morcom continued. "Who's to say that you won't renege on the deal as soon as you're in power?"

The screen was filled of montage of Devon-related images: Brownly-Smith first tucking into a pasty with a top crimp, followed by Sully's film of him constructing a cream tea in the Devon style.

"You can trust me because I have the ear of the Prime Minister. He is sympathetic and is willing to contribute most generously to your cause." He felt that he had them on side now. "In addition, David Cameron is willing to review the whole Duchy of Cornwall business. He feels it unreasonable for a whole county to be owned by one man."

"Who?" came a voice from the crowd.

"Prince Charles, the Duke of Cornwall of course," he said a tad too patronisingly.

"But he doesn't. He rents a few holiday cottages, has a few castles that don't even have roofs, and built a couple of housing estates."

Flummoxed by the response, and the silence in the auditorium, he felt best not to challenge. "There has also been the promise of increased funds to help expand the tourist industry on the Isle. In exchange for a reciprocal working agreement on eco-town development there is the offer of airport expansion to allow more regular flights in and out." This was complemented by the projected image of Martin Brownly-Smith beaming into the camera lens, sporting a shorty wetsuit – completely unaware that it was on back to front. More titters from the auditorium.

"What the hell does that mean, Lloyd?" Jake whispered to Lloyd who was sat in row in front of him. "Reciprocal working agreement on eco-town development?"

"I think it's an underhanded way of saying – *tell us your eco-town secrets of success, and we'll build you a fancy new baggage carousel at the airport.*"

"They won't be allowed to get away with this, really?" Jake said, exasperated.

"Who knows. But it sure as hell won't happen if Roger's in charge."

He talked further about the income streams that Whitehall were offering in return for Brownly-Smith being voted in as Governor, and with each offer of cash or assistance there was something removed. What the Isle of Kernow had to lose as a result of this generous additional funding was never clearly addressed, but Roger was a politician, he knew the language. He knew the game, and this was a game where, by degrees, everything that the British Overseas Territory status had given them would be eroded, until eventually they would be back where they started. Except this time not only removed culturally, but geographically. The intimation was subtle, and unless you understood the intricacies of the policy, all you would be hearing was money in, money in, money in. Roger shook his head in despair.

Roger was pushing the Beamer to the limit on the switchback roads. "Slow down for god's sake, Roger," Aggie admonished. He slowed slightly but drove in silence.

"What is wrong? I thought it went well."

"What bit of *money, grants, funding, blah, blah, blah* did you think went well?"

"The bit where you gave an incredible, heartfelt speech, and the audience could see that you genuinely care."

"But I can't compete. He has something tangible to offer them. I don't have access to such financial support."

"But you don't need to. Do you really think that London's money will turn their heads?"

He shrugged sulkily.

"The beauty of your speech was that you showcased all that we have achieved through the hard work of the Cornish, despite the machinations of Whitehall. We have a long memory, Roger. The reason that all is going so well is that for once we're doing it our way, and you have been instrumental in that."

"But no one even asked a question that I could respond to."

This was true, and Aggie had found it frustrating. "That was because they know what you can offer. They know how you work. They were grilling the outsider, seeing if they could find a chink in his armour."

"Which they evidently didn't."

"Well maybe not. I'm just hoping that images last longer than words."

"What do you mean?"

"Didn't you see what photos they ended on?"

"No."

"I guess not. You were facing the audience. Oh Roger, you're going to love this. When Ash asked you each to get up and take a bow, when you stood they showed you accepting your role of Governor, but when he stood up they showed the video of Brownly-Smartarse slapping Mitch's bum and Mitch decking him in return."

He slowed right down and turned to look at her. "No way!" he said incredulously. "I couldn't work out why the audience were all in stitches when he rose to his feet. Bloody hysterical!" he said cracking a smile. Maybe it didn't go so badly after all.

Chapter 34

Isle of Wight

Meg and Elle arrived at Southampton Airport but instead of being directed to a waiting car they were escorted to a VIP lounge and told to wait whilst their luggage was transferred. They sat nervously and were asked by a waitress what they would like to drink. "I don't think we're here for very long," Meg replied.

"The helicopter won't be ready for another half an hour so the drinks are complementary during your wait. We also have some snacks if you are hungry?"

The girls exchanged glances. "Two dry, white wines please?"

"No problem. I'll bring them straight over."

They waited until the waitress was out of earshot when Meg said with panic in her voice, "Where do you suppose they are taking us?"

"The Isle of Wight I'm hoping. It was an old army base so I'm sure it's more than equipped to land helicopters."

"I always wanted to go on a helicopter, but I didn't think it would be a flight where I was scared whether I was being abducted or not."

"Chill out, Meg. They need us more than we need them right now."

"Maybe so, but I'm not convinced."

They arrived into a bustling paradise. It looked like the set of a film with men rushing backwards and forwards carrying unlikely props. 'This,' Elle thought, 'is exactly what is wrong with this venture'. She could see the difference between the evolved community approach at Pentwen where real people got together to make their place a better place, and were then willing to share it with others. This, by comparison, was a theme park, the theme being making money by presenting a facade of sustainability. Her first impression of the place vindicated all that she was about to do. Not only for the underhanded way that they had treated her and Meg, but by the lack of collegiality. Why not approach Pentwen and ask Jake and Lloyd to share their experiences? Because this was a financial venture and not a community approach to living.

They were shown to their quarters – a very spatial apartment in the main hotel block. Their hostess asked them to get settled in and suggested they get ready for dinner at seven where they would meet the directors and chat about the week ahead. As she left the room Elle opened her mouth to say something but Meg quickly put her fingers to her lips suggesting silence. Then giving Elle a theatrical wink, she said, "Well let's get unpacked. Which bedroom would you like?" As she said this she pulled her notepad from her bag and scribbled 'it might be bugged – no talking about our plans'. She showed it to Elle who nodded in agreement. She took the pen from Meg and replied 'we'll need to find somewhere to talk as we need to get Holly and Ray active at some point'. Meg gave the thumbs up, "Yes, I think I'll take this room if that's OK with you, Elle?"

"Super. I'm happy with this one."

The hostess picked them up at seven and took them to a waiting golf buggy where they sat and were given a quick tour around the gardens on the way to the restaurant. There was a chill in the air and they pulled their jackets tighter around their shoulders, unused to the coldness of the UK. They were introduced to CEO and his wife who doubled as the director of operations, Thomas and Fiona Grant. They appeared as they had in the photo Lloyd had shown them; both tall and elegantly dressed, and impossibly glamourous. It seemed that the casting director was as Hollywood as the props department. They were each given a glass of bubbles that Elle knew to be something more expensive that her regular Prosecco. They made small talk as they were shown to a private dining room away from the main restaurant. The décor was exquisite; understated but evidently expensive. They were shown a menu with several choices for each course, with far too much French than Meg was comfortable with. They ordered and the conversation turned to business. Whoever this couple were they did not seem connected to Messrs York, Warwick, Oxford or Stafford. They were the business end of the deal, and seemed unaware of what the girls' true mission had been. The Grants really seemed to believe that the girls were there in a consultative capacity, having been through such an inspection previously. Elle found this disarming. The whole place had an unnatural feel to it, reminding her of the Truman Show movie, where Jim Carey was the star in the ultimate reality show – his entire life being a lie lived out on a film set, and he the only one unaware of the falsity of the situation.

They chatted knowledgably about the sorts of things that the inspectors looked for, and how they would like to work with the staff directly to ensure that all was going to plan. They finished their meal, and Elle made of show of stifling yawns, not least she was tired of the pretence. As they were escorted from the dining room they noted another couple leaving at the same time. Fiona Grant waved the couple over and set about introductions. "Meg and Elle, this is Natalie and Dominic Foster from The Times. They are doing an article on the Wight-Green eco-town."

They all shook hands politely, Meg unable to make eye contact with Ray in his photographer's corduroy and newly grown goatee beard, and Holly sporting a black bobbed wig. Introductions over, Fiona suggested that Meg and Elle meet up with the journalists to give them some of the technical details of how eco-towns are assessed. Numbers were exchanged and they all went their separate ways.

Their time at the Wight-Green eco-town was split into two phases; preparation and assessment. Throughout the preparation phase Meg spent time working with the manager of their eco-pods and glamping facilities based on her experiences working with Holly in Pentwen. Meanwhile Elle focused her attention on the luxury hotel and serviced apartments mirroring her work at the North Bay Hotel. At the end of each day they would meet in the bathroom with the shower running so that they might talk without being overheard – still untrusting of their paymasters.

Having Ray and Holly pose as journalists gave them the opportunity to bring over crates of supplies that they needed to put their plan into action. The crates were labelled as delicate photographic and recording equipment, and were swathed in security tape to prevent anyone poking their nose in. The supplies that they had sent with Ray and Holly were the residue of paraphernalia left in Pentwen after their move to more eco-friendly lines of supplies. Meg relieved the Surf Shack of the boxes of plastic bags that she had found in the stock room. These she distributed to the various shops at Wight-Green explaining how these silicon-based alternatives were entirely biodegradable and had a very low carbon footprint. As the retailers working in the shops were employees of Wight-Green they did not question, nor argue the point, but accepted what the girls said as truth.

"You wouldn't get this sort of compliance in Pentwen," Meg exclaimed to Elle as she offloaded the last box to the last retail outlet.

"Hell no! Could you imagine Julie Ward putting her fruit and veg into one of these without wanting to see documentary evidence."

Meanwhile Elle was replacing the new linen in the Wight-Green laundry cupboard with that discarded from the North bay Hotel. Elle made sure that she made up a couple of bedrooms in the hotel, apartments and eco-pods with this linen, taking careful note of the room numbers ready for the arrival of the inspectors.

As well as bringing the surplus stock into Wight-Green undetected, Ray and Holly were also responsible for switching the eco lightbulbs with the redundant stock Elle had found in the hotel's attic. Elle gave them the numbers of the rooms where she had used Jake's old sheets, and The Times crew asked if they could use these rooms to film and do interviews for their article. The hospitality crew were happy to oblige, giving them access to wherever they needed. It was whilst Ray and Holly were in the middle of replacing the bulbs in one eco-pod that they were interrupted by a maintenance manager doing a final inspection. Ray and Holly froze mid-action as the man walked in with his assistant and caught them with bulbs in their hands. "Who the hell are you, and what the hell do you think you are doing?" he bellowed.

Ray and Holly were speechless for a second, when the assistant intervened. "They're the film crew. You know, the ones from The Times doing the big article on us. You remember. Dave told us they would be on site."

The maintenance manager looked them up and down suspiciously. Holly grabbed the initiative. She walked forward, hand outstretched. Ditching her south African accent for received pronunciation she shook the maintenance manager's hand firmly, saying, "Hi, yah, hi. I'm Natalie Forest, yah. And this," she said gesturing towards the goatee-faced Ray, "is my husband and photographer, Dominic Forest."

Ray stepped forward and shook the man's hand, following Holly's lead. "Good to meet you. Fine job you're all doing here. Fine place."

Holly continued, knowing vanity conquered all, "So you are?"

"I'm Peter Simpson, maintenance manager."

"Yah, Peter. Good to meet you. So we're just doing some cue sequencing, but after that I'd really like to spend some time with you, Pete," Holly continued, putting an arm around Peter's shoulder. "Get to know the nuts and bolts of how this all came together and the role you've played in its creation. How do you feel about that? Possibly over a drink and nibbles," Holly continued gradually guiding him to the door.

"Um, well yes. I suppose that would be alright. Um, yes, what time then?" he mumbled.

"Say, half an hour?"

"Um, yes. Fine. I'll meet you where?"

"In the tropical bar?"

"Yes. Excellent choice."

She had just about got him and the assistant through the door when he walked back in, and as if an understudy for Columbo he asked, "Sorry. I just need to check. Um, what are those bulbs you've got there. I mean they don't look like eco-bulbs?"

Ray looked him square in the eye, and holding out the old eco-unfriendly bulb he said, "This is an accent light, and" gesticulating to the one Holly was still holding, "that's a background filter light. It's essential when shooting in these types of interior to make the place look cosy, not dark. So we use a range of light types to achieve this. Amazing what you can achieve by increasing the yellow end of the lumen spectrum," he finished, nodding with admiration at the bulb in his hand.

"Okay. Well as long as you take them with you when you go."

"The price these babies cost, you can guarantee they're coming with me."

At last the two left the room and Holly and Ray fell on the bed laughing hysterically. "What the bloody hell is a lumen?" she whispered through her laughter.

"Well you can talk. Cue sequencing?"

Holly stood up, wiping tears of laughter from her cheeks. "We better get a move on, it looks like we're doing an interview in an hour."

"You're not actually going to do the interview, are you?"

"Hell yes! I might get some real gossip from Pete the maintenance manager. Like yah, baby."

Having interviewed Pete the maintenance manager, Ray coming along to get some shots to make it look more realistic, Holly took it upon herself to interview anyone of interest. She recorded them onto her phone and emailed them to Lloyd each evening so he could have a listen through. Anything he thought sounded dubious he contacted Jeanette O'Loughlin for advice, sometimes asking Meg and Elle to confirm whether what was being said in the interviews actually reflected what was being done in practice. By the end of the week Lloyd had compiled a running document of contraventions to the process that he felt the inspectors may find enlightening.

The second phase of their visit was the inspection itself. Meg and Elle were invited to the Grant's executive suite to meet the inspectors. They entered and exchanged pleasantries with the Grants. Meg noticed something move in the shadows of the back wall. She strained her eyes against the glare of the light streaming in through the windows either side, and a man stepped forward. Almost silently.

"Ah," Fiona Grant started, almost having forgot he was still here. "Let me introduce you both to Mr Warwick."

Meg stepped forward, unsure if she was meant to indicate that she had met him before, so she hedged her bet. "Very nice to meet you, Mr Warwick."

"Likewise," he replied squeezing her hand tighter than she felt necessary.

"Anyway, I shall leave you to your business," Mr Warwick said, shaking the Grants' hands briefly before exiting. Meg and Elle exchanged confused glances, confused as to what the purpose of his visit was.

The door opened again and the hostess escorted the inspectors in. Ian Philips honed in on Meg and Elle, shaking their hands enthusiastically, explaining how good it was to see them again. Mr Merton, on the other hand, stood back and waited to be introduced to Thomas and Fiona Grant, showing no interest in rekindling his acquaintance with Meg and Elle, a feeling that they reciprocated. Although they had hoped that Philips and Merton would be the inspectors sent to assess the Isle of Wight venue, this had been in no way guaranteed, so they were relieved at this turn of events. Whilst Merton talked business with the Grants, Philips turned his attention to Meg. "How is the project going? We must find time to chat about what you have found so far. It might be that any data you collect could be of value to the Agency."

"Really?" Meg exclaimed, "The European Environment Agency might be interested in what we may have found?"

"Absolutely. Remember, we only get a snapshot in time. Whereas you are on the ground on a daily basis, so can make objective observations as you are only temporarily connected to the community."

"Good point." Meg replied. "Would you mind if we accompanied you again on your inspection. This way we can get a consistent view of the standards, and pick up on anything we may have missed from the Kernow inspection?"

"Absolutely. We would be delighted." Meg and Elle were pleased to hear this, although they predicted that Mr Merton would not be quite so delighted.

As soon as they got out of the office and were alone walking in the grounds, Meg asked Elle on her thoughts of Mr Warwick being there. "I think it was for our benefit. I think it was a warning to us to remember our role here. I mean, it's not like we've seen him here before, or even heard mention of his name."

"He just leaves me with the heebie-jeebies," Meg replied visibly shivering.

They stopped to take a break, sitting beside what looked like a newly created lake sipping cold drinks from the cans. They had kicked off their shoes and were enjoying the sunlight reflecting on the water as swans cruised calmly by. Elle lay back on the grass and closed her eyes, listening to the sound of lapping water and buzzing insects. Conversely, Meg's mind was reeling, she was so excited by the invitation that Ian Philips had made about using their data. "Can you imagine, an authority like that being interested in what we have found?"

"Hmm, very exciting," Elle replied, sounding anything but.

"Well you don't sound very excited?"

Giving up on her relaxing moment in the mild sunshine, Elle propped herself up on her elbows, and thought for a moment. "It's not that I'm not excited. It was just something else that Ian said that made me think."

"What?"

"Well, it was the reason that they would be happy to take our observations seriously."

"What? That we were objective observers. Well he's right, isn't he? We can be objective."

"But the reason he gave for our ability to be objective was the problem."

"I don't remember what he said."

"He said it's because we are not members of the community at Pentwen," Elle explained sadly, meeting Meg's gaze.

"Well we're not," Meg shrugged.

"Aren't we? Have we not just compromised our fees for next year in order to remain loyal to the place and its values. And what about Mitch and Jake, not to mention everyone else who's made us welcome?"

Meg sat silently reflecting. "I guess so," she replied, feeling like a child admonished for a selfish act.

"I mean, Lloyd should have berated us for what we came to Pentwen to do, but instead he stuck by us and helped us put right our wrongs."

Guilty silence.

"And what about when all this is over, do you want to go back to Southampton? What about Mitch? Are you ready to give that up?"

"I've tried not to think about it really. Are you going to stay on?"

"I'm not sure. I think one huge deciding factor will be how Jake reacts to what we've, or what I've done."

"You really care for him that much that you'd stay on in Kernow without finishing your degree?"

"Maybe. I've not really thought the full implications through yet."

They sat in silence, staring out to the lake, wishing life was as easy as the tranquil swan's.

The inspection went well as far as the Isle of Wight interlopers were concerned. Elle directed the inspectors to the venues that they had sabotaged, ensuring that all elements had been sufficiently compromised, and maintaining a deadpan expression as they examined each property. Meanwhile they met Ian over coffee to discuss elements of the process, under the guise of their research projects. Elle managed to slip into the conversation how she had found it difficult to compare the experiences of the two ventures as there did not seem to be any business owners at Wight-Green, therefore she was bemused as to how this would relate to the community engagement aspect the sustainable tourism. Subtly they sowed seeds of doubt by throwaway comments, letting him draw his own conclusions.

It was their penultimate day on the Isle of Wight when Elle received a text from Lloyd:
PACKAGE AWAITING COLLECTION AT HOTEL

"What the hell am I meant to do about this?" Elle asked Meg frustratedly.

"Not sure. How can we get offsite without transport and without drawing attention to ourselves?"

"Ah, but Holly and Ray have transport. Maybe they could go?"

Ray and Holly set off in their hire car under the pretence of getting some background shots and Islanders' perspectives on the eco-town. Meg gave them directions to the hotel they had stayed at on their previous visit, and Ray and Holly were delighted to meet up with Maxine and John who they had known when they had owned the hotel in Pentwen all those years before. After some catch-up beers, leaving John and Ray a little the worse for wear, Holly drove back to Wight-Green and delivered a large padded envelope to Meg and Elle. Inside the package was a thinner sealed manila envelope with name MR IAN PHILIPS typed on the front, and PRIVATE & CONFIDENTIAL typed on the bottom righthand corner. There was a handwritten note accompanying it:

Prior to departure ensure that this envelope is put into the possession of the addressee anonymously. Good luck. L

"It looks like Lloyd has been digging up some dirt, and is ready to spill the beans," Meg said satisfied with the bulk of the envelope.

"So how are we going to get it to him without him knowing it's from us?"

"Thinking caps on!"

*

Fiona Grant was sipping her breakfast tea at her desk and going through the daily feedback from the staff who had accompanied the inspectors on their tour. This morning she noted that the hotel housekeeper had mentioned that Mr Merton had commented in passing on the corporate look of the rooms, and that they could look a little more inviting. She pondered on this for a moment. 'Well this could be a quick fix' she thought. She rose and pulled a pile of magazines from a rack and placed them on the desk. She flicked through them until she found the ones she was after, a pile she had saved on interior design ideas. She opened The Times Colour Supplement and leafed through until she found the article *Looking Chic on the Cheap* by Natalie Forest. Her eye moved down and was struck by a photo that stopped her in her tracks. It was not of stunning interior, but of a woman with a black bob, but this woman did not capture the essence of the Natalie Forest who was doing their article. This one was rounder in the face, maybe she had lost some weight. This one was also rounder in the eyes, a change that Fiona Grant could not account for. She left her office at a brisk walk and headed outside.

Holly and Ray were up and about. She had sent Ray for croissants while she had a shower. She was blow drying her hair when there was a knock at the door. "Idiot forgot his key card again," she muttered under her breath as she opened the door. Opening the door she was surprised to come face to face with Fiona Grant, who looked equally surprised to see her.

"Terribly sorry to interrupt you, I've got the wrong door," Fiona said, and walked briskly down the corridor.

At first Holly did not realise the enormity of the event. She returned to the bedroom and as she picked up the brush and hairdryer and looked in the mirror it struck her – no wig. They'd been rumbled. She grabbed her mobile and called Ray, then listened with a sinking feeling as she heard the chirruping of his phone in the bedroom. Next she called Meg as she ran around the room wildly stuffing any belongings into their bag.

"Hi, Holl" she replied sleepily.

"No time to talk. We've been rumbled. We need to get out of here. Be outside your door in five."

"What?" Meg asked blearily.

"Now!" Holly shouted. "Dressed and out!"

As Ray came through the door he was met by a tornado of activity, with Holly in the eye of the storm. "What the hell is going on?"

"They've caught us. We need to get out of here. And now."

"How do you know they've caught us?" Ray stood rooted to the spot.

"I'll explain later, Now, move it. I've told the girls to be ready in five," she said zipping up the bag and thrusting it at Ray.

"He grabbed the keys to the hire car and bolted out of the apartment. They heard rapid footsteps coming up the stairs so turned in the opposite direction and down the fire escape. They bundled into the car and took off at speed, ignoring the one way system and 'twenty is plenty signs'. There was no one outside the hotel block where Meg and Elle were staying, so Holly started to get out of the car. Ray put his hand on her arm to stop her, "Ring them."

There was panting from the other end of the line. "We're coming. Where are you?"

"Outside the hotel. Hurry, they're coming."

The doors burst open and chaos emerged. They leapt in the back and Ray took off again. Elle looked out the back window. "They're following us I think."

A security van was in pursuit, but some way behind them. As Ray neared the exit he saw two golf buggies pull in front trying to block their way. "Are you kidding me?" Ray said, almost laughing at the stupidity of the situation. He dodged between them, clipping the one to the left and tipping it over. The security guard on the gate stepped out of his office to intervene but realised just in time that Ray was not going to stop.

"Duck everyone. Keep down!" Ray shouted as they went under the lowered barrier. Luckily the barrier was more for show than deterrent. "Thank Christ they didn't keep the old army barrier!" Ray said, relieved.

Now they were on the open road Ray put his foot down and sped away. "What now?" he shouted to the bewildered passengers.

"Ferry port?"

"Okay. Anyone know what direction it's in?"

"I'm looking it up. Just waiting for maps to open."

"Meanwhile someone look up what times the ferries are."

"On it."

Whatever advantages their pursuers may have had in knowing the island were confounded by Ray's lack of knowledge, and his choice of random routes.

"The next ferry leaves in fifteen minutes," Elle informed.

"And how far away are we?"

"It says twelve," Meg replied.

"So we've got to get their without getting lost and hope they let us on."

"What exactly do these guys think they can do if they catch us?" Holly said reflectively. "I mean have we broken any laws?"

"Well probably less laws than they have. Which is half the problem I guess."

"But they can't arrest us. They're not the police or anything."

"Then it's even more worrying that they are chasing us," Ray concluded, taking a roundabout a tad too fast.

They arrived at the ferry port and were relieved to see that the ferry was still in dock. "No, look the door is raising. We can't get on!" Holly cried.

Ray was not to be put off. Looking in his rear-view mirror the security van was still on his tail. "Right, on the count of five Holly and Elle jump out and run for the port. Stall the boat if you can. Meg stay put until I say." He pulled the wheel sharply to the right, sitting at right-angles to the road with the passenger side facing the ferry. Holly and Elle fled without closing the doors behind them. Seeing they were clear of the car Ray stuck the car into first and sped away, then pulling on the handbrake the car swung across the carriageway, blocking the road to oncoming traffic, this time with the driver's side facing the ferry. "Run Meg, run!" and both jumped from the car and followed Holly and Elle to the foot passenger entrance. They darted up the gangplank and the ferry steward lifted the rope for them to enter, unimpressed with the tardy passengers. Ray bent over, hands on his knees to catch his breath.

As the ferry pulled away from its moorings they looked back towards the shore. The security van had been joined by a dark Mercedes, against which Mr Warwick was leaning, arms crossed across his chest, and shaking his head as he glared at them.

Chapter 35

Pentwen

"How was your trip home?" Jake asked as he hugged her. She pulled back slightly, and his expression changed to that of a kicked spaniel. "What's up?"

"We need to talk, but not here. Follow me," she said taking him by the hand and leading him up the hotel staircase. He was bemused as she dragged him to the top floor, then passed the penthouse suites to the corridor and up the narrow staircase to the attic storeroom.

"Well this is a naughty welcome home, I must say," he joked in a lecherous voice.

"We'll see,' she said noncommittally.

They entered the attic and she felt around for the light switch. When the room was illuminated she stood and waited for a reaction.

"What the -? where's all the crap gone?" Jake asked, looking at the empty shelves where the old linen used to be.

"I stole it."

"Stole it? What the hell for?"

"I needed it for a project I was working on."

"Project? What project?"

"You need to her me out on this," she said holding his gaze to reinforce the seriousness of the issue.

He shrugged in agreement.

"So," she faltered, finding it hard to start. "You need to hear the whole story before you comment. Okay?"

"I guess," he shrugged.

"So," she started again. "We didn't come here to do a placement year – that was a lie. We were sent here by people in power to find out about starting up an eco-town. Well, that was what they told us. They said- "

"Who's they?"

"I said you'd have to hear me out first. But in answer to your question, we are still not entirely sure. Whoever they are are powerful people with money and influence. And it wasn't long after we accepted their offer that we realised that. They said if we came here and found out how to start an eco-town then they would pay our expenses and pay our uni fees next year. If someone made you that proposition, what would you say? I mean, on the face of it, there's nothing wrong with the offer, is there?"

Jake looked confused. "So are you students or not?"

"Yes. We just took a year out because of this offer. Wouldn't you have done the same?"

"I guess so."

"Then once we got here and started to settle in, our contact started to move the goal posts. He was all, *change in mission*, and *HQ need you to blah, blah, blah*. We weren't happy with the change but he was sort of scary."

"What change in mission? I don't get it?"

"So now he says that they want us to do more than just find out about how to start an eco-town. Now they want us to sabotage the Pentwen inspection, and then help them get through their inspection."

"Their inspection of what?"

"Of their new eco-town. On the Isle of Wight. That's where we've been for the last week," she said looking down. Breaking eye contact as the shame started to rise.

"What the hell have you been doing there?" Jake said shaking his head with confusion.

"I'll explain when I get to that bit. I promise." She took a breath. This was more difficult that she had imagined. "So Meg and I were scared and confused. Like, we felt guilty because everyone here had been amazing and we were meant to cheat you out of it. So we made a decision. We were not going to do what they wanted, but we didn't know how to turn it back on them without some help, so we asked Lloyd."

"Lloyd?!" Jake exclaimed. "He was part of this plan to ruin what we'd created?"

"No, no," she said putting a calming hand on his arm. "Lloyd helped us make it right. We pretended to the guy that we were doing all we could to gather information, and Lloyd helped us write it into a report that sounded genuine, with figures that were out enough to tip them into the fail category of an inspection. Then we learnt everything we could from your inspection to scupper theirs."

"So where did all the stuff go?" he asked pointing at the empty shelves.

Grinning she said, "We replaced their eco stuff with your old non-eco stuff."

He made a range of faces which started with confusion, then realisation and finished on amusement. "Cool. Two birds, one stone. How did you get to do that?"

"They thought we could help get them set up for their inspection, so we went to the Isle of Wight to help them, based on all we had learnt from yours."

"Wasn't that a bit dangerous?"

"Well, yes. But we had help."

"Who from?"

"Well Lloyd helped us from here, looking at data and information we were sending in order to compile a report that would ruin their chances. And the Jordans came too, posing as a journalist and photographer."

Jake looked a little hurt. "What? They weren't taking a break in Portugal?"

She shook her head without making eye contact.

"So basically everyone knew about this but me and Mitch?"

"No. It wasn't like that. It was just Lloyd, but then he felt we needed backup so he sent the Jordans to help." She sighed, and contemplated the backs of her hands for a moment. "I didn't want to tell you until I'd put it right."

"And have you?"

"It's a good question," she replied quietly. "I don't suppose we'll know until the inspection results come through, but be assured, we did everything in our power to screw theirs' up."

*

The sun still seemed incredibly high in the sky for seven o'clock, but it was the height of summer. On the sand sat two lit barbeques, one loaded with chicken and burgers, the other with swordfish steaks and veg on skewers. Jess had taken control, once a chef, always a chef, and Meg was opening cartons of coleslaw and packets of pitta breads.

"Meg, when I've got the veg off, can you give the bread a quick blast on the fire."

The boys were kicking a ball around, with no apparent rules or teams, and Holly fished in her rucksack pulling out a bottle in a cold sleeve, "Fizz time, ladies?"

"Oh yes," Elle exclaimed rooting around for suitable glasses. "This is the life."

"Grubs up!" Jess shouted to the boys, who lined up in a flash, plates at the ready.

After they had all had their fill and the sun was slowly dropping into the ocean. Holly poked at the embers of the fire they had built and asked, "What was in the envelope you sent to the Isle of Wight, Lloyd?"

"All sorts really," he reflected, taking a sip of red wine from a plastic goblet. "There were documents that showed that someone in government had sold MOD land *after* it had been converted at the public's expense."

"What? That's stealing, surely?" Mitch exclaimed.

"You'd think. I suppose they thought that no one would ever tie up the time lines of the building and purchase. And there were documents that showed ownership of Wight-Green being owned solely by Sustineri Estates, therefore it was not a community effort, but a commercial venture, so the best they could have got out of the inspection was eco-park status." Lloyd continued.

"So technically they were not a threat to us?" Jake asked.

"I don't think they would ever have been a threat to Pentwen. I mean they have the English climate, they're not even coastal, and at the end of the day – they are still the Isle of Wight." There were chuckles from around the fire.

"Anything else?"

"Oh yes. There were the photos that Meg took when she strayed onto their land."

"Attacked by their fence more like," she said defensively.

"They showed that this was not a community build -"

"Not unless the community was in Riga." Meg interjected.

"Riga?" Ray questioned.

"Yes, all the workers on the build were from Latvia. It saved them a fortune in local wages," she continued.

"And it turned out that the sustainable materials they claimed to be using were not as documented. The photos Meg took showed that the apparent solar rooftiles that they claim to have used on all the rooves were in fact cheap replicas made in Russia."

"It means that really they had failed the inspection before we even added our own twist," Meg added.

"But to be fair, if it wasn't for you taking the photos the inspectors may never have realised that," Lloyd said, eager that they take credit for the role they played.

"So what was the result?" Sully asked.

"We don't know yet. We're waiting for the report to be published, but it won't be for a few weeks yet."

"And what about the pompous git that I scammed a twenty from in the car park?"

"Ah, the delightful Mr Brownly-Smith. Well, I left him with a parting gift of photographs and video footage that you guys took in the car park at Padstow. I don't think we'll be hearing from him again in a hurry."

Chapter 36

Truro

"Here we go a-bloody-gain," Roger moaned as Aggie attempted to do up his tie. "I mean, it seems like only ten months ago that we last did this."

"That was because it was only ten months ago," she replied mimicking his sarcastic tone. "How about – it was so much fun last time you were made governor that we thought it would be fun to do it again?"

He stepped back from her slightly and held her hands, "But seriously Aggie, what if I lose? God knows what I'd do for a living and now you've given The Anchor to Stewie and Carrie what would you do with your time. I feel responsible for the fact that we may both be destitute by this evening."

She leant over and kissed him. "Stop going on. It's not going to happen. And even if it did, I'd rather be destitute with you than anyone else."

"You say that now, but one week of living in a cardboard box and you'd be running off with the first man with a tent."

"Oh, how little you know me, Governor Stiles. We could always utilise one of our untapped talents."

"What, like busking?!"

"No, fair point. I've heard you sing in the shower. You're terrible."

So for the second time in recent history the County Hall was a hive of activity. Roger and Aggie popped in at seven to help set up and had then returned to the flat for a quick bite to eat and get changed. They returned to County Hall just before ten when the ballot would close, and then the long and arduous count would begin. There was no sign of Brownly-Smith until after eleven when he arrived looking like an extra from a Bugsy Malone film in a black and white pinstripe suit with shoulder pads. He shook hands with several people that were milling around the hall as he made his way over to Roger and Aggie. "Well hello, Aggie. You look as radiant as ever," he said, taking her hand and kissing it. She squirmed inwardly.

"Likewise, Martin," she replied curtly.

He grabbed Rogers hand in both of his pudgy paws, and whilst pumping it vigorously he leant in and said, "It didn't have to be like this, Roger. I did warn you."

"Like what, Martin?"

"I take no pleasure in winning such battles," Brownly-Smith said, almost apologetically.

"Who says you've won this one?" Roger replied forcefully, in a threatening whisper.

Brownly-Smith stood back, and now in a voice audible to anyone who cared to listen he said, "Well good luck, old man," before sauntering off.

"He could curdle yoghurt," Aggie said, visibly shivering.

They continued to mingle, chatting with council employees, members of the public and local dignitaries. Roger was chatting to Robert Ash when he noticed Aggie trying to catch his attention, nodding her head towards Brownly-Smith with a questioning look on her face. He followed her gaze and saw Brownly-Smith huddled away in a corner in deep conversation with someone he did not recognise. He shrugged in reply to Aggie's questioning look.

Roger walked over to the canteen hatch that was doing a roaring trade in coffee, keeping the vote counters alert. He didn't need any more caffeine but he had spotted someone to chat with, Rick Mantel the County Chief Fire Officer. "Hey Rick, when you said you were an election junky you weren't kidding were you?"

"Hey, Rog!" Rick exclaimed, slapping Roger forcefully on the back. "Never missed an election yet."

"You counting tonight?"

"Sure am."

"What's this all about, Rog? I mean we only just got overseas territory status less than a year ago and then we're having another election?"

"Not my choice, mate. This was a Whitehall call."

"I didn't think they could tell us what to do any more. I thought we'd severed those ties?"

"Oh, if I get through tonight I can assure you this will not be happening again," Roger said forcefully.

"Nah, you'll be fine, Rog. You've got nothing to worry about."

The count was finished. As they mounted the stage Martin Brownly-Smith gave Roger a smarmy smile. It was a look that Roger was at pains to decipher, so he chose to ignore it, although something niggled at him. He knew Martin of old and knew he never went into a battle unless assured of victory. Maybe Brownly-Smith was convinced that the money shot would win every time, maybe that was why he seemed curiously confident – but Roger was not convinced.

For the second time in ten months they watched the returning officer stand up and proclaim, "I, Peter Blizard, Chief Returning Officer, am announcing the results for the election for Governor of the Isle of Kernow." He looked down at the piece of paper he had clutched securely in his hand. "There was eighty percent turnout with two percent spoilt ballots." There were nods from the audience impressed with the high turnout. "The results are as follows: Roger Stiles, incumbent Governor of the Isle of Kernow, 240,576 votes."

There was a huge intake of breath as people tried to mentally calculate whether quarter of a million votes was sufficient on eighty percent turnout. The Chief Returning Officer hesitated for effect before continuing, "Martin Brownly-Smith, challenger, 103,104 votes. I therefore declare Roger Stiles as the Governor of the Isle of Kernow."

The noise was incredible, the cheer rattled the windows, and Roger felt himself breathe out, the relief flooding through him as if he had been holding his breath for six weeks. He looked down at Aggie who was beaming up at him from the floor, tears starting to form in her eyes. Roger turned to Martin Brownly-Smith to shake his hand and was disturbed to see that he was smiling, a smile that looked genuine.

The Chief Returning Officer waited for quiet, and as he started to introduce Roger to make an acceptance speech there was a disturbance at the rear of the hall, the crowd gradually parting to allow a man through who was trying to make himself heard – the same man that Brownly-Smith had been deep in conversation with earlier in the evening. Everything about this man reeked of civil servant. From his poorly cut charcoal suit, to his grey hair and the grey pallor of someone that doesn't leave the office enough. The Chief Returning Officer looked concerned at this intervention, and all had surprised looks on their faces as the grey civil servant crossed in front of the stage and made his way up the steps. All that was, except Martin Brownly-Smith.

The man made his way to the centre of the stage, and taking the microphone from a flabbergasted Chief Returning Officer, he flourished a sheath of paper, and said, "I call into dispute the results of this election."

There was a murmur of disapproval from the crowd. Roger felt sick to his stomach. He knew this was not a madman, this was the work of

Brownly-Smith. This explained why he had been so confident all along. This was the stich-up.

"I call into question the right of Roger Stiles to stand as a candidate as he does not meet the criteria."

People looked quizzically at each other.

"In order to put yourself forward for the position of Governor, Her Majesty's Government requires the applicants to be of Cornish descent in order to respect the cultural heritage of the Isle."

More glances were exchanged by those gathered. Roger stood dumbstruck.

The uninvited man continued. "Roger Stiles, can you confirm whether you are of Cornish heritage?"

Roger just shrugged, baffled by the turn of events, "No."

Turning to his opponent, "Can you confirm that you are of Cornish descent."

Grasping his hands in front of him and lowering his head in an almost pleading manner, Martin Brownly-Smith replied, "I can indeed confirm that I am of Cornish descent."

"On this basis I request that the Chief Returning Officer declare Martin Brownly-Smith the new Governor of the Isle of Kernow."

Chapter 37

Truro
The newly elected Governor entered his office in New County Hall and sat at his desk, taking in his surrounds with great satisfaction. The First Lady entered the office putting two cups of coffee on the desk and walked behind his chair to massage his shoulders.

"Are you ready to get on with some hard work?" she asked.
"I'm ready to pick up exactly from where I left off," Roger replied.
"Thatta boy!"

The night of the election was the worst of his life, Roger had never before felt so impotent. He had shrugged and walked from the stage humiliated. Aggie ran to meet him. He grabbed her hand and started for the exit, tugging her along with him. They got into the car in silence. He rested his head on the steering wheel and cried deep, heartfelt sobs. He had known from the outset that he had been set up to fail, but had hoped that natural justice would win through. This was destined from the outset, and he had been a fool to pursue it. Aggie was feeling equally impotent, in shock and clueless how to console the man she loved.

Meanwhile mayhem ensued within County Hall. The Chief Returning Officer remembered that he was in change and asked the interloper for evidence of such a ruling. The civil servant furnished him with the relevant paperwork containing the government seal. The Chief Returning Officer read through the policy, and all seemed to be as the man had said. He returned to the microphone and explained to the expectant crowd that this did appear to be true.

"Just because that's true doesn't mean that he's Cornish," shouted an angry man at the front. The Chief Returning Officer decided this was a fair point, turning to Martin Brownly-Smith to explain himself.

Brownly-Smith grabbed the microphone, "I can confirm that my direct ancestor, Hugo Brownly was born in Bridgerule in 1844."

"Where's the evidence of this?" Brian Clough shouted.

The Chief Returning Officer nodded at his comment, turning to Brownly-Smith. "Can you furnish us with such evidence?"

"I can indeed, dear man," he replied smugly pulling a long envelope from his inside jacket pocket. The Chief Returning Officer opened the envelope and inspected the contents, nodding as he did so. "I can confirm that Martin Brownly-Smith does have evidence to support his claim, therefore should be declared Governor of the Isle of Kernow."

There was uproar from the crowd, but as it died down one voice could be heard repeatedly saying, "But what month was your ancestor born?"

The crowd turned to see Callum, mobile phone in hand, calmly repeating his question. The Chief Returning Officer asked whether this has any bearing on the matter, and Callum said that the answer may be crucial.

"According to the evidence just supplied by Mr Brownly-Smith, Hugo Brownly was born in December of that year. Does this have a bearing?"

Callum looked down at his screen, and looked back up beaming. "Oh, I believe it does." All eyes were on him now. Grinning, he continued, "Bridgerule was transferred to Devon earlier in that year, which means that his ancestor was Devonian, and not Cornish!"

Brownly-Smith glared at the civil servant, who shrugged nervously. There was absolute silence in the hall, then there was a muttering. The bemused Chief Returning Officer clambered down from the stage to look at the website that Callum had consulted, nodding in agreement with his findings.

"Well it appears, Mr Brownly-Smith, that you do not have Cornish ancestry. And therefore your claim to the position is also rejected." He stood awkwardly for a moment, unsure of what to do next. He looked down at the sheath of paper that the civil servant had passed earlier. He flicked through some pages. Then looking up he asked to the crowd, "Is Mr Stiles married to a Cornish woman?"

Brownly-Smith replied decisively, "No he is not."

"Ah, that's a shame as this is also a criteria -"

He was interrupted by a shout from the crowd. "Yes he is."

"Since when?" Brownly-Smith spat.

"Since two weeks ago," Stewie shouted, and holding up Carrie's left hand, "We had a double wedding, me and Carrie, and Aunty and Roger."

Realisation started to dawn on the crowd, voices uplifted.

"We were going to have a celebration when the election was over."

The double marriage had taken place the week before with just the bare minimum of people present. Roger had been surprised when Aggie had first suggested it, but riding on the tide of relief that she had not been having an affair with James he was in a particularly romantic mood. Not wanting to spoil the romance Aggie decided not to mention that her idea for a double wedding was not due to romantic ideals, but more to spare Carrie, and more importantly Stewie, the wrath of Jim Downs when he found out that Carrie's expanding waist was not due to increased cookie consumption.

On realising the game was back in Roger's favour Brian nudged Callum, and they darted out, sliding down the corridor and into the carpark. Callum took the lead and bounded up to the Beamer, banging on the window, making Aggie and Roger jump with fright.

"This isn't a good time," Aggie spat vehemently from the partly opened window.

Panting, Callum nodded. "Yes it is," not fully able to catch his breath.

She scowled at him.

"It is. It's yours, I mean Roger's. He's won."

"Look," Brian interrupted pointing to two men walking across the car park. One wearing a grey suit, with his head down being berated by another larger man in pinstripes.

Roger looked quizzically at Brian and Callum, who both had their heads poking through the lightly opened window.

"Congratulations Governor, and Mrs Stiles our returning First Lady."

So sitting again at his desk Roger was primed and ready for action. "At least I can get back to the running of the Isle without distractions from Whitehall," he pondered.

"Did you ever get to the bottom of why they tried to regain control of the Isle from you?" Aggie asked.

"Not a clue," he said, picking up the first piece of post from the pile. He opened the envelope and read, a huge smile spreading across his face.

"Good news?"

"Yep, Pentwen passed their sustainable tourism inspection with flying colours."

Epilogue

Buckingham Palace, London

David Cameron sat nervously waiting for the arrival of His Royal Highness. He had had a sleepless night trying to decide how he was going to break the news to Prince Charles, and he had still come up blank.

"Ah, excellent. Cameron. Good news I hope?" Charles said on entering.

Cameron bowed, a suitable mask for the cringe he was feeling at that moment.

"Well, it depends on how we define good?"

Charles looked at him askance. "Good news would be that the whole Kernow thing has blown over, and normal biscuit sales could resume."

"Well, not entirely."

Charles crossed his arms and looked down his nose at Cameron like a petulant schoolboy.

"We had a good plan, but Brownly-Smith rather put a spanner in the works?"

"How so?"

"Something to do with pinching a man's posterior and eating a pasty with cutlery, I believe."

"Buffoon. Well that's his knighthood down the swanee."

"Not to worry about him. He has resigned from politics, so I've sent him to the Isle of Wight to rectify a little problem we have down there."

"Well you better make sure you don't screw up this daft EU referendum that you promised in the election. Mummy will be furious if she has to start paying duty on her gin."

"Oh, do not concern yourself about that. It's a dead cert - we won't be leaving the EU any time soon."

ACKNOWLEDGEMENTS

My heartfelt thanks go to many who helped in the creation of this sequel. Firstly to Sarah Joselyn for access to her collection of beautiful books celebrating the Cornish fishing industry. I would also like to thank Sim Harris for his random information on aspects of Cornwall that I would have otherwise been unaware of.

Thanks go to the myriad of local Cornish brewers and bakers for giving the county its own authentic taste, most especially Atlantic Brewery & Distillery and Malcolm Barnecutt Bakery.

And if you are in Cornwall I highly recommend a visit to Athelstan House which is based largely on Trewidden House, although you will need to go to Penzance to take in their amazing gardens.

ABOUT THE AUTHOR

Cathy-Ann Child has been a psychology lecturer for over twenty years and is now turning her hand to fiction rather than academic writing. The Isle of Kernow Fights Back is her second novel about her adopted home of Cornwall.

Keep in-touch or up to date at
cathy-annchild.com

Printed in Great Britain
by Amazon